MW00479594

THE LAIRD AND THE SASSENACH

ASHE BARKER

Copyright © 2017 by Ashe Barker

Published by Stormy Night Publications and Design, LLC.
www.StormyNightPublications.com

Cover design by Korey Mae Johnson
www.koreymaejohnson.com

Images by Period Images, 123RF/Eric Isselee,
123RF/Christopher Smith, and 123RF/ciarada

All rights reserved.

1st Print Edition. January 2017

ISBN-13: 978-1542327473

ISBN-10: 1542327474

FOR AUDIENCES 18+ ONLY

This book is intended for adults only. Spanking and other sexual activities represented in this book are fantasies only, intended for adults.

PROLOGUE

"Lady Eleanor is here, from Duncleit."

Roselyn shot her mother a glance but did not answer. There was no need, they both understood clearly enough the implications. Lady Margaret, mistress of Mortain Castle, was dying.

"I wonder how long Lady Eleanor will be staying? Until the end, I daresay…"

Roselyn reached for her mother's slender hand. Even at just ten summers the child well understood her mama's sadness at the imminent loss of her lifelong friend. Roselyn, too, would miss the gentle lady with the ready smile and fondness for sweetmeats which she would distribute freely to her smaller guests.

"Shall we see her?" Roselyn harboured mixed feelings on this. Lady Margaret bore little resemblance of late to the gracious chatelaine who used to stride through her domain with such confidence, such quiet authority. Her illness had taken hold swiftly and her descent had been rapid. She had plummeted from rude health to become the shell of a woman who now lay still and fragile in the great master

1

chamber.

The entire episode had terrified Roselyn. Lady Margaret's rapid decline undermined the child's previously unshaken belief in the immortality of herself and those around her. Even the death of her own father just two years earlier had not affected Roselyn so deeply, though of course he had been a virtual stranger to his tiny daughter.

Her mother offered her a wan smile. "You may remain downstairs in the hall if you wish. I expect Joan will be here with her mother and she will no doubt be pleased to see you."

Roselyn hoped so, though she did not share her mother's certainty. In truth, she barely knew Joan McGregor, daughter of Lady Eleanor. The two girls saw each other rarely since Joan's home lay far away to the north, in the Highlands of Scotland. Even when Joan did visit Mortain and their paths might cross, Roselyn found it near enough impossible to decipher the other girl's pronounced Highland brogue. Despite this it would be pleasant, she supposed, to spend time with her, though on balance she wished to say her farewells to Lady Margaret also.

"May I come to Lady Margaret's chamber with you? Just for a few moments?"

"Of course. You may remain as long as you wish. I believe that I might stay until… Until…"

Lady Eleanor did not finish. There was no need.

"I am glad ye're here. 'Tis so gloomy, everyone so sad…"

Roselyn regarded her occasional friend with some surprise. How could Joan expect the mood at Mortain to be otherwise when all here loved the lady who was not expected to survive the night? "I know, but…"

She abandoned her admonition when she saw the tears clouding Joan's eyes.

"She was always kind tae me." Joan made no attempt now to conceal her grief. "I shall miss her so," she sobbed. "I had always imagined that she would be here when…

when I…"

"What? When you what?" Roselyn took a fortifying nibble of the dried apple which the Mortain cook had slipped into her hand as the pair scuttled through her kitchen on the way to the rear stairs that led down into the storerooms below. She considered offering a bite to Joan but decided against it and instead wrapped her friend in her small embrace and held her whilst she cried. Only when Joan quieted, her sobs now reduced to hiccupping gulps, did Roselyn resume her questioning.

"When you what, Joan? When did you expect Lady Margaret to be here?"

"When I come tae live i' this keep. Forever."

Had she heard correctly? Roselyn was never quite certain with these Scots and their strange form of speech. "You will live here? At Mortain? Why?"

Her friend lifted her chin and adopted a haughty, superior air, her efforts somewhat undermined by her continued gentle weeping. "Why, when I am wed to Edmund, o' course."

"To Edmund?" Roselyn gawked, her jaw dropping. Edmund was heir to Mortain, the son of Lady Margaret and her husband, Archibald, the laird. "But you cannot marry Edmund. He is old."

"He is but a few years older than I," countered the other girl defensively. "And we shall nae be wed for several years yet. Eight years, in fact, when I am nineteen years old. 'Twill be a long wait, but my father insists upon it."

Roselyn considered this news in slack-jawed horror. "You should be thankful for the wait. Surely you cannot wish to marry. It is… It will be…" Roselyn was not entirely certain what marriage would be, but she had no doubt that it was not a state to which any sane female should aspire.

"All women must wed. 'Tis our duty."

"I know, but… are you not afraid? You will have babies, and… and…" The precise details escaped Roselyn, but she was convinced that the matter was dire indeed. Babies were a dangerous business for women.

"Edmund is kind tae me. I shall be happy. I ken that I shall."

Roselyn had no desire to quash the other girl's optimism though she considered it to be misplaced. Her own experience of the married state was sparse, she would readily acknowledge that, limited to just her own parents whose union was both distant and cold. She harboured the most profound of doubts regarding Joan's future, but could not find it in herself to dampen her friend's apparent enthusiasm, especially not on such a dark day.

"We shall be neighbours, after I am wed. Ye must visit here regularly. It will be so good tae have a friend here i' the borders, especially wi' Lady Margaret gone."

Roselyn flattened her mouth, her smile wan and disappointed. "I cannot. We are to move soon, to Etal. My brother insists upon it."

"Yer brother?"

"Yes, the Earl of Ingram. My half-brother, in fact. He and my mother, his stepmother, have never been friends, and since he inherited the title he has ignored us and allowed us to live with my mother's kin here in the borders, at Beauchamp Manor. However, he has written to insist that I must present myself at his keep near Berwick to be brought up within his household. My mother has no desire to go, she says she always hated it there, but will not allow me to go alone. We leave within a few weeks."

"Oh, I see. But ye will be back, surely?"

"I hope so. I do not know."

"Berwick? That is in England, across the border. 'Twill not be so easy to remain in touch…"

"I know that, but I am English, so—"

"That doesnae count," insisted Joan. "We shall still be friends."

"Yes," agreed Roselyn. "We shall. Of course we shall." She dusted off her thick woollen skirt. "Come, we should go back up to the hall. Lady Margaret does not like us to play down here, she says 'tis not safe."

Roselyn scrambled to her feet and shoved the last of her apple into her mouth.

Joan also made to rise, but the pair stiffened at the sound of masculine voices approaching. They dived back into the cranny they had been huddling in, between two huge sacks of grain.

"'Tis Sir Archibald," hissed Roselyn, recognising the low tone of the laird who ruled Mortain.

"Aye, an' he has my Edmund wi' him," added Joan.

Her Edmund? Perhaps there was some merit to this marriage plan after all. Roselyn shimmied back and concentrated on making herself as small as possible in order to escape notice. She did not fear the laird, she had no cause to, or his son for that matter. Mortain was a benign, easy-going household but their disappointed censure at her disobedience to Lady Margaret's rules would pain Roselyn and embarrass her mother. She had no wish to be the cause of further distress in this unhappy keep. Not today.

The pair watched in silence as the men strolled the length of the storage chamber, passing within two feet of the girls' hiding place. The laird and his son conversed in low tones, their voices subdued, but their words carried in the confined space and were easy enough to hear.

"It will not be long now. The physicians have said…" The older man bowed his head, his strong voice almost breaking in his grief.

"Physicians have been known to be wrong. She may yet rally." Edmund patted his father's arm, though his words of comfort lacked conviction to Roselyn's young ears.

To the laird's also, it would seem. "Nay, she will not. Not this time. She will not last the night." He paused and heaved in a ragged breath. "I shall miss her so. She has been my companion these last twenty and five years, my closest friend, my confidante. How shall I cope? How shall any of us manage when she is not here?"

"I do not know, but we shall. We have to."

"Aye, ye're right. We must do it, for her. An' this is why we must sign the contract this evening. It is her wish."

"My betrothal contract?"

"Aye, lad. It is your mother's desire to see it done, to have the contracts signed which will bind you to her sister's daughter. It will bring her peace, at the end…"

"Aye, I know this. Lady Eleanor has the authority to sign on behalf of her laird, Joan's father. Very well, we should get on with the matter. I… I do not believe we should delay unduly."

The laird offered no further comment. His son's meaning was clear enough, to the laird as well as to Roselyn and Joan who listened unseen. If Lady Margaret was to witness Edmund formally and irretrievably betrothed to Lady Joan, it had better be soon.

"So, why are we down here, then?" Edmund eyed his surroundings with displeasure. "Should we not be in the solar putting our seal to the contract?"

"A betrothal gift is customary. Margaret will expect it, as will the McGregors. I have several pieces of fine gold plate I have been keeping for this very occasion."

"Ah, I see. Very well, let us press on." Edmund strode on, toward the stairs below the buttery. He paused beside the stone staircase. "Would you like me to open the strong room?"

"Aye, lad, if you would." The older man followed him, and as the distance increased Roselyn found their voices difficult to hear. Curiosity got the better of her and she poked her head out from between the sacks to further observe their actions. As she watched, Edmund ran his hand, palm flat, up and down the stonework at the side of the staircase.

His father leaned over and pointed to a precise spot. Edmund nodded at his sire and pressed hard on the stone indicated. Before Roselyn's astonished eyes the entire side of the staircase swung outward to reveal a cavity concealed beneath the steps. Both men bent their backs to enter, disappearing into the space beneath.

"A secret room," breathed Roselyn. "There is a hidden chamber. Did you know?"

Joan shook her head, her mouth forming a perfect 'o.'

"I wonder what is in there." Roselyn started forward, intending to follow the men under the stairs. Joan grabbed her arm.

"Nay, we must nae. 'Tis a secret and… ye must promise ne'er tae tell. Ye must swear it."

"Tell? Who would I tell?" Roselyn regarded Joan in astonishment. "I merely wondered…"

"'Tis none o' our concern. Come, we must be away, afore they come back out." Joan scrambled past Roselyn and reached back for the smaller girl's hand. "This way, we shall take the main stairs back up tae the hall, the way they came down. And remember, ye must tell no one o' this. Not ever."

CHAPTER ONE

Isle of Skye, Scottish Highlands, 1482

The crisp thud of his stout leather boots striking the stone flags echoed along the draughty upper hallway as Blair Andrew James McGregor headed for the stairs which led down to his great hall. He had yet to break his fast and the day beckoned, his duties as laird unrelenting. Even now, at the height of summer, the days were never long enough to accomplish all that needed to be done to ensure the safety and security of those who depended upon him.

Blair took the stairs two at a time and strode across the hall. Servants who left their beds even earlier than he did had already piled the high table with nourishing bread, meat, and ale. He nodded at Elspeth, the cook of indeterminate years who had prepared his meals for as long as he could recall. In the absence of a lady to manage his household, Elspeth tended to take charge of the running of Duncleit Castle, commanding a bevy of serving wenches and lads to ensure his stomach was kept full, his bed remained clean and dry and his floors likewise. The woman sketched a quick curtsy in his direction before she bustled back across the rushes freshly strewn over the floor. She was headed back to the domain she ruled with absolute authority, the hot and heaving kitchens beneath his keep. Laird or no laird, Blair knew better than to delay her.

He selected a plump loaf and broke off a hunk of the soft bread, still warm from Elspeth's ovens. Next he drew his dirk to spear a slice of venison which he dumped on his bread, then took a bite. He chewed as he reached for the jug of ale to swill down his food. Blair didn't bother to sit; there was too much to be done today, he could not afford the luxury of a leisurely breakfast.

He turned at the sound of footsteps behind him. "Ye're late, Robbie. The morning'll be half gone by the time we reach Dunisburn wood."

The giant of a man ambling across the hall to join him offered a toothless grin. "Lad, ye'll kill yerself an' all that ride wi' ye. The dew's not even warm yet an' that stag's goin' nowhere. We eat, aye, then we hunt."

Blair returned the smile. He knew the captain of his guard was right, though he'd not be admitting that any time soon. "Is there ever a time ye *stop* eatin', Robbie? I swear, Elspeth can't keep up with ye."

"It'll be a cold day in Hades when I'm beat by the likes of this brainless brute." Elspeth nudged Robbie with her pointed elbow to shift him from her path. "Now, out of me way, the pair of ye."

They both grimaced at the irritated tone of the cook as she scuttled between them, this time bearing a steaming bowl of oatmeal porridge. She deposited that among the already heaped serving dishes and turned to regard her laird. "Did I hear ye say ye were going' huntin', Laird? If so, we could do wi' a nice bit o' pork to salt for the winter."

Blair groaned. He hated hunting the wild boar but he knew better than to quarrel with Elspeth on any matter pertaining to her kitchens and their storerooms. He had long since resigned himself to the reality of their situation—it was his task to supply the food, hers to make sure it reached his table succulent and steaming. The arrangement worked well.

The clatter of feet from outside heralded the arrival of more of his clansmen intent upon satisfying their growling stomachs. He and Robbie returned polite greetings as men and boys pushed and shoved in their haste to reach the table. Blair swallowed the last of his bread and meat then grabbed a couple of apples and rammed them into his pocket before striding for the door.

"We leave in ten minutes," he yelled over his shoulder. "Any man not ready to ride with me can stay and tend to the fields with the women." A chorus of groans followed him from the hall, but as he blinked in the dawn sunlight Blair knew there would be no male backs bent over their crops that day.

He was halfway to the stable block when a shout gave him pause. The call came from the high wall shielding the eastern face of Duncleit Castle, the McGregor keep which overlooked on the western shore of the Isle of Skye. Blair stopped to shield his eyes as he peered up.

"What is it, Archie?" he yelled.

"Riders, Laird. Three, and approaching fast from the south."

"Can ye make out who they are? What colours do they wear?" Blair was already sprinting toward the stone steps leading up to the parapet which surrounded the keep.

"Nay, Laird, not at this distance." The man was still peering into the dawn haze as Blair arrived beside him. "Look, sir. Over there." The lookout pointed to the three specks on the horizon.

Blair picked the horsemen out at once, but he couldn't discern their identity either. It wouldn't be long though. The men were galloping at full pelt in the direction of Duncleit.

"Raise the drawbridge and station guards on the walls." The curt command was aimed at Robbie, who had followed him up onto the battlements. "Take no further action though until we know who they are and what they want." Blair McGregor would fight to the death to defend what was his, but he was never a man given to needless aggression. He remained on the wall as his men hastened to take up their positions, their alacrity the product of long years of hard training. Every man knew his duty and would do it, Blair had no need to direct them in this.

"Shit, those are Mortain colours. They must be Edmund's men." Blair turned and bounded down the steps, then crossed the bailey at a run. "Lower the drawbridge, give them entry." He reached the outer portal as the gate was opened to reveal the approaching riders, now just a mile or so from their fortress. Blair watched in stony, tense silence as the early morning visitors closed the distance. He knew this could not bode well. To arrive at this time the men must have ridden all night. This was no social call.

Sure enough, the men who clattered across his drawbridge to come to a halt not a yard from where he stood were dusty and exhausted as they slithered from their sweating mounts. Blair clicked his fingers to signal the stable lads to attend to the horses, then extended his hand to the nearest of his unexpected visitors, a man he did not recognise but instinctively knew to be a loyal retainer.

"Welcome, friend. Ye bring news from my cousin?"

Edmund of Mortain was three years older than Blair and held lands in the borders just north of the Tweed. His mother, Margaret, had been sister to Blair's own mother, Eleanor McGregor and the boys had spent the better part of their early years together cavorting in the Lothian hills before the elder McGregor recalled his son to Skye to train for his future role as laird. The cousins remained close though, a bond strengthened two years earlier when Blair's sister, Joan, married Edmund. The last news he had received from Mortain Castle had informed Blair that he was to be an uncle by the end of the summer.

The man staggered toward him and Blair noticed the blood for the first time. "Ye're wounded." He clasped the man around the waist to lend his support and Robbie moved to grasp his other side.

"Nay, no time. Leave me," wheezed the injured man. "Ye must go. At once. Our laird is attacked, he sent us to summon aid. Ye must leave now, afore it's too late."

"Mortain is under attack?" Blair waved his arm to summon more assistance in order to carry the man into the keep. "But who would do this? We are not at war."

The wounded man snorted. "There are always those who will try to take what is not theirs. The English attacked us, the Earl of Ingram. He has besieged Mortain and demands the surrender of the keep. Sir Edmund cannot hold him off much longer and sent us to seek your aid. Ye will come, aye?"

"Aye, we'll be there." Blair half carried the man to the entrance of the great hall, where he handed him into the care of a bunch of female servants. "Tend him well, and the others too. They have ridden hard and are exhausted." He turned to Robbie. "We'll need at least fifty men, our finest. Leave just enough to see to the safety of Duncleit, the rest ride with me. Ye stay here to command the fortress in my absence. Aiden will be my second in command on this foray."

As Robbie hastened to do his bidding Blair closed his eyes and drew in a long, slow breath. He had a bad feeling about this. A really bad feeling.

• • • • • • •

"It took Edmund's men two full days and nights to reach Duncleit, and we have taken only slightly less on the return journey. Already this bloody earl has had four days in which to wreak his havoc." They had slowed their horses to allow the mounts a much needed rest and Blair took the opportunity to offer his grim observation to Aiden Montgomery, the knight who rode at his side.

Aiden was of Irish origin but had arrived in Scotland as a lad of five following yet another famine in his home country. He had travelled the Highlands before settling at

Duncleit in return for an opportunity to be apprenticed to Robbie and train as a knight. Blair had never had cause to regret his father's investment in the itinerant lad. Aiden was a fine addition to their garrison. His formidable skills with the claymore and bow were matched by his keen intelligence and avid interest in everything that happened in Scotland and the borders. Blair had long since abandoned any attempt to understand how his captain-at-arms was always so well informed, but he was the one he always turned to when he needed information.

"I do vaguely recall my father had dealings with the previous Earl of Ingram, though 'tis a name I have not heard mentioned for years. He offered one of his sons as a match for Joan but she was promised to Edmund since we were all children together so the alliance was never seriously considered. What do we know about the current earl? Why would he attack Edmund? And what is his strength?"

Aiden narrowed his eyes in concentration. "The current earl is a younger son who inherited when both his older brothers perished at Piperdean. It was the oldest lad, Arthur, I believe, who sought your sister's hand. He subsequently wed an heiress from Chester though the match was childless. The younger son who eventually inherited the title was meant for the clergy I gather so he is untrained for battle but he does not allow that to dissuade him. Perhaps that does not matter since he is favoured by Henry Percy, the Duke of Northumberland and enjoys his protection. The earl's keep is close to Berwick but he desires to extend his lands and cares little in which direction he turns. For obvious reasons he chooses not to provoke Northumberland, the most powerful noble in the north of England. He has two hundred men under his command, well trained I gather but unpaid for some months. He will be seeking wealth, and is already attempting to marry off his sister to acquire influence and power."

"He can raise a dowry?"

"A modest one, perhaps. But he seeks powerful allies

and hopes to wed the girl to Percy's half-brother. I gather the negotiations are progressing well, despite the girl's reluctance. She is currently residing in the convent at Kelso and has expressed a fervent desire to take the veil."

"A pious woman with a murderous, greedy bastard for a brother. God's balls, what a family." Blair resisted the urge to dig his heels into his stallion's flanks to gain a fraction more speed. Every moment might count in their dash across the Scottish borders to come to the aid of his kinsmen, but they could not do so on ruined horses. "So ye believe he is seeking money then, as well as lands? He intends to plunder Mortain's coffers?"

"Aye, I daresay. And he will be familiar with the likely pickings as his older brother was a friend to your cousin, despite the business over Joan's hand. 'Twas nothing personal, I gather."

"But this is personal. The faithless, opportunistic bastard attacks his friends in his greed."

"It would seem so. He can't hope to take and hold the keep itself, not without the support and endorsement of King James, which is unlikely to be forthcoming. Also, he must know that we will come to the aid of our clansmen and that our numbers likely exceed his. Ye have a formidable reputation in battle, Laird, so he risks much in crossing The McGregor. My guess is that this is intended to be a swift raid motivated by greed and he will likely have a mind to seize any livestock, along with anything else of value."

"Hostages?"

"Probably, if he can get his hands on any."

"My sister is pregnant. If he has laid so much as a finger upon her, I'll—"

"Laird, let us not borrow trouble. We shall be at Mortain within two hours, then we will know what we are to deal with."

Blair glanced over at his companion, just a few years older than he was and perhaps his closest friend after Mortain. "Ye're right, as ever. I appreciate your counsel.

And your knowledge."

"You are welcome to both, sir."

They kicked their mounts into a full gallop and pounded across the barren moorland in the direction of the besieged keep.

• • • • • • •

Blair had feared the worst, but the sight that met his eyes as he crested the last hill which lay between his troop of Highland warriors and the besieged fortress of Mortain exceeded even his worst imaginings. It was almost dawn and the acrid smell of burning hung on the stagnant air. Smoke still rose from the smouldering remains of the castle's wooden outbuildings, and the stone keep itself stood stark against the lightening sky. Here and there figures moved around, but they were few. Far, far too few. Of the conquering army which had wrought this havoc there was no sign.

"Sweet Jesus," murmured Blair. "We are too late."

Aiden did not reply. They urged their horses to yet greater speed and hurtled down the hillside to the ruined castle.

No one offered any resistance or any greeting as they thundered across the meadow which stretched before what remained of Mortain. His men at his back, Blair cantered over the drawbridge to come to a halt at the steps leading up to the castle entrance. He stood up in his stirrups to peruse the ravaged bailey but saw no one he recognised.

"Hey, you. Yes, you man." He captured the attention of an elderly individual, his breeches tattered, his hair stained with the blood which still seeped from a head wound. "Where is your laird? Where is Edmund of Mortain?"

The man shrugged and turned away. Blair slid from his mount to grab the man by his bony shoulder. He forced the peasant to turn and face him again. "I asked ye a question. Where is Lord Edmund? Lady Joan?"

"Dead. All are dead." The man gestured to their ruined surroundings as though the devastation were not perfectly obvious. "Can ye nae see? Burned. Destroyed. All are gone."

"I said, where are they? Show me." He lowered his voice, his tone little more than a growl.

"Gone. I told you—"

"He took them? As hostages? Captives?" A glimmer of hope flared. Where there was life…

The man shook his head. "No hostages, no prisoners. They slaughtered all who were here, everyone they could find… dead."

Blair groaned, struggling to comprehend such senseless destruction. It was obvious that Ingram had not come here solely to rob and to plunder. His intent was seemingly not to take the keep for his own since he had departed almost as quickly as he had arrived, having quashed all resistance. He could have breached the castle walls and taken anything of worth, yet still left Mortain standing and its residents alive. There was no need for this.

"The bodies? Where…"

"There, in the chapel. It was stone, so would nae burn." The man pointed to the small single-storey structure in the corner of the bailey. "All the dead are there, at least, those that could be found."

Blair was already striding in the direction of the tiny church, Aiden at his heels. He stepped through the doorway and immediately gagged. No stranger to the battlefield, Blair had encountered death before, but not usually on this scale. And not encompassing women and children as well as soldiers.

Ingram's violence had been indiscriminate. The stench of death permeated every nook and cranny, and the entire floor was covered with bodies, not all of them even intact.

Blair stepped forward, cautious, unwilling to step on any of the bodies yet finding no unoccupied space to put his feet. He picked his way through, wincing on those occasions he felt a lump beneath his boot. He resolved to see every single one of these poor souls laid decently to rest before he departed in search of the bastard who did this.

He reached the altar and it was there he found them. His family. The man he thought of as a brother, Edmund of Mortain, had died of a sword wound, the blade driven under his armour and into his heart. He must have been already down when the death blow was struck. And beside him, her deep chestnut curls half-concealing the destruction wrought to her once-beautiful face, he discovered his sister. He could see at a glance that Joan had been hit on the side of the head by a blow from a mace; her devastating injuries would have been instantly fatal, but he drew little comfort from that. She was a woman, heavily pregnant at that. They had no need, none at all…

Blair knelt beside her and took her cold hand between both of his. He kissed the chilled skin, touched his lips to each finger in turn before lifting his gaze once more to her face.

"I will avenge ye, sister. I will make him and his pay for what has been done here. I swear it, on your life and that of the child ye should have borne. Ingram will regret this day's bloody work."

● ● ● ● ● ● ●

Forty-eight hours later Blair leaned on the spade he had used to help dig graves. He and his men had worked tirelessly to ensure that the victims of Ingram's bloodlust had at least the benefit of a decent, Christian interment. He had despatched troops to secure the services of a priest from the nearby abbey at Jedburgh and the man had intoned the necessary blessings over each burial. Blair hoped this would suffice to ensure the salvation of these poor souls, but for himself he required something more tangible in the way of vengeance.

He caught the eye of Aiden who toiled a few yards from him and tipped his chin to indicate he wanted to talk. The two men strode to the edge of the meadow and surveyed the scene before them. In all, they had dug sixty-seven graves, though some held more than one occupant. Where the survivors of the massacre were able to identify families, these had been buried together. The total number of dead was close to ninety, and might yet rise further.

The members of the laird's household—Edmund, Joan, and Edmund's elderly mother who had perished many years earlier, were buried in a vault beneath the chapel where the bodies had been found. Blair had passed much of that night on his knees before the tomb, promising vengeance for the senseless destruction of so many precious lives.

"We'll leave a handful of men to rebuild the gates and walls and do what they might to secure the keep. I have already offered the survivors sanctuary at Duncleit, though the journey there will be arduous."

"I believe most will opt to remain here, Laird."

"Aye, me too. But I had to offer. Edmund had no brothers or other male cousins, and with the death of his unborn child I am his heir so they are my responsibility now. I will need to appoint an agent to manage this keep until a better arrangement might be found, unless James decrees otherwise."

"The king has concerns of his own. He is too busy seeking to subdue the Livingstons and Black Douglases to bother about the fate of a borders fortress."

"Then he is a fool. Mortain occupies a strategic location and must be defended. First, however…"

"Ingram." Aiden met his laird's stony gaze.

"Aye, Ingram. He will pay for this carnage with his life."

"We go to Berwick, then?"

"We do. Round up the men who will accompany us. We leave within the hour."

• • • • • • •

The journey to the Ingram stronghold at Etal, a village

to the west of Berwick, took them the best part of two days. Blair saw no cause for haste; Ingram would have no reason to expect pursuit so quickly since he had slain all who might have given chase. Even if Ingram had anticipated aid coming to Mortain from further north, the troop from Duncleit had made fast time and had not lingered long at the ruined keep, despite his men's fatigue. All were eager to settle this bloody business as quickly as might be achieved, but Ingram was not to know that. Let the bastard enjoy the peace of his own hearth for an extra day or two, it made no difference to Blair. He would exact retribution for that vile day's work soon enough.

He and Aiden surveyed the quiet scene from vantage points atop their destriers. The fortress in the valley below appeared quiet, just a few wisps of smoke from the ovens and the scurrying of peasants in the village itself betraying the day-to-day activity of the small, isolated community. Of the lord himself there was no visible sign, but that meant nothing. He would be inside, languishing in his hall, no doubt exchanging stories with his men at arms extolling their victory at Mortain.

"There is but one main gate, and that is poorly guarded. If we can reach the castle unseen we shall have little difficulty in gaining entry."

"Aye, Laird," agreed Aiden. "Those trees to the west will provide ample cover to bring us within a hundred yards of the walls. I see no archers on the battlements."

"That does not mean there are none within. We need to approach swiftly and overcome their defences before they can properly react. Ye shall lead the advance through the trees. Take thirty men and signal when ye're as close as ye can get without alerting the castle guards. Once your flank is in position I shall charge from the east to draw any fire from their archers and lure their guards away from the main gate on the western side. Ye shall attack their unguarded portal. I shall see ye in the castle bailey, my friend."

"Aye, that ye will. The signal shall be a single whistle,

easily mistaken for the hoot of an owl."

Aiden nodded once and wheeled his mount away. This would be swift. And decisive.

• • • • • • •

There were archers on the Etal battlements, perhaps a couple, but their aim was poor and their range utterly ineffective. Other defences amounted to little more than token resistance by a band of elderly retainers and a handful of villagers with pitchforks. It would have been laughable were the puny reaction to the attack by the Highlanders slightly less ominous. Blair knew before he'd even charged across the drawbridge to reunite with Aiden in the castle bailey that the lack of any significant resistance proved that Ingram was not at Etal. His second-in-command had arrived at the same conclusion.

"He has fled, sir. Already."

"Could he have had word that we were approaching?"

"Perhaps. We are in England now and none hereabouts owe us any allegiance. Our quarry might have been forewarned."

"Craven coward. He has not the backbone to stand and account for his deeds, let alone to defend his own." Blair glanced about him as his men rounded up the castle occupants, herding them together in the centre of the courtyard. His jaw was set as he regarded them, his gaze cold. "Make sure all are assembled. Leave no one inside."

"Laird?"

Aiden appeared troubled by that order, but Blair raised a hand to forestall any argument. "Do it. I want every man, woman, and child to be brought here and lined up before me. And search the stables, the storerooms, the butteries, the lord's private quarters. If there is any evidence of the spoils from Mortain to be found here I want to know about it."

Aiden nodded and set off to do his laird's bidding.

Satisfied, Blair nudged his destrier's flanks with his heels to guide the animal forward. He approached the entrance to the keep, intending to urge his horse up the short flight of steps then to enter the great hall itself. He reined his stallion to a halt as a slender figure emerged from the darkness within.

"Madam…?" He knew Ingram to be unmarried and had expected to find no noble females here, yet this woman was clearly of gentle birth. She wore a pale apple-green kirtle of fine quality linen, belted with a band of velvet in a darker shade which put Blair in mind of the waves which lapped the shores of his island home. Her hair was covered by a shawl in the same apple green as her kirtle, but a few wisps of reddish-blond hair escaped to frame her delicate features. His position astride his horse placed him at eye level with her as she hovered in the castle entrance, one hand clutching the stone to her right as though scared to relinquish her hold on her home. She would lose her grip soon enough, he promised himself silently.

"Your name, madam?" His tone was clipped, uncompromising. The girl was lovely, he would concede that, but he had no doubt that she was his enemy and could expect no gentle courtesy from him.

She tilted her chin in his direction, shifting her gaze until it settled on his chin. The wench might well baulk at looking him in the eye. He had no such compunction, studying her face at his leisure as she stood framed in the doorway, the noontime sun bathing her in a pool of light whilst it probably dazzled her. It was her eyes which caught his attention. They were stunning, quite beautiful in a shade of lavender he had never encountered before. Not quite blue, yet not purple either, they glittered with tears she had yet to shed.

"I asked ye tae identify yourself, lady. Must I ask ye again?" His tone had hardened further, and he did not miss the slight flinch as she heard it too.

"I am Roselyn, Roselyn of Etal." Her voice shook.

"What is your position here?"

"I am sister to Alan, Earl of Ingram."

"Ah," Blair acknowledged. He recalled mention of the sister who would be a nun, though a less likely looking bride of Christ he had yet to see. This wench would be wasted behind the cloister walls, though she might soon wish with all her heart to find the cool sanctuary they might offer her.

"Where is your brother, madam?"

"He... he is not here."

"I had arrived at that conclusion without your aid, lady. I ask again, and for the final time, where is he?"

"I do not know. He received word late last evening that a force was approaching from Mortain, and..." Her voice trailed off and she tilted her chin again, though still failing to meet his gaze. "I am to advise you to return to your own keep, but I realise that will not happen unless I surrender the castle to you." She lowered her hand to rest it upon the keys fastened to her waist.

"I care not for your English fortress. The place will be ashes soon enough in any case. I only want your craven cur of a brother, and those who rode with him to lay waste to my cousin's home and who murdered his family. Where did he go, my lady?"

She shook her head and stepped back. "I... I cannot tell you. I have no idea, other than that he rode south, deeper into England."

"To Alnwick? To seek the protection of Northumberland?" Blair was guessing, but that theory made sense.

"Possibly, though I do not believe the Percys harbour a great deal of fondness for him. He will not find shelter there."

"He will find shelter nowhere," growled Blair. "I shall seek him out and slaughter him, just as he did my kinsmen. And my sister."

The girl paled and reached once more for the stonework at her side. She would have spoken again, but Aiden interrupted them.

"The castle occupants are all assembled, and the search is ongoing, as you ordered. Already, though, we have discovered two horses from Mortain in the stables here, and several bolts of McGregor tartan. It is clear that the spoils of the robbery found their way to this keep."

Blair's lips flattened, his resolve hardening. "As we expected. Very well, locate whatever carts ye may and load all that is ours onto them. We shall return the plunder to Mortain along with stock from the fields hereabouts to replace what was destroyed. It will aid our people in re-establishing the prosperity of their estate. Once ye're satisfied that nothing of value remains, set every building here tae the torch. We will leave nothing standing." He lifted his chin to survey the doomed castle. "The Earl of Ingram will never again pose a threat to his peaceful neighbours."

"Burn it to the ground, Laird? Are you sure?"

"Aye, ye heard me. I am quite sure."

"And them?" Aiden raised his arm to indicate the throng of terrified peasants and servants who huddled together in the middle of the courtyard.

Blair turned his mount to regard the fearful group, his brow furrowing.

"No!" The cry from behind caused him to twist in the saddle to look back at the lady in the doorway. She had taken a pace forward, her hand outstretched in entreaty. "No, you cannot harm them. It was none of their doing. It is me you want."

"You are quite correct, Lady Roselyn. I do indeed want ye, an' your freedom shall be part of the forfeit to be paid for your brother's evil work. As for your servants—"

"They are innocent. It was my fault. I caused my brother to go to Mortain. I am responsible and you must not harm anyone else."

Blair pulled on the reins to wheel his mount around to face her once more. "You, Lady Roselyn? And exactly how might ye have been responsible for the massacre of almost a hundred men, women, and children, one of them my own sister?"

Still the wench refused to meet his eyes. "I... I knew about the gold in the Mortain coffers. It was the Lady Joan's dowry and... I told my brother where it might be found. He went to Mortain to take it."

Blair's eyes narrowed. It was true that Joan's dowry had been a generous one, fifty gold crowns. The settlement was large because it was destined to remain within their family. Blair's father had negotiated the sum, and though the marriage took place after the elder McGregor's death Blair had seen no cause to seek a reduction to the agreed amount. The money meant little enough to him now, though, in the face of such a tragedy. Even so, it would irk him to know that Ingram had profited so richly from his barbaric act.

It seemed to him inconceivable that this trembling wench would have knowledge of the strong room situated in the foundations of Mortain Castle. It was true that the fortified room had been empty when he and his men had managed to gain entry beneath the rubble and burning timbers, but surely Ingram would have found the stash of gold coins by systematically searching the premises once he had killed those who protected it. He leaned down over his horse's neck to regard her more carefully as he continued his questioning.

"So, lady, where *was* the gold to be found? Exactly?" Blair's tone was deceptively soft. He waited for her response.

Roselyn's voice was low also, little more than a whisper. "It could be found by descending into the storage rooms. A... a concealed entrance beneath the stairs at the rear of the buttery led to another chamber, and here was where the Lord of Mortain kept his valuables."

His eyes widened at the accuracy of her account. Blair was incredulous. "How? How could you know that?" he breathed.

"I... Lady Joan was an acquaintance of mine. And I

visited Mortain often as a child so I knew the castle well."

"Ye knew my sister?"

Lady Roselyn nodded. "I did, slightly."

"Ye told your brother all of this? About the dowry, and the strong room?"

"Yes. I… I am sorry, I never expected that he would… would—"

"By God's holy bones, what the hell else did ye imagine he might do?" Anger caused him to roar at her, his grief resurfacing now that the demands of conflict were over. "Did ye expect my cousin to just stand to one side and invite your murdering, robbing bastard of a brother to step inside? Was Edmund to just hand over his family's wealth without protest? Of course there would be a battle, and of course there would be casualties."

"Yes, I realise that, but—"

Blair slashed the air with his hand. "I don't have time for this. Ye shall pay also for your part in this bloodbath, and pay dearly. But first, I intend to track down your brother and haul him back to face good Scots' justice at the end of a claymore." He leaned toward her and beckoned her with his fingers. "Come here, madam. While I decide exactly what I intend to do wi' ye, ye can wait under guard with the rest of your household."

The woman remained motionless, her lavender gaze fixed on a spot close to his right shoulder. Blair's patience was at an end. He urged his horse forward and mounted the steps. Lady Roselyn recoiled as the huge beast bore down upon her, the horse's flaring nostrils puffing air into her startled face. She stumbled in her haste and crumpled to the floor with a pained cry. Blair hauled on the reins to prevent his destrier from trampling her under his powerful hooves then slid to the stone flags to lean over the prone figure.

"Take my hand," he instructed, his gloved palm outstretched. The woman raised her hand but didn't take his. Blair grabbed her by the wrist and dragged her to her feet. The English wench winced and let out a startled squeal though he had not struck her. He noted that the top of her head barely reached his shoulder. "Come," he commanded and turned to stalk down the steps, tugging his captive behind him.

"Wait, I—" The girl lurched forward to bump into his back, then she grabbed his leather tunic and held onto it. "Please, may I take your arm?"

"My arm? What...?" He peered down into the frightened features, her eyes closed now as she fumbled to grasp his elbow. And at last it made sense. "My God," he exclaimed. "Ye're blind."

CHAPTER TWO

Roselyn managed a nod. "Yes, my lord, that is correct. I usually manage unaided, but I confess I am feeling a little disoriented, so if I might just take your arm... only to the foot of the steps..."

She flinched at the obscenity he breathed, but was glad enough when he grasped her numb fingers and wrapped them around his elbow.

"There are four steps down, though I daresay ye know that. Two paces ahead."

"Thank you." Roselyn tightened her grip and allowed him to lead her down the steps, then hung onto his sleeve as he continued across the cobbled bailey.

"Ye will remain here until I deem it otherwise." Her captor's words were curt and delivered in a soft Highland brogue. He disengaged her hand from his arm. "See that she does." The final words were presumably addressed to one of his men.

"Aye, Laird," came the response, as the heavy footsteps of the conquering lord receded.

He was gone, and thus far she still breathed. Roselyn did not dare to believe this happy state would continue for long. His sister... Dear sweet Lord, what had she done?

"Milady, are you injured? That brute did not hurt you, did he?"

The voice came from her left and Roselyn recognised the worried tone of Betsy, one of her brother's servants. The woman normally took care of linens but sometimes tended the fires in the lord's chamber and Roselyn knew her to be a kindly enough sort. She turned in the direction of the voice.

"No. No, he just startled me, is all. His horse…"

"Aye, the rampaging devil looked as though he would gallop right through the hall itself. Let us pray that is all he intends this day."

Another voice broke in, this one shrill, on the edge of panic. The words came from close behind Roselyn's shoulder. "Nay, there will be more. Much more. My cousin was at Mortain. He told me what happened there. Dead, all of them, an' this lord'll be wanting vengeance for his kin. He means to kill us, I know he does."

"Now Martha, we don't know that." Betsy's own tone faltered but she seemed intent upon calming the younger maidservant.

"We do. They be murdering scum, all of them. The Scots are heathens, barbarians, everyone knows what they be like."

"How many of our men died defending us? Was it very bad?" Roselyn reached for Betsy's arm, interrupting the gloomy conversation.

"No, milady. None are dead that I know of. Mind, there was hardly any left here to put up any resistance. The castle fell almost at once."

"No guards? None at all?" Roselyn could hardly believe they had been abandoned, left defenceless by her brother.

"Sir Alan took all his able-bodied men with him when he fled last night, leaving behind but a handful of old men or young lads, as well as the injured. Maybe it was for the best, I don't think we would have stood much of a chance even if fully garrisoned. The Scots attacked so quickly…"

"We shall be murdered, just like those poor souls at Mortain. I need to find my Edward. Have you seen him?" It was Martha again, her shrill tone betraying her mounting panic.

"Nay, lass, but I think the lads were set to work loading carts over by the stables. He'll be here soon, you'll see."

Martha was not reassured and her voice rose again to a near-hysterical shriek. "No, he's dead, I know it. I want to go to him, he might need me, He's but a boy, not yet twelve summers…"

Roselyn was jostled from behind and stumbled forward as the distraught Martha shoved her way past in search of her missing son. Roselyn clutched at thin air and would have fallen to the ground but for a strong arm encircling her waist.

"Steady, my lady. And you, get back with the others."

Roselyn regained her balance and murmured her thanks to the soldier whose quick action had saved her from ending up sprawled in the courtyard. Meanwhile Betsy seemed to be taking charge of the weeping Martha, ushering her back past Roselyn.

"Now Martha, calm yourself and stay still. You do not need to attract that guard's attention again. I can see your Edward. He's over there with my brother, John. They are both on their feet, look." She sounded exasperated, but her words seemed to penetrate Martha's rising panic. Roselyn could hear the woman's dejected weeping which had replaced her frantic screeches.

"He's only a baby," wailed Martha. "Our Rodney told me they killed even the little ones in Scotland. What's to become of any of us if this lord wants blood in exchange for those he lost?"

"He won't. I shall tell him it was none of your doing, any of you." Roselyn hoped her words would reassure her companions, though Martha continued to whimper her predictions of doom.

"Let us hope this Scottish warlord is in a mood to listen

to reason then, milady," was Betsy's final comment on the matter.

• • • • • • •

A heavy tread approached. Roselyn instinctively knew it to be the Scottish lord who had led this conquering force to such an effortless victory who now stood before her. She had to speak to him, must find a way to convince him not to harm the defenceless people huddled around her.

"Sir? My lord, I wonder—"

"Be quiet. I shall deal with ye soon enough."

More footsteps approached.

"The carts are all loaded, Laird, and ready to leave."

"Right. Apart from the drivers, bring the men and boys back to join their womenfolk then. Is everyone here, in the bailey?"

"Aye, sir. We searched all the buildings, there are none left within."

"Torch it then. I want every part of this cursed place aflame by the time we leave."

"Please, you cannot do this—" Roselyn reached for him, her fingertips brushing the leather of his jerkin.

"Can I not, madam? I disagree." His tone was unrelenting. "Mortain is burnt to the ground, still smouldering days after your brother's vicious blood-letting. Why should Etal Castle fare any better?"

"Please, these people have done you no harm. Have mercy, I beg of you."

"What does Etal know of mercy? What mercy was shown to my family? To the weak and the innocent at Mortain?" He shook his arm to dislodge her grip. "Aiden, you have your orders."

"Aye, Laird."

Roselyn cringed and hugged her stomach as the other soldier yelled his commands to their men. No part of their keep was to be spared.

"As for ye, I have unfinished business to resolve with ye, my lady. Ye may be assured that ye will regret bitterly the part ye played in the death of my sister and her family. Your hands, if you would."

"My hands? Sir…?"

"Hold them out."

"You mean to bind me?"

"Aye. Ye're a prisoner now, an' will be treated as such. Ye may consider yourself fortunate indeed that I do not drag ye behind my horse all the way back to Duncleit. Now, your hands."

Roselyn flinched as her captor bound her wrists together before her. Her restraints were tight, though not to the point of pain, but even so she felt more vulnerable and isolated than usual. Her hands were her main means of finding her way, of knowing her dark world. Without the ability to touch she was at a loss. The stern Scot who now held the power of life and death over her was unrelenting though. He grasped her bound wrists and tugged her behind him as he walked across the bailey, then she was unceremoniously lifted and tossed onto what she quickly realised must be one of the loaded carts. Instinctively Roselyn twisted her body but failed to prevent the stab of agony that shot through her ribs and winded her momentarily. She failed to stifle her cry of pain.

"Did I hurt ye, madam?" He sounded surprised. And concerned. "I apologise if I did so, 'twas not my intent."

"Nay, my lord. I was startled, is all."

"Then make yourself as comfortable as ye may. Ye have a long journey ahead."

She listened to his crisp, heavy tread as he strode away from her. As the footsteps faded Roselyn cautiously arranged herself in her new surroundings. Coarse sacking rubbed her hands as she scrabbled for something to grab hold of, and the scent of milled flour filled her nostrils. These must be supplies from the Etal stores, now pillaged and about to be carried off by the victors.

Was that what she, too, had become? The spoils of war?

No, it was worse than that. At least as an innocent captive, a hostage, she could expect decent treatment and eventual release. This harsh Highlander had a score to settle and now that he knew of her involvement he would kill her. Of that she was quite certain.

And he would be right to do so for she did not deserve any better.

"Make sure she reaches Duncleit safely. I will deal with her there. The rest of your cargo is intended to relieve Mortain. I bid you a safe journey."

"Wait! Please, wait…" He might be already gone, though Roselyn thought not. She had heard no footsteps, and could still sense his presence close by. "May I know your name?"

There was a short pause, then, "You may. I am The McGregor, Laird of Duncleit."

The McGregor. As a woman of Northumbria Roselyn was familiar with the custom north of the border for chieftains to assume the name of their clan. And of course this warlord was a McGregor, for that was the clan Lady Joan hailed from prior to her marriage.

"Where…? Where are you taking me? What about the others? Please, you cannot harm them, they are innocent, and—"

"Enough. I have said where ye are bound. You will be taken to my keep at Duncleit. There I shall establish the extent of your guilt in this matter, and the appropriate penalty."

Roselyn jerked as though he had struck her, though he laid not a hand upon her. She knew full well the extent of her culpability, and there could be but one outcome.

• • • • • • •

Roselyn became intimately acquainted with the sacks of flour and grain with which she shared the small cart. Over the next two days she clung to the rest of the cargo to gain such comfort as she might, but still she was bumped and jostled ceaselessly as the procession of loaded horse-drawn wagons made their way across the hills, lanes, and meadows of the Scottish borders. She knew they were bound first for Mortain because the Scot had said as much, there to unload the supplies retaken from Etal. He had also mentioned another destination, his keep at Duncleit. She recalled Joan having mentioned her childhood home in the Scottish Highlands but Roselyn had no idea how long the journey to reach there might take.

How much farther was this Duncleit? What manner of a place was it, and once there would she be imprisoned in the dungeons? She might be left there, forgotten until someone eventually got around to meting out the punishment she deserved. Roselyn cared not about the dark, but she hated to be cold. Most of all though she feared the vermin she could not see but imagined would scurry all over her body were she to be incarcerated below ground.

What manner of death would her captor consider fair and just? Would it be swift, a merciful end? Or might he decide to drag it out, to ensure she had the time to properly repent her misplaced and selfish act? What had possessed her to disclose to Alan details of the rich pickings to be had at Mortain Castle?

She had been desperate, not thinking straight, but regardless of her reasons, she should never have resorted to such wickedness. There was no excuse, and now she was to pay for her stupidity. She had been a fool, and others had suffered mightily for it. Even if her captor was inclined to show mercy, how could she ever forgive herself?

Roselyn lay in the cart, bewildered, disoriented, adrift from the familiar scents and sounds of Etal or Kelso. She was accustomed to her world of darkness and normally managed well enough, but she had never before been so alone and so frightened. She willed herself to remain calm, to listen, to absorb what she could of her new surroundings.

Soon her keen ear was able to discern five distinct voices

among the guards assigned to escort their small convoy, though they spoke in a tongue she could not understand. Occasionally they uttered words in English, though their dialect was almost as impossible to decipher as their native speech.

The Highland warriors treated her well enough. She had been given food, a little watered ale to drink, and allowed to leave the cart for brief periods to relieve herself in the bushes at the side of the lanes. She had no illusions that she was afforded privacy at those times. She knew that at least one of the men entrusted to guard her would be close by, but she had no choice in the matter and did what must be done. Her hands would be unbound and she was led a few paces from the cart, then instructed to be quick. She was, wasting no time in seeking comfort after the bumping and buffeting of the journey. Each time she stood and straightened her skirts a hand would take her elbow and guide her back to the cart. She would be assisted back onto her perch on the sacks, usually offered something to eat. The fare consisted of bread in the main, with occasional pieces of meat if one of the guards had managed to take any game as they made their way through the forest. A rabbit, perhaps, or a few mouthfuls of pigeon. Roselyn appreciated that they did not intend to starve her and thanked the guards for their kindness.

The only other conversation she had was with the peasant from Etal assigned to drive the cart. His name was Wilfred, and he was not known to Roselyn prior to this. In an undertone he explained that his usual labour was in the fields. He and his family lived in the village beyond the castle walls and rarely ventured within the confines of the keep itself. He appeared to harbour no real fondness or loyalty for her brother and had not been unwilling to embark on this excursion with The McGregor's men. He was unable to offer any reassurance regarding the fate of the rest of their household as their convoy had departed Etal just as the flames began to lick the base of the stable walls. He admitted he had looked back when they crested the first hill and had seen most of the castle ablaze by then. He doubted much would remain by the first nightfall.

The guards discouraged conversation so much of the journey took place in silence. Apart from when she ate or saw to her personal needs, Roselyn's hands remained bound. She knew their caution to be unnecessary, but made no protest.

They reached Mortain on the third day. The acrid stench of burning hung in the air as they approached and Roselyn shivered despite the warmth afforded by the blanket she had been given on their first night sleeping in the open. She pulled the woollen rug up to her neck and inhaled the dispiriting odour which pervaded the atmosphere all around. Mortain smelt of death, of grief and sadness and suffering. And she was responsible.

It would not have surprised her had she been hauled from the cart and handed over to the survivors of this unfortunate keep for them to exact retribution as they saw fit. That was apparently not their intent however, because the guards allowed her to remain in the cart as they, the drivers from Etal and the Mortain villagers unloaded the cargo. If any of the remaining inhabitants of that troubled settlement harboured curiosity about the presence of a captive noblewoman in their midst they did not express it, at least not in Roselyn's hearing. For the most part, she was ignored to glean what information she could from snatches of conversation and the shuffling of feet as people passed by her lonely perch.

They were soon on their way again, though she could hear no rumbling of wheels from other carts as she had on the way to Mortain. She could only surmise that all but the cart wherein Roselyn rode had been left behind at the burned-out keep. Wilfred, too, was no longer with them and one of the guards took over the reins of the small wagon. The ride was even less comfortable now that the sacks of grain were gone. Roselyn sat on the bare planks of the cart, her knees bent up by her chest and her arms hugging them. She yelped as they bounced over one particularly vicious rock in the road.

"Ye may ride up here alongside me if ye wish, lass."

Roselyn was surprised at the offer, but nodded in gratitude. The man halted the wagon and aided her onto the narrow bench at the front. It was scant improvement, but better than her previous seat.

She listened to the conversation around her, or at least those brief snatches which took place in a version of English, as the five Scotsmen continued on toward their home. From the banter which they tossed to and fro she gathered that one had a wife called Meg of whom he was heartily afraid, especially when the woman became riled, as she was inclined to on those occasions when her husband had imbibed too much fine whisky. Another was married to Agnes who was about to bear his third child. He had two daughters already and hoped for a lad this time. A third man was yet to wed, though the rest of his companions seemed to believe he had his sights set on the daughter of the ghillie who cared for the McGregor lands. Their light-hearted ribbing helped the journey to pass, though with every turn of the wheels beneath her Roselyn sensed her fate coming closer and closer.

The men slept on the ground, leaving Roselyn to herself in the cart at night. On the second night after they left Mortain the rain started, and soon settled into a cold, penetrating drizzle which drenched everything. The guard who usually sat beside her produced a length of sacking for Roselyn to wrap around herself. She was pleased and a little surprised when she felt the texture of her covering to realise that it was waxed and therefore offered decent protection from the elements. When she thanked the guard he just grunted and reminded her of their laird's instructions. She was to arrive at Duncleit safe and well, which to his mind meant ensuring she did not succumb to some ague on the way there.

At one point the cart rolled to a halt and Roselyn was helped to clamber to the ground. She stood, clutching her waxed sacking around her shoulders as she shivered in the chill northerly breeze, listening to the soft lap of waves close by and inhaling the salty tang of the sea. Gulls shrieked overhead and male voices conferred in low tones, in a tongue she could not understand. The ground beneath her feet shifted, she stood on soft sand rather than solid earth. They were at the coast.

One of the guards lifted her in his arms and set her in a boat which rocked and swayed beneath her. She huddled on the floor of the vessel as the motion became stronger, the breeze harder. The splash of oars, the sense of motion, of movement, the grunts and sighs of the oarsmen as they pulled the craft across the waves told her they were afloat, bobbing about on the water. It was the first time Roselyn had experienced such a mode of transport and she whimpered in fear, convinced that she would surely be tipped into the cold water to drown in the inky depths. This must be the end The McGregor planned for her.

"Be not afeard, lassie, we shall see ye safe across." The guard from the cart sought to reassure her. His words did little to ease Roselyn's mind, and the crossing seemed to her to be interminable.

At last, though, she was violently jolted as the bottom of the boat struck sand. The oarsman brushed past her then there was a splash as he vaulted into the water to haul the craft onto the opposite shore. The guard lifted Roselyn from the floor of the boat and carried her back onto dry land. Roselyn curled her numb fingers into the rough wool of his plaid, terrified lest he might even now drop her into the frigid deep.

He did not, and soon she found herself perched once more upon a small cart, though not the same one as that which had brought her this far. This conveyance was higher, smaller, and considerably less comfortable. Within moments they were on their way once more.

"Are we getting close to Duncleit yet?" Roselyn had resisted seeking information as the men who accompanied her clearly preferred to talk among themselves. The only words directed at her were in the main instructions or concerned her basic needs, and she was content to remain silent. But the journey seemed never-ending, she was exhausted, afraid, chilled to the bone, and every part of her ached. Surely they must be close.

"We'll be there soon enough, lass," came the taciturn response.

Roselyn huddled back within the thick plaid they had supplied for extra warmth at night and resolved to ask no more questions. What did it matter in any case? The outcome was inevitable.

"We should be there by tomorrow evening." One of the guards on horseback took pity on her. "Just one more night on the road, then we'll be at Duncleit."

"Thank you. You will be glad to be with your family again, I expect." She knew from the man's voice that it was the guard with two daughters and a third child due any day who had spoken to her.

"Aye, that I will. An' I expect ye'll be glad of a proper roof o'er yer head again, lassie."

"Yes," murmured Roselyn. "Very glad." He had not mentioned the castle dungeons, but even so, given what awaited her at Duncleit she was not sure that the road was not a better option.

• • • • • • •

They clattered across the drawbridge into the Duncleit bailey at nightfall the following evening. Roselyn knew they had arrived at their destination by the pounding of running feet and cheerful shouts of welcome from all directions. She sat on the bench at the front of the cart, her body hunched against the plummeting temperatures and such other terrors as she could not quite bring herself to imagine. Her teeth actually chattered as the soldier who had made most of the journey at her side assisted her to the ground. Her wrists were bound, as they had been for almost a week now, but Roselyn no longer noticed or cared. It was with some effort on her part that she lifted her chin and sought to absorb such clues as might be there to help her plot her new surroundings.

Voices, footsteps, the clip-clop of hooves as horses were led away to the stables, the scrape of iron on stone as the drawbridge was raised against intruders. She could not count how many people now bustled about the castle forecourt, but had the sense that this was a busy place. Roselyn stood, rooted to the spot, afraid to move in any direction.

Was he here, waiting for her? The McGregor?

"So, what's this then? Who have we here?" The woman's voice rang across the bailey and Roselyn turned in the direction from which it had come. "An' how go matters at Mortain?"

The guard checked Roselyn's bindings as he answered. "It were not good, Elspeth. Not good at all. We were too late."

"Too late? What do ye mean? The Lady Joan…?" The voice came from somewhere much closer now, slightly breathless as though the speaker had been hurrying.

"Dead, lass, an' her bairn too, along wi' her man and most o' their household. The McGregor has gone in pursuit of the murderin' villain who did it."

"All of them? All…" The woman's voice trailed off on a sob. "But how could that be? Why? Why should anyone do such a thing?"

"I dunno, lass. It were a terrible sight, I can tell ye. An' meanwhile we have a prisoner. This here's the sister o' the devil who murdered our folk an' the McGregor intends to question her hissel'. His instructions are to hold her secure until his return."

"Sister, eh? An' what might ye be knowin' about the

goings-on at Mortain, then?"

Since the question was clearly addressed to her Roselyn moistened her dry lips before attempting a reply.

"Nothing…" she began, only to break off. That was not true. She might not have been present at Mortain when the bloody deed was done, wielded no weapon herself, but without doubt she knew much more than she should about the entire affair. And here she was, in the lion's lair itself, just waiting for the great beast to return and devour her whole.

Roselyn's knees turned to jelly and she started to collapse. At once the guard caught her and held her upright. "It's been a long journey and the lass needs to rest."

"Take her to the small chamber off the laird's solar. It has a lock, an' is handy for the kitchens so I can keep an eye on 'er."

The guard seemed less than convinced. "What about the dungeons for 'er? She's The McGregor's prisoner, not 'is guest."

"The McGregor can have her moved when he gets here, if he sees fit. Come wi' me, lass an' I'll see to ye for now." The woman apparently expected her suggestion to carry the day, and indeed the guard seemed ready to defer to her. The invitation seemed genuine enough so Roselyn took a cautious step forward.

"Wait," yelled the guard who had driven the cart. "Ye'll 'ave tae lead her. She's nae sight, ye ken."

"Ach, the poor wee thing. And you wanted to shove her down in the dungeons? Shame on ye. And why is she bound up like a side o' salt pork? The lass'll be goin' nowhere."

"The McGregor's instructions. He said—"

Elspeth made a clucking sound in her throat which seemed to indicate her general contempt for her laird's orders in this matter. She tugged at the ropes binding Roselyn's wrists and in moments her hands were free.

"Thank you," murmured Roselyn, almost overcome with gratitude for the woman's kindness.

"Come wi' me, lass. We'll get ye rested, an' some decent food in ye. Then ye can tell me how all this came about."

• • • • • • •

Roselyn stirred and rolled over in the bed. She listened for a few moments, confused at the silence. No rhythmic clopping of hooves reached her ears, no raucous chatter of male voices, no rattle of wheels on the hard-packed earth. Instead she detected just stillness, peace. And blessed warmth.

Reluctant to move, still she sat up as the events of the last few days hurtled back to fill her consciousness. Etal. Mortain. Duncleit. She was safe, for now, but how long that happy circumstance might last was impossible to know.

Roselyn cocked her head to one side to listen. At first she had thought the castle to be silent, but now she realised it was not. Voices carried from outside, faint but her hearing was acute and she could discern them nonetheless. And closer, she could pick out footsteps elsewhere in the stone keep, the clank of metal as servants scurried about their tasks in the kitchens which she recalled the woman Elspeth had said were right below the chamber selected for her. Much closer still the crackle and spit of a fire in the grate.

Roselyn turned her face toward it, knowing at once she must ascertain the exact location of the blaze in this unfamiliar room. Her greatest fear was that she might inadvertently brush her skirts into the flames and set her clothing alight. She tended to avoid fires, preferring to endure the cool of the evening despite hating the cold, rather than take the risk of serious burns or even death.

As she debated whether she dared to get out of bed and explore further she was saved the trouble. Roselyn heard the lock scrape, then the sound of the door opening. She turned her wide, empty gaze in that direction.

"Ah, ye're awake then. I brought ye some more food. It's just a spot o' porridge, but warming. Even though it's still the height of summer there's a chill in the air this mornin'."

"Elspeth?" She was fairly certain she recognised the voice.

"Aye, it's me. Elspeth Brodie. I look after most things hereabouts, including the laird's prisoners now it seems. Did ye sleep well, lass?"

Despite her stark words there was no malice in the woman's tone. Roselyn believed her to be well-meaning if somewhat blunt. She nodded. "Yes. I must thank you for the comfortable chamber. Is it morning now? Have I slept the entire night through?"

"Ye have nae sight at all then? Not even light and dark?"

"No. None, I am afraid. Please, is it daylight outside?"

"It is. Ye slept all night an' half the mornin' too. Ye do look a mite better for it, though." The aroma of oats and warm milk reached her and Roselyn's stomach growled. "Ach, ye're famished. Here, let me arrange this tray on your lap."

Roselyn sat still as the woman fussed to set her breakfast before her. She had rarely enjoyed the luxury of having food brought to her chamber, and considered it ironic that she had to become a prisoner of a Scottish warlord before being afforded such treatment.

Elspeth pressed a spoon into her hand and guided her other hand onto the side of the bowl itself. "There, ye can manage for yourself now, I expect. Is the room warm enough?"

"It is, yes, but I wonder, could you tell me just where the fire is? I need to avoid getting too close…"

"Oh, o' course. Aye. Well, it be opposite the foot o' yer bed, maybe three paces. The window is to your left. The door is on the wall straight across from that, though ye'll not be needing to find your way out as ye'll be confined to this chamber." The woman paused. "How do ye normally manage?"

Roselyn took a tentative taste of her porridge. It was

stronger and richer than she was accustomed to eating, but she enjoyed the earthy flavour. "This is good. Thank you." She laid down her spoon. "I like to explore my surroundings, by touch mainly, and contrive to commit every detail to memory. As long as nothing is moved afterwards, I can get by. In a strange room though, or where there are a lot of people… I become confused."

"I see. I shall arrange to have a screen placed before the fire so ye need not be afraid as ye move about in here. Then ye may set to exploring this chamber."

"That is very kind. Thank you."

"They said ye had something to do wi' what happened. Over there at Mortain. Is that right?" The woman's tone had hardened, the change barely perceptible but Roselyn's hearing was acute, and she was sensitive to such subtleties. She had to be.

The porridge turned into a lump in her stomach as Roselyn nodded. The woman's kindness would be short-lived when she learnt the awful extent of Roselyn's culpability.

"An' that'll be why The McGregor has taken ye prisoner, then?"

"Yes. He… he will…"

"He's a fair man, though 'tis true that he adored his sister. We all did, she was a sweet girl an' will be mourned by all here."

"I know," whispered Roselyn. "I'm sorry. So sorry."

"Ye'll have to tell your tale to our laird, it's him you need to convince. But if you want to start by telling me how this all came about, maybe that will help. A chance to think through just what ye need to say to him."

Roselyn was puzzled, and wary. "Why would you do that? Why would you wish to help me if you loved Lady Joan too?"

"Because I'm no fool an' I reckon I know people well enough. It seems to me that all is not as it seems here, an' I wish to know the truth afore making up my mind. Our laird will too, so the clearer that truth is to ye, the better your chance of makin' him see it. I would nae wish him to make a bad decision in anger an' live to regret it."

Roselyn hung her head, desolate. "I do not believe it will make any difference, whatever I say to him. He will order me to be killed, might even do it himself. It… It is what I deserve."

"Only the good Lord knows what each of us truly deserves, lass. If you wish to talk, I'll be right glad tae hear your story."

"Thank you." Roselyn meant it. Already she ached to unload her story on someone who might actually listen, though she doubted that she could ever convince the fearsome clan chief to show mercy, even if she was minded to plead for such.

"So, ye'll be finishing your breakfast then. I need to be getting on but I shall be back later, for the bowl an' we can talk then if ye wish it. An' I'll bring ye some warm clothes to wear—your flimsy English gown will be nae use to ye here."

Footsteps and the firm click of the door closing marked the woman's exit. Roselyn returned to her breakfast with a heavy sigh. Despite the dire circumstances in which she found herself the porridge was still good and she ate the wholesome fare with an enthusiasm she had not experienced for weeks.

· · · · · · ·

"So, ye were at the root o' the killin' at Mortain then? How so, lass?" Elspeth did not hesitate to come to the point. As well as decent food she had returned to Roselyn's lonely chamber with warm clothing as well as a few necessaries for Roselyn's comfort—aired water to wash in, and even a porcelain pot for her more personal needs. The Duncleit cook appeared to consider these kindnesses entitled her to be blunt, and Roselyn could find no reason to dispute that logic.

"I was. I am. I wish… I wish it were not so."

"What's done is done, lass. So, tell me how this came about." The woman settled on the edge of Roselyn's bed, clearly in no rush to leave.

"I do not know where to start." Roselyn brought her knees up to her chin and leaned forward. She started as her companion patted her leg.

"Sorry, lass, I didna mean tae startle ye. Is it all right to touch ye?"

"Of course, yes. I just… I was not expecting it, is all."

Elspeth cupped Roselyn's knee and squeezed. "Just start at the beginnin' and we'll see where that gets us tae, shall we?"

Roselyn nodded. "My brother is Alan, Earl of Ingram. It was he and his soldiers who attacked the castle at Mortain."

"I ken that, lass."

"He did it because I told him there was gold there, wealth to be stolen. He… My brother is in dire need of coin because he owes money to the king. The Duke of Gloucester, brother to Edward of England, had become most insistent that the debt be repaid to help finance the costs of the border wars with Scotland. Alan was desperate and he arranged a marriage for me to one of the Percys. The husband he selected is John of Hexham, a half-brother to the duke, a man of forty-five summers who has been wed twice already but both his wives died in childbirth. He was willing to overlook my obvious flaws in return for a young and he assumed fertile bride, and would even forgo the usual dowry. Alan was determined upon the match. He saw it as the means to secure an alliance with the Percys and thus bring about a shift in his fortunes. But first he had to placate Gloucester and the king, and to do so he required funds."

"I take it the match was not tae yer likin'?"

Roselyn shook her head, emphatic. "John of Hexham is a brute, a vile man. My brother came to Kelso, the priory where I normally reside, and he told me of the match. I pleaded with Alan to select a different husband for me if I must wed, but he would not shift. Sir John holds sway with Northumberland so his brother-in-law Alan would be able to draw on his support. My brother is an ambitious man, and power-hungry. A female relative, even a blind one who has spent the last several years in the cloister, is a commodity to be bartered and he would not listen to me. So… I struck a bargain with him."

"A bargain?"

Roselyn nodded, and made no move to check the tears which streamed down her cheeks. "I offered my brother information in exchange for his agreement to release me from the betrothal to Sir John. I used his need for money as leverage, and told him I knew where he might acquire a small fortune in gold." She paused, drew in several shaky breaths, then continued. "Of course, he seized on this information and demanded I provide the details. Immediately I regretted my offer and I refused to tell him what he wanted to know. I even agreed to marry the repulsive Sir John if he would drop the matter, but he just laughed and told me that the wedding was to take place within the month whatever I might wish. I had betrayed my friend and played into his greedy hands, and for naught."

"Your friend? You refer to the Lady Joan?"

"I do, though she was perhaps more of an acquaintance. We met a few times as children and Lady Joan visited us at Kelso Priory on occasions, most recently to pray for the safe delivery of her son. She was kind enough to read to me during the evenings whilst she was under our roof and I very much enjoyed her company. We spoke, and she confided that her husband was so delighted with the news of her pregnancy that he had gifted her the entire sum of her dowry. She told me the fifty gold crowns remained untouched even after two years of marriage and that she intended to bestow a proportion of it on Kelso Priory as a mark of her gratitude for the holy sisters' prayers and good wishes."

"So that is how you became aware of the wealth stored at Mortain. Yet, ye say you refused to share that knowledge with your brother?"

"I did, but once he became fixated on the prospect of acquiring the gold he was having none of that. He was aware of my acquaintance with Lady Joan, and he knew that I had spent time at Mortain as a child so might claim familiarity with the layout of the keep there, all of which lent weight to the notion that I was indeed privy to the details I had claimed to know. He became quite… insistent."

"He threatened you?"

Roselyn nodded. "He not only threatened me. He beat me too. I was on the floor and he was kicking me, screaming at me to tell him the secrets of Mortain. I believed he would actually kill me before he was done, but he suddenly stopped. My ribs were broken, I am certain of it. I could hardly breathe for a week, and every movement was agony. He had not given up though, simply changed tack. He threatened to harm the holy sisters instead, swearing he would burn down the convent with me and the sisters locked within if I did not tell him exactly where to find the coins. I… I could not allow that to happen. So, I told him what he wanted to know."

"You say you visited Mortain when you were younger and knew the castle, which was why you could describe just where to find the coins? Why did you go there?"

"Alan and I share a father, but we have different mothers. My mother's kin, the Beauchamps, lived just a mile or so from Mortain and I would spend time with them as a child. The Beauchamps were regular visitors to the castle, and I would accompany them. I played with the castle children, including Lady Joan when she was there, and we would explore all the secret places. I recall the cellars quite vividly. There were storerooms and butteries filled with wondrous things and we loved to play chasing and hiding games in the dark and winding corridors. One day I was down there with Lady Joan and we observed Sir Edmund and his father moving through the rooms. We followed them and watched as they unlocked the door to the strong room beneath the stairs at the end of the buttery. It was the day of Lady Margaret's death, and of Edmund and Joan's betrothal. The laird opened the secret chamber because he had gold plate secreted there and intended to make a betrothal gift of it to the McGregors. Later, when Joan told me of her dowry, I surmised that if her husband did indeed have fifty gold coins within his keep it was most likely kept in that strong room. And I was right."

"And this is what you told to your brother? You gave him directions to find Lady Joan's money?"

"I was scared, convinced he would set light to the priory. But that is no excuse. I know I should never have breathed a word of Lady Joan's confidences to me. I should have just obeyed my brother and agreed to wed Sir John, and if I had done so Mortain would have remained untouched. But I swear, even in his greed and avarice, I never contemplated that my brother would perform such a bloody act. I expected him to attack the castle and force his way in to seize the gold. I never imagined he might... he might..."

Roselyn buried her face in her hands and gave way to sobbing. "Oh, dear Lord, what have I done. I am sorry, and if there was anything, anything at all that I might do to atone for the harm I have caused I would do it gladly. But there is nothing, nothing I can do to bring back those who are lost."

CHAPTER THREE

It was a weary band of McGregors who clattered into the bailey at Duncleit, their laird riding at the head of his men. Blair dismounted by the stables and tossed the reins to the bleary-eyed lad who came stumbling from the hayloft to greet them. Others followed on the boy's heels and soon all the men were walking toward the keep, their mounts in safe hands.

"We missed him this time, Blair, but we shall have the bastard. Eventually." Aiden uttered the words with deadly certainty, a sentiment shared by his laird.

"Aye, I shall not rest until that vicious cur has paid in blood for the evil he has done. We paid out enough in bribes, and promised far more for information if and when he dares to slink back to his seat in Etal. There's little enough loyalty for him thereabouts, someone will come forth and tell us."

"They will, sir, we can be sure if it."

"And meanwhile… ah, here is Robbie to greet us." Blair paused to hug the older man and smiled at his heartfelt welcome home. "'Tis good to be back, Robbie. Is all well here?"

"Aye, Laird. All is quiet."

"Good. And did my prisoner arrive all right?"

"Ye mean the borders lass? Aye, she's been here this last sennight."

"I'll take a bite to eat, then I'd like you to bring her up to my solar. I daresay a week in our dungeons will have impressed upon her that I mean business, if such were needed."

"Dungeon, sir? I wasnae aware ye expected her tae be in the dungeons."

Blair halted mid-stride. "She's a fucking prisoner, an enemy, seized in connection with the murder of my kin and likely to die for her crime. Where else would she be kept?"

"Er, well, ye see, Elspeth—"

"Elspeth?" Blair growled the servant's name. "How in the name of God does my cook come into this? At what stage did I appoint Elspeth Brodie custodian of my prisoners?"

"Now, Laird, ye know how she can be. It's not easy to gainsay our Elspeth."

"But *my* orders can be disregarded at will? Is that it?" Blair rounded on the hapless captain of his guards. "Am I not The McGregor? Am I not master here?"

"Aye, but—"

"Where is she then? If not safely ensconced in chains in my fucking dungeon, where may I ask has this English wench been housed?"

"In the guest chamber, sir. The one leading off your solar. Elspeth thought—"

"Elspeth thought? It seems to me that Elspeth thinks, and presumes, far too much." He raked his fingers through his hair, dragging the inky black strands back from his forehead. "I want food, then have the girl brought before me. She shall soon be set straight as to her status here. Guest chamber indeed." He stalked off into the keep, his temper barely in check as he took the stairs leading to his private quarters. Once there he glared at the door to the small guest chamber and seriously contemplated kicking it off its hinges. He might have succumbed to the temptation but for the timely intervention of the female he had placed second on the list of women with whom he had scores to settle.

Elspeth entered the room without knocking, bearing a tray of cold meats, bread, and various cheeses. One of her bevy of kitchen wenches followed bearing a jug of ale, and a panting lad dragged a large wooden bathtub across the floor.

"'Tis good tae see ye home, sir. I have food here, and ale, and I shall have water brought up that ye may bathe." She addressed him with a wide smile as though nothing at all was amiss. One would think for all the world that this infernal woman had not taken advantage of his absence to tuck up his despised enemy in the guest quarters next to his own. What on earth had possessed her?

"Put the food and drink down. I'll bathe later. For now I'll be knowin' what ye're thinkin' of, setting up that treacherous English wench in my solar? Were my instructions nae sufficiently clear?"

"I wasnae aware of any instructions, sir. I merely acted as I believed to be right. The lass has been ill-used."

"Has she? Has she indeed? Well, I daresay she shall feel somewhat more beset by the time I am done with her."

"Ye should hear her side of it afore ye take any action, Blair. There be more tae this tale than meets the eye. That lass is as much a victim of her brother as the rest of 'em."

He considered taking issue with his servant's use of his given name but decided to let that go on this occasion. He was not about to be deflected from the matter at hand. "I hardly think so. If she was, then she would also be lying dead, buried with the rest beneath the good green earth."

"If it were up tae her brother then I daresay she would be. He beat the poor lass near enough senseless, did ye ken that?"

Blair paused as he reached for the ale jug. "He did what? Why?"

"Ye need tae be askin' her that. Shall I fetch the wee

lassie in now?"

He poured himself a mug of the frothy ale and drank deeply, as much to allow himself a moment to collect his thoughts as to quench his thirst. "Thank you, but I daresay I can manage to locate the wench. You may leave, Elspeth."

"Now, Blair, I—"

"Elspeth, please be so good as to close the door on your way out." He fixed her with a stony glare, and thankfully that was sufficient incentive to convince the meddling cook that he meant what he said. She bobbed him a quick curtsy and scuttled from the room, though she omitted to close the door.

Bloody woman! He slammed it shut himself, then stalked across the room to the door leading to the small guest chamber wherein Lady Roselyn, sister to the Earl of Ingram, awaited his pleasure.

• • • • • • •

"Elspeth? Is that you?" The wench sat on the edge of her narrow bed and swung her blank gaze in the direction of the door as he opened it.

Blair regarded her in silence for a few moments. By the saints, but she was lovely, especially with her beautiful dark blond hair uncovered and falling in loose waves about her shoulders. The sunlight pouring through the window played across the golden tresses, bringing out the titian highlights. Her features were delicate, but he had noticed that on first meeting her on the steps at Etal castle. He did not, however, recall that her mouth was quite so full, nor her brows so elegantly arched. And the lavender-blue of her sightless eyes was quite wondrous, he decided. Neither had he properly appreciated the slender curve of her waist, nor the gentle swell of her breasts beneath the snug woollen gown she now wore. The deep aqua colour suited her. It somehow deepened the shade of her eyes and complemented her lustrous hair.

"Elspeth?" she repeated. Her tone was nervous, apprehensive.

"Nay, 'tis I. The McGregor. We need to talk."

She scrambled to her feet. "Of course, my lord. I... I am ready."

Blair doubted that. "Are ye?"

"Yes, my lord. I heard the clatter of hooves, voices, and I was sure that you must have returned. I was expecting you to send for me."

"Send for ye? An' why would I be needin' tae send for ye when ye are right here, takin' yer ease i' my private apartments?"

"Oh." She appeared nonplussed by his observation.

"Ye did nae ken where ye be?" Blair pressed her for a response.

The girl before him paled visibly, then proceeded to gnaw on her lower lip, becoming more agitated by the second. Blair's patience was thin already, his temper simmering dangerously, and the Sassenach wench seemed to be taking an inordinate amount of time in answering even the most basic of questions. He had far weightier matters to address with this conniving little English bitch, as she would soon learn.

"Answer me, Sassenach." he demanded.

The strangely alluring lavender eyes widened, their colour deepening to a glorious shade of amethyst. Tears streamed unchecked down her cheeks and she stepped back, her fear evident. "I cannot... Please, I do not understand..."

"What are ye blatherin' about, wench? 'Tis a simple enough question. Do ye ken where ye are?"

"My lord...? What...? I do not understand your speech. Please, is there someone—?"

"What?" Blair peered at her, only now starting to comprehend her dilemma. "Have ye no' heard a Highland brogue afore, lass?"

His prisoner shook her head, her expression uncertain

as she continued to chew on her lip and wring her hands though she did appear to have at least grasped the meaning of his last question as she had managed to answer him. Blair was raised in the Highlands and among those in his household he usually spoke the native Gaelic. He would not have expected an English noblewoman to understand that tongue so had addressed her in English, though with no attempt to modulate his dialect. Clearly his speech was incomprehensible to the girl.

Blair drew a deep breath. He was a Highlander but far from uneducated. He could draw on a more orthodox form of speech though rarely found it necessary to do unless called upon to present himself at court. However if he was to have any sense out of this prisoner he would need to at least make himself understood.

"I asked, did you not know where in my castle you had been housed?" He spoke to her more slowly, enunciating the words with care.

Comprehension dawned in her beautiful eyes and she shook her head. "I was brought to this chamber by Elspeth. I never thought to ask…"

"No matter. We will talk in my solar. Come."

"Sir?" She remained where she was.

Blair stepped forward and took her hand. He placed her fingers on his arm just as he had in the bailey at Etal and led her from the small chamber into his much larger solar. He considered inviting her to sit, but reminded himself just in time that she was his prisoner and guilty of a heinous act of greed and treachery. She could bloody well stand in his presence.

He disengaged her fingers from his sleeve and slumped into the heavy oak chair which he preferred. He stretched out his long legs and considered his next move. Elspeth had been keen that he talk to the wench, and despite his irritation with the cook who had served his family for as long as he could remember he was accustomed to heeding her advice.

He dispensed with any preamble. "Tell me what happened at Mortain, and your part in the affair."

"Sir?"

"You have a story to tell, I gather. Now is your chance, Lady Roselyn. I advise you not to squander it as you may not be afforded another opportunity to be heard."

The girl drew in a breath, tipped up her chin in a manner he found engaging rather than defiant, and she began to speak.

Blair listened, for the most part in silence. He prompted occasionally, seeking clarification here, more detail there, but in the main he allowed her to explain the circumstances in her own way. Eventually she was silent. He was too as he considered the account she had given.

He leaned forward, his elbows on his thighs. "You say you watched my cousin and uncle open the strong room to remove valuables from there, and that is how you knew where the secret chamber was located. You were not always without sight, then?"

"No, my lord. I lost my sight four years ago in an accident. I fell from my palfrey and hit my head on a rock. I lay unconscious for two days, and when I regained my senses I could not see. My brother's physicians could find no cause for my blindness, but it is a fact."

"That must have been hard to accept." His sympathy was genuine. Blair could not even start to imagine losing his own sight.

"Yes, at first. But it was the will of God. I have accepted my lot and I have adapted."

Blair nodded. Privately he could not help but admire her resilience. "And your brother beat you, you say?"

Roselyn nodded. "He did, and he threatened to put Kelso priory to the torch. I truly believed that he would do so…"

"And this is why you sent him to Mortain? To save yourself and your priory?"

She was sobbing now, her features stricken. "I am sorry.

I bitterly regret what I did, and what happened as a result. If I had known, if I could have imagined…" She brushed away her tears and lifted her chin once more. "I truly had no notion, none at all, that my brother would be so brutal, so ruthless. There was no need, and—"

"On that we agree. Your brother's brutality was beyond belief, but as his sister, his closest relative, you surely knew him well enough to have anticipated it."

"I did not, I swear it. Alan and I are not close. We are half-siblings and have rarely lived together, and although I know him to be self-serving and lacking in either kindness or empathy, I had never known him to be violent or cruel. Not until recently, at least. His debts have weighed heavily upon him I fear."

"Indeed. And that is what passes a justification for such an act, does it, my lady?"

"Of course not. I did not mean to imply such a thing. I just… I want you to believe that I regret what has happened and if there was anything I could do to help make it right I would do it, my lord. I do not seek to excuse his actions, or mine, but I would hope you will at least be able to understand why I acted as I did. I have no evidence to offer you though, just my word. And I realise you have no cause to accept my account alone."

Blair stroked his chin, replaying the events at Etal in his mind. Some details which had puzzled him then were starting to make sense.

"There is evidence, or there might be. You have said that your brother knocked you to the ground and kicked you, injuring your ribs. This took place at Kelso? Were there witnesses to the assault?"

"Yes, of course. The prioress herself was present. The Reverend Mother pleaded with Alan to cease but he ignored her. She was kind enough to care for me afterwards though, once he had left. She aided me to my bed and prepared poultices for my injuries."

"I see. Kelso is almost a week's ride from here,

however."

Roselyn bowed her head, her expression bleak. "I know. 'Tis too far away. And I was there for only a short time after in any case. My brother sent men to escort me back to Etal two days after he attacked me. By then though he had already left for Mortain. He returned briefly to Etal, but fled as soon as he learnt of your approach. You know the rest."

"How many days prior to my arrival at Etal did the attack on you take place?"

"It happened almost a sennight earlier, my lord."

"You were still in pain when we met. You screamed when I put you on the cart. I thought I had hurt you, but in truth it was the result of the battering you had from your brother, was it not?"

"Yes, my lord. I was still quite sore."

"Why did you not say so at the time?"

"I… I did not dare to, my lord. You were so angry, so terrifying…"

"I am only slightly less angry now."

"It… does not seem so, my lord. And Elspeth said that you would be fair and hear my story."

He let that comment go unremarked. "So, the beating was what, near enough three weeks ago now? Is that correct?"

"Yes, sir."

"If your injuries pained you so badly and left you struggling for breath your ribs might have been cracked. At the very least there would have been severe bruising, however effective the Reverend Mother's poultices."

"I suppose that is true, my lord. It certainly felt so though of course I could not see it."

"But I could. There is a possibility that the marks might still be upon your body."

"My lord?"

"I shall have to trouble you to remove your gown, Roselyn. And your shift. I require you naked to the waist."

Her eyes darkened to a shade close to violet. "I cannot.

You cannot ask that of me."

"I am not asking. It is not a request, it is a command. You will remove your clothing, or I shall summon a couple of my guards and they will remove it for you." He stood and reached for her thin shoulder. Apart from offering her his arm to lead her into the solar this was the first time he had touched her and he was oddly pleased that despite her predicament and obvious fear she did not shrink away from him. He squeezed gently. "I do not intend to harm you, Roselyn, and this will be easier for you if just the two of us are present. If you require assistance I shall be pleased to aid you."

She turned her face in his direction. "You really believe there might still be bruises."

"It is possible, aye. Shall we find out?" He deliberately gentled his tone, sensing that she was willing to do even this if it would help to bolster her case.

There was a brief pause. She chewed on her lower lip and twisted her fingers nervously. Moments passed, then she raised her face to grant him a tremulous smile. "Very well, my lord. Thank you."

"Thank you?"

"For your offer of aid. I believe I shall require it for my hands are shaking."

Fuck. He took no pleasure in that knowledge, though why he should care was beyond him. Blair turned her to face him and with a few deft movements untied the laces which held her kirtle closed at the neck. The garment was simple enough, and practical. He was glad of that as he separated the two halves and slid it off her shoulders and down her arms. Beneath she wore just a woollen leine, loose enough not to require any fastenings. The lower portion disappeared into the skirts of her kirtle, still held at the waist by her belt made of plaited leather. Blair loosened the belt to free the fabric beneath, then pulled the leine up out of the confines of her outer clothing. Despite her acquiescence Roselyn made a grab for the garment as he started to lift it higher.

Blair paused. "Roselyn?"

She released her grip on the soft wool and raised her arms obediently in order to allow him to draw it over her head. She was naked beneath.

She was his enemy, but that was no reason not to speak his mind. Blair made no pretence of not observing what was displayed before him.

"You are quite lovely, Lady Roselyn."

She gulped and laid her hands over the plump mounds. "Please…" she whispered.

He leaned in to murmur in her ear. "Do not be afraid. I mean you no harm here. I will touch you now, and if I hurt you, you must say so. Do you understand?"

"Yes, sir." Her lovely eyes were closed and she continued to worry her lower lip between her small white teeth. Despite his reassurances she was plainly terrified. The view was delightful but even so he opted to conclude their business as quickly as he might.

"Turn to the right, if you please, to better catch the light from the window." Not that he particularly required the benefit of improved illumination; the yellows and faint purplish smudges on her skin were plain to see. Blair was familiar with injuries acquired in battle and in training. He had sustained enough himself and had no difficulty in recognising the remnants of a severe battering. Both sides of her slender torso were similarly marked from just below her arms almost to her waist. He could not accurately date the original attack, but saw no cause to dispute her account of it.

He stroked the contours of her ribs on her left side, careful to exert no pressure. Even so, she winced. "Does it still pain ye, lass?"

"Your hands are cold, my lord."

Blair chuckled. "Ah, I apologise." He stepped around to better examine the right side also. This time when he laid his fingers on her she remained still.

"Are there bruises, my lord?"

"Aye, there are."

"Then this will prove my account? You believe me?"

"It helps, without doubt. 'Tis a pity we have no witness to support your story, though I daresay I could dispatch men to Kelso to question the Reverend Mother."

"You would do that?"

He was surprised to realise that he would. Indeed he would, for he found he badly wanted to prove the mitigating circumstances which might help excuse Lady Roselyn's actions. He was not a fool, Blair knew his people well. He would have to present convincing evidence of coercion in order to satisfy the members of Clan McGregor who would demand retribution for the deaths of their kinsfolk. As matters stood they would expect him to hang the English wench and would consider that a merciful end. It might yet come to that, but despite his earlier intentions he now found he had no real stomach for heaping his vengeance upon this fragile wench.

His real quarry was her brother, the earl. He would have no hesitation whatsoever in killing him.

Was it her blindness? Had he allowed that to affect his judgement? He thought not though her vulnerability brought out some protective instinct in him. That would not be enough to save her though, not if he deemed her truly culpable. At this moment he was simply not sure. Maybe he did need to send men to Kelso.

"There were witnesses at Etal also." Roselyn's words broke into his thoughts. "I was still in a lot of pain when I returned to my brother's keep. Our steward assisted me to my chamber when I first arrived as I was unable to manage the stairs, and Betsy attended me there."

"Betsy?"

"One of our servants. Elspeth reminds me of her, a little. But Betsy cannot help me either, not from beyond the grave."

"She is dead?"

"You should know, you had her killed along with the rest of our household."

"I beg your pardon?"

"You had them all assembled in the bailey in order that your men could cut them down." Roselyn choked back a sob. "She did not deserve that. None of them did."

"I agree."

"Then why? You warlords are all the same and you, sir, are no better than my brother."

He regarded her through narrowed eyes. "Have a care, madam, lest I lose my patience with you after all. Your servants are not dead, or if they are it was not my doing. I offered them a choice, that is all."

"A choice? What choice did you put before them?"

"We set Etal to the torch, you know that."

"Yes," she responded bitterly. He noted that despite her obvious distress she did not relinquish the pressing business of shielding her luscious breasts from his view. Perhaps he might insist…

He quashed that impulse. He would not ill-treat his prisoner out of annoyance at her harsh judgement of his honour. "I offered those who wished it the choice of remaining at Etal to rebuild their homes. Some opted for that and we left them some supplies to see them through the coming lean weeks. It will be hard, but their survival is in their own hands." He paused to regard her stunned expression with a degree of satisfaction. "It was a better option than that granted to my people by your brother."

"You left them there? Alive?"

"Aye, some. Those who wished to remain. I also offered your people the choice of going to Mortain to make new homes there. It would be several days' journey, but the land there is fertile and will support them if they are prepared to work hard. I believe that the majority found that an attractive proposition. They will have reached their new home by now."

"Oh."

He was gratified to have near-enough silenced the little English wench. But he was not yet done. "There was a third option, that of making the long and rather more arduous journey to Duncleit. Those who choose to make the trip will find a welcome here."

"Here, my lord? You invited people from Etal to come *here*?" If she had seemed surprised before she was utterly incredulous now.

"Aye, we can always use willing workers in the Highlands."

"But it is much too far, and in unknown terrain. How would they even find this place?"

"They have directions, and they can ask those they meet along the route. Duncleit is well known."

"Directions? You mean some would actually contemplate it? They would attempt to make their way here, across the whole of Scotland, on foot?"

"They are made of stern stuff, your countrymen, more so perhaps than you give them credit for. And yes, a group did decide to make the attempt."

"But—"

"We passed them as we made our return from Alnwick where we lost your brother's trail. There were perhaps six or eight, two families as far as I could tell though I did not enquire closely. They had reached the southern shore of Loch Lomond when we caught up to them."

"How much farther…?"

"They had covered perhaps half the distance and it had taken them over a sennight."

"They will never make it. 'Tis too far…"

"I am not so sure. We left them a horse and coin with which to purchase a cart, as well as food. I believe we could expect them within two days, three at the most. If they are not here by then I shall send out men in search of them."

"You would do that, for your enemies?"

"They are not my enemies now that they no longer serve Ingram. When they decided to come to Duncleit they shifted their allegiance to me. They are *my* people now and I look after my own."

"You regard me as your enemy, yet you have been kind enough to hear my case."

He moved around to stand in front of her and cupped her chin in his palm. "I am not certain how I regard you, Lady Roselyn. The coming days will be telling, for us both." He lowered his face and brushed a kiss across her hair. "Do you require my aid to replace your clothing?" He could not believe he was actually offering to help her dress.

"I would, sir, but first... may I make a request?"

"A request? Aye, ye may ask, though I may not grant it."

"You have seen me, rather more of me, in fact, than any man has before. I wonder, may I see you?"

"See me, madam? I do not understand."

"With my hands? My fingers? If you would allow me to touch your face I might explore your features and form a picture of you in my mind."

"You wish to touch me?"

"It is intimate, I understand that. Some people are uncomfortable with it so if you prefer that I do not..."

"I shall make a bargain with you, my lady." He knew he was about to take outrageous advantage of his prisoner but somehow he was beyond caring. "A bargain based upon fair exchange."

"Please explain your terms, sir."

"You may explore my face to your complete satisfaction, and indeed any other part of my person should you feel so moved, but I expect the same in return. You will allow me to touch you in like manner."

"My face?"

"Aye, your face. And your shoulders, your back, your breasts, your belly. But I shall not venture below your skirts unless you invite me to do so. Do we have a bargain, madam?"

"I am still a little sore..." God's sweet bones, she was about to agree. His cock lurched within his braies, tenting the soft linen of his underwear. He adjusted his woollen hose accordingly, somewhat relieved that she was unable to observe his response to her.

"I shall not hurt you, I swear it." He kept his voice low and gentle, determined not to alarm her now.

She hesitated, but only for a few moments. "Very well, sir. I accept your terms."

He lowered his face to kiss her again, this time on her forehead. Then he cradled her face between his palms as he brushed his mouth over hers. Her lips parted on a small gasp but she made no protest.

Blair stepped back toward the chair he vacated minutes earlier, drawing Roselyn with him. She followed, her trust precious to him. He located the oak seat and sank into it, pulling her into his lap.

"Please feel free to make your explorations, my lady."

"You will remain quite still? It is better if you do not move, or speak."

"Very well."

He sat, immobile, as she lifted her hands to lay them on his cheeks. She used just her fingertips at first, drawing them slowly over the planes and hollows of his face. She caressed his jaw, his forehead, his chin, and his lips. Her eyes remained closed, her brow furrowed in concentration as she learnt the details of his features.

"You are handsome," she announced at last. "You have a strong jaw and a firm mouth, and I find a small cleft in your chin. I believe you to be a man accustomed to command though you are younger than I had assumed."

"I am thirty years old."

"How long have you been laird here?"

"The last eight years."

"You wear your authority with ease, my lord. May I ask what colour are your eyes? And your hair?"

"My eyes are blue and my hair near enough black."

"You have long eyelashes, for a man, that is." She feathered her touch over his eyelids before running her fingers through his shoulder-length locks. "And your hair, too. You have no beard though there are whiskers here." She scraped her fingers over his jaw.

"I prefer to be clean-shaven, though I have had no opportunity to address the matter since Alnwick."

"I am keeping you from seeking your comfort."

Blair groaned. If she but knew. "No, madam, you are not. Not exactly. Can I assume, since you have asked me questions, that I may now speak? Have you formed your impressions?"

"Yes, sir. Thank you for your patience."

"You are most welcome. Now, it is my turn."

Her response was a brief nod. She lifted her hands to cover her naked breasts again. Blair allowed himself a smile; he would soon deal with her modesty.

"I would like you to turn slightly and rest against me. You may lean on my shoulder. And place your hands behind your back, if you would."

She hesitated for but a moment, then her eyes remained closed as she arranged herself as directed. Blair was pleased at her ready obedience, he loved a woman to accept his commands. He especially appreciated such an attitude from a half-naked woman lying in his arms.

He started at her throat, caressing the slender column briefly before he once more kissed her lips. She appeared to enjoy the experience for she opened her mouth and poked the tip of her tongue out to moisten her soft lips. Blair groaned inwardly before he leaned in to lend his efforts to hers by licking her lower lip. After all, he had not promised to only touch her with his fingers.

"Oh." She let out a startled exclamation, but that was as far as the protest went.

Blair deepened the kiss, slipping his tongue between her lips when she parted them to allow him entry. He twisted it around hers, intrigued at the manner in which she returned his enthusiasm. He was willing to bet the little Sassenach had never been kissed before and she appeared to rather like the new experience.

He cupped her full breast in his hand and squeezed gently. She arched her back, thrusting the plump mound against his palm. He shifted the angle a little, enough that he could brush her budding nipple with his fingers. It hardened at his touch, swelling and lengthening. He took it between his finger and thumb and pressed, soft at first, then harder. She made a purring sound in her throat and Blair wondered that she did not feel his cock, the hard length solid against her hip. Maybe she did but had no notion what it might be. Was she indeed so innocent?

He switched his attention to her other breast to bring the nipple there to the same state of pebbled arousal. He dragged his mouth from hers to work his way down her neck and shoulder, to fasten his lips around one swollen pink bud. He flicked it with his tongue then scraped with his teeth.

Roselyn writhed in his arms, but still she kept her hands behind her back and remained in the position he had set for her.

He shifted to suck on the other nipple whilst maintaining the pressure with his fingers. He squeezed harder, but relaxed his grip when she stiffened. He had sworn not to hurt her, though he sensed ambivalence in her response. Some women enjoyed pain, just as he enjoyed inflicting it on a willing female. He feasted on their submission, relished their freely offered surrender. Was Lady Roselyn of such a bent? It was early in their acquaintance, he barely knew her, but he sensed she might be.

He trailed moist kisses across her stomach until he reached the barrier of her leather belt, still secured about her narrow waist. He ached to loosen it, to shove the remaining fabric of her kirtle down her hips and away. He desired unfettered access to her body, but the choice must be hers. And despite her obvious pleasure in his touch, it was too soon to ask more of her. Worse, she might mistake his desire for coercion. He could not forget that he held her life in his hands as well as her body, and he would do well not to confuse matters further than he already had.

"Roselyn, would you like me to aid you to get dressed?"

"My lord?" Her eyelids flickered as she turned her lavender gaze on him. "Is that…? I mean, are we finished?"

"Finished? I doubt that, my wee Sassenach. But for now it will have to be sufficient."

"Please, what does that word mean? What do you intend to do to me?"

"Be easy, 'tis not a threat. Sassenach is merely a Gaelic word. Here in the Highlands we use it to mean a lowlander or English."

She nodded slowly. "I understand. It is not a pleasant word, I think?"

"No, not entirely," he conceded though he was damned if he would offer an apology for any perceived insult. She was still his prisoner, even if her situation was more complicated than he had initially assumed. "We still have much to resolve, you and I."

He eased his arm behind her to help her into a sitting position then stood with Roselyn in his arms. He set her feet down on the oak floor and held her until she steadied. "Remain there. I shall retrieve your undergarment."

She stood quite still as he pulled her leine back into place and eased it under the waist fastening of her skirts. Then he rearranged the bodice of her kirtle before refastening the ties at her throat. He had barely finished when there was a knock at the door.

"Come," he commanded.

Elspeth entered. "Do you require more food, Laird? Shall I have the hot water sent up for your bath?"

"What? Nay, I'm nae hungry. But I shall have the bathwater, if ye would." What had he been thinking, pawing at Lady Roselyn like some randy farm lad while still covered in the grime of his travels across the country?

"Robbie tells me that the poor wee lassie is tae be removed tae the dungeons. Ye'll be requirin' guards, then tae take her down there?"

The startled gasp from his prisoner was not lost on Blair. Mentally he cursed the cook. "Nay, no guards will be necessary. Lady Roselyn may remain in the chamber ye selected for her, at least for the time being."

"Ah, well, that's all right then. Mind, if she's tae be spendin' her time in here too we shall be needin' a screen across the fire. The lassie is nervous around flames."

Blair looked from one female to the other as he tried to work out just where he had managed to lose control of the situation. He abandoned the effort and waved his hand at Elspeth. "See to it, would ye?"

CHAPTER FOUR

Roselyn was nothing short of baffled by The McGregor. He reminded her constantly that she was his prisoner, yet he permitted her the freedom of his quarters. Despite the intimacies which had occurred between them during his initial interrogation he had not touched her since. He was polite, courteous, concerned for her comfort and safety but no more than that.

Following Elspeth's remark the fire screen was installed at once, and thus reassured she had explored every inch of the solar. She now knew the lord's chamber intimately. She knew where her captor kept his writing implements, his clothing, his sword belt when he slept.

She continued to make use of her own adjacent chamber to sleep in but her days were spent in the larger, more comfortable room. The laird was rarely there during the day since his responsibilities demanded his presence elsewhere in the castle or out on his estates which she gathered were extensive. The McGregor was lord of the whole of Skye, and several smaller isles in the Inner Hebrides also paid him obeisance though he left them pretty much to their own devices. He was an influential and much respected northern chieftain, and Roselyn quickly came to appreciate her brother's folly in crossing such a powerful warlord. Alan had had no notion what fury he would unleash in attacking Mortain, though Roselyn was under no illusions on that score now. The McGregor might be restrained in his treatment of her currently, but once he determined what penalty should be paid for her crimes he would extract it without mercy.

She might well hang, or worse.

But for now he clearly chose not to make reference to the future. The McGregor usually exchanged a few words with her in the mornings, but she might not see him again until after the evening meal. The laird usually ate with the rest of his household down in the great hall whilst Roselyn's meals were brought up to the solar for her and she ate alone. She surmised that he had no other close family here as no one else made use of the lord's solar or apartments. There appeared to be no Lady McGregor, nor any lusty dark-haired bairns. For the most part the apartments were silent and she was left to ponder her fate in solitude.

She did not complain. It could be so much worse.

The McGregor would often bring a jug of wine up to the solar in the late evening and share it with his prisoner. Conversation was stilted, though Roselyn appreciated his consideration in moderating his manner of speech when he spoke with her and she found his Highland burr easier to comprehend with each passing day. Neither Elspeth nor Meggie made any effort to control their strong Scottish brogue and she was becoming accustomed to the lilting dialect.

She was astonished to find she greatly enjoyed the laird's company, his gentle humour and courteous manners. She particularly appreciated his kindness in not banishing her to much less comfortable surroundings. He seemed to be allowing her the benefit of the doubt, at least until the travellers from Etal arrived and he might determine once and for all what her future was to be.

Or even if she had a future at all.

• • • • • • •

Roselyn's stomach growled. It was early evening on the third day since the laird's return and she had not eaten since noon. For the entire day she had awaited news of the arrival of the travellers from Etal but she heard nothing. Roselyn was determined not to assume the worst, that they had become stranded or injured, set upon by brigands, or met with some awful mishap. She tried, but it was difficult to maintain calm when so much was at stake. She had no desire to irritate her captor but saw no alternative; she would have to press The McGregor to send out men in search of her missing countrymen and women.

Meanwhile, she was famished. She expected one of Elspeth's horde of minions to arrive at any time with her tray so was not surprised to hear the scrape of the lock in the outer door leading to the upper hallway. The hinges creaked a little as the portal opened. Roselyn had been seated in her preferred location at the window the better to discern any encouraging sounds from outside, but stood and took a pace forward. She knew the small table which she would use for her meal was just five or six feet in front of her.

"Thank you. If you would leave the tray on the table I shall be able to serve myself."

"Excuse me, milady, but the laird requests that you join him in the great hall this evening." The voice belonged to Meggie, one of the scullery maids. A cheery little soul, the lass was usually the one sent to bring her meals and clear away afterwards. But not this evening, it would seem.

"In the hall? I am to eat downstairs?"

"Aye, milady, I understand so. He said to make haste as the rest are waitin'."

"Oh, but I am not dressed. I had not expected—"

"He were most particular, milady. Ye may take a few minutes tae straighten yer hair an' such if ye wish, but ye are tae make haste. An' ye look just fine in any case."

"He…? Is he angry?" A thought occurred to her, an awful, terrifying idea. "Have the people from Etal arrived?"

Maybe Betsy was not among the new arrivals, nor anyone else who might bear out her tale. Perhaps the proof the laird required was not after all to be forthcoming. Roselyn started to tremble. She had hoped…

"Nay, milady, no one is here but the usual clan members an' our own household. An' the laird is nae out o' sorts as far as I ken. I am tae aid ye in finding yer way downstairs." The girl crossed the room. "Would ye like to take my arm, milady?"

"Thank you." Roselyn fitted her chilled fingers around the girl's elbow and allowed herself to be led from the room. They turned to the right as they left the solar. "How far is it to the stairs, please?"

"Perhaps a dozen paces or so, milady."

Roselyn reached out with her free hand and found the cool of the roughly plastered wall. She took comfort in the solid feel of it as she gingerly followed the smaller girl's lead. Soon the lass halted.

"Here are the stairs, milady. Shall I go first?"

"What nature of staircase is it, Meggie?"

"I beg yer pardon, milady? Stairs is stairs."

"No, not to me. Tell me, is it a spiral staircase, and does it curve to the right or the left?"

"'Tis a spiral, and curves to the right."

"How wide are the treads? Is there a handrail? How many steps are there?"

"The staircase is wide enough for one person, though two couldnae pass upon it. There is nae rail but ye may hold on tae the wall. I have ne'er counted the steps but I could do so if ye wish. Shall I go down first?" The serving wench appeared anxious to proceed, but Roselyn drew back.

"Please, might we take the other route? The one which uses the straight flight of stairs?"

Roselyn recalled that when Elspeth led her up to the

laird's solar that first day they had ascended a straight flight of stairs, with a rail to the right-hand side. She had anticipated she would encounter the same stairs on her way back down, not the hostile and dangerous obstacle she was now expected to negotiate.

"Aye, but it is a longer way tae go an' the laird did particularly say that ye were to come immediately. He will be waitin'."

"Please, Meggie, guide me along the other route. I... I had a fall once when I missed my footing on a curving staircase and I prefer to avoid narrow spiral stairs. I shall explain to The McGregor why we did not take the more direct way."

The wench gave a heavy sigh, but seemingly knew when she was defeated. She turned to offer her arm again. "Aye, verra well if ye say so. We shall have tae go around by the main entrance hall and the outer stairs. Come, we should hurry..."

Conscious of the need not to delay the laird's meal longer than necessary, Roselyn quickened her step alongside the hurrying servant. She managed the stairs without great difficulty and memorised the total number for the next time she might take this route. Twenty-seven steps, then five paces to cross the outer lobby, and she found herself at the main entrance to the great hall.

"The laird's table is on a dais at the far end, maybe thirty paces." The girl started forward.

"Wait, please."

"Milady?"

"Is the way clear? Will I collide with furniture? Are there people moving about?"

"Aye, milady. There are servants, an' a few hounds. I shall nae let ye crash into anything though. Have I no' brought ye here safe enough?"

"You have, and I thank you for it. Very well, lead on." Despite the girl's assurances Roselyn was nervous as she progressed down the hall. The chatter which had assailed her ears as she entered subsided to just a few murmurings as she made her way past the assembled McGregors. She might only guess at what they thought of her, the English woman who had betrayed their precious Lady Joan and brought about that lady's death. They would hate her, surely. How could they not?

"We are at the steps up onto the dais, milady. Eight of 'em, straight ahead, then at the top we shall turn to the left."

"Thank you, Meggie. You have been most helpful and competent."

"Indeed she has, an' I too thank ye for it, lass. I shall take over now." The low tones of the laird greeted her as he took her hand and settled it in the crook of his elbow.

"Sir." Meggie stepped away and Roselyn heard her light tread as she scampered back down the hall.

"Lady Roselyn, I am so pleased ye could join us, eventually. Did Meggie not explain that I wished ye tae make haste? Why are you coming through the public lobby rather than down my private staircase?"

Roselyn turned her face toward him.

"My apologies, sir. I confess I found the steps somewhat daunting. I had Meggie show me here by a different route. I hope I have not kept you waiting."

The laird did not respond at once, instead he led her up the eight stairs and onto the dais. There was a scrape as a chair was shoved across the floor. "You are here now. Be seated, madam. 'Tis the feast day for Saint Mungo and I wish ye tae join us for it."

"Of course. Thank you for the invitation." Roselyn was pleased to observe that she no longer found his dialect so difficult to follow though she was aware that he still made an effort to speak more clearly to her. His servants however did not, and her quick ear had served her well as she had learned to piece their lilting speech together. She reached for the chair and eased herself into it.

"We have meats, puddings, and Elspeth has outdone herself with the roasted sturgeon. You shall share my trencher, my lady?"

"That would be most kind of you, my lord."

Delightful aromas wafted past her nostrils and Roselyn inhaled hungrily. The fare at Etal was poor in comparison, and at Kelso they had eaten plainly. She had already come to realise that the McGregors enjoyed good food and that none went hungry here, but this was better than anything she had enjoyed thus far.

"I have selected some fish for us, some baked apples which are my favourite, some plump breast of swan, and a slice or two of roast hare. Please, help yourself. Would you like a little mead, or wine perhaps?"

"Wine, please."

Her companion murmured to a servant who Roselyn assumed must be stationed behind them and she listened to the gentle splashing as her goblet was filled. Roselyn stretched out her hand to locate the vessel, then took a tentative sip. The rich flavour exploded on her tongue.

"This is very good, my lord."

"Yes, so I am told though I prefer a good ale myself. Or a decent whisky. Please, eat."

Roselyn picked up a piece of meat and chewed on it. The swan, she surmised. Despite her hunger though she could not enjoy the meal until she knew more of the fate of those she awaited so eagerly.

"My lord, have the travellers from Etal been sighted yet?"

"Nay, they have not."

"But—"

"I would have hoped to see them here by now. I have given instructions that a party will leave here at first light to search the route they would be expected to take. If there is news, we shall discover it soon enough I daresay. There is nothing tae be done tonight, so I suggest ye enjoy this fine repast and put them from your mind for now. If ye must chatter, perhaps ye might like to tell me what quarrel ye have with my private staircase."

He was right, she knew that. Roselyn set aside her concerns for a while and concentrated instead on explaining her fears regarding falling down the narrow, winding staircases so prevalent in keeps such as this.

"Ye must be restricted in your movements, I suspect, if ye canna manage stairs."

"At Kelso the Reverend Mother was kind enough to arrange for a handrail to be installed on the main curved staircase so I could go up and down well enough. The main stairs at Etal are—were—straight and quite wide so I could use them safely enough. I should be relieved, I suppose, as I do not believe my brother would have been sensitive to my needs in the matter."

"Aye, I daresay ye're right there. Is something amiss with the sturgeon?"

"No, my lord. It is delicious."

"Then perhaps ye might manage to eat a few bites rather than poking at it as though ye expect it to up and swim off at any moment."

She nodded and returned her attention to the food on the trencher but still Roselyn struggled to properly appreciate the delicate flavours and rich textures of the food before her. She nibbled at the fine fare, complimenting the skill of her friend Elspeth whilst doing little justice to the products of it. She lifted a particularly succulent morsel of suckling pig to her lips then thought better of it and lowered her hand.

"Oooh, what was that?" The tidbit was snatched from between her fingers before she could fathom what was happening.

Blair chuckled. "Ah, the hounds have taken a fancy to ye, my lady. Or at least, to the food ye seem intent on pushing around our trencher." He swung around in his chair "Archie, chase these greedy mongrels off, will ye?"

Roselyn placed her now empty fingers back in her lap, and was surprised at the warm, wet sensation which assailed her senses.

"Oh, it is licking me." She turned her hand and the rough tongue scraped her palm. "I believe I must taste of fine pork."

"Aye, no doubt. Have no fear though, Freya is gentle enough."

"Freya? That is her name?" Roselyn brought her other hand around and found the huge head now wedged in her lap. She fondled the hound's ears, noting the rough and rather long coat. "I have always loved dogs. Horses too, though I am not permitted to ride any more. This is a large animal, I believe?"

"Aye, Freya is a wolfhound, though not a particularly useful one as I recall." The laird sounded amused. "She suffered a broken hind leg as a pup so has not the speed needed for hunting. She bears fine litters though, so has earned her place in our hall."

"I believe she likes me." The dog continued to rest her massive head across Roselyn's thighs and submitted to a gentle ear-tugging.

"Freya likes everyone," observed her host dryly. "She is sweet-natured enough if a trifle over-fond of the hearth. Is she bothering you, my lady?"

"No, not at all. May she stay here?"

"If you like," granted the laird, "but please dinna feed her all our finest morsels. She has bother enough stirring herself without putting on more fat."

"She feels perfectly lean enough to me, sir," countered Roselyn. "I believe that Freya and I shall be friends."

Roselyn was correct. The wolfhound remained at her side during the rest of the meal, and even tried to follow her and the laird back up to his solar when the feasting was over. The McGregor was having none of that.

"Archie, hang onto this hound, will ye. I'll not be sharin' my bed wi' a bloody dog." He escorted Roselyn back out into the public lobby and up the main stairs. Once back in his solar he saw her safe into her chamber then offered to summon Meggie to help her undress.

"I believe I can manage, my lord. I prefer to shift for myself."

"As you like, madam. Good night." The door clicked shut and Roselyn was alone again.

• • • • • • •

Two days passed, and there was still no news of the group from Etal. The search party had left as promised the morning after the feast of St. Mungo and The McGregor assured her he would send word at once if they were sighted. He urged Roselyn not to worry unduly, there were many reasons why travellers might be detained on such a long and arduous journey and it was much too early to be seriously concerned. Roselyn smiled and managed a brief nod of agreement, but still she paced the solar and fretted constantly as soon as the laird departed to be about his daily business.

On the third day she could no longer conceal her fears. "My lord, could you perhaps send more men in search of them?" She made her plea as they broke their fast together in his solar.

He squeezed her elbow. "'Tis early yet, but if they are not here by the sennight's end I shall mount a bigger search."

"The sennight? But—"

"Patience, Roselyn. And have faith, aye?"

The laird returned to his solar at noon, surprising his apprehensive guest. "Sir? Is there news?"

"From Etal? Nay. But I thought ye might like to spend some time down in the hall today. You must get lonely tucked away up here."

"The hall, sir? Yes, of course, but..."

"Come, I shall escort ye down." He placed her fingers on his sleeve and Roselyn grasped the now familiar soft leather of his jerkin. In the hallway he turned to the right.

"My lord, I wonder if we might—"

"This way is the quickest. Trust me, Lady Roselyn."

"But—"

"And whilst I think of it, I should prefer you to use my given name since most do hereabouts."

"Your given name? But I do not even know it, sir."

He paused to cup her chin. "Blair Andrew James McGregor, my lady. At your service. But Blair will do just fine."

"Blair? Then you must call me Roselyn."

"I believe I already do, my lady, much o' the time." He resumed walking and Roselyn clutched at his arm. He halted at the top of the stairs. "Give me your hand, Roselyn."

"Sir?"

"I believe we just discussed this," he admonished. "But your hand, if you please?"

Roselyn held out her right hand and his larger one closed around it. Blair drew her forward then placed her fingers on a round pole which appeared to be attached to the wall.

"What is this?" She ran her palm along the length of wood which ran vertically at about the height of her waist.

"'Tis the handrail ye set such store by. Two paces ahead the stairs start, and the rail descends the entire length, though on the steps themselves 'tis made of stout rope to follow the curve of the wall. Ye should be able to make use of this route now. Would ye like to try it?"

"A handrail? You had a rail installed, especially for me?"

"I have not yet determined your fate, but for as long as you are here in my charge I will ensure that you are safe. This is the first such rail, but I have instructed the castle carpenter to install a similar device on every staircase. I have also asked Elspeth to ensure that all fires in the castle are protected by a screen so ye may move about without fear."

"Oh." Roselyn inched forward, her hand on the rail, until she reached the edge of the first step. "Oh." She could think of nothing more erudite to say.

"I shall go first, backwards, so ye may be assured I shall be there to catch ye if ye miss a step. But if ye hold onto the rope ye should manage well enough. Are ye ready?"

"Yes," she whispered. "Yes, Blair, I believe I am."

It was a triumphant Roselyn who emerged into the great hall several minutes later. She had picked her way with care, but the rope offered all the reassurance she needed. Only once did she waver, but held on tight to her new rail and was able to right herself.

"My private stairs bring you out onto the dais where my table is located so ye must remember that if ye decide to wander around. The rail has not yet been installed on the steps down to the main hall but soon it will be safe like the rest. In the meantime, Elspeth has spared Meggie tae act as your guide. Ye like the lass, aye?"

"Oh, yes, very much. Is she here?"

"I shall summon her before I leave. Your other friend is here though."

"What? Oh… Freya." Roselyn giggled as the huge head nudged her waist. "Is it you?" She bent to scratch the dog's wide head. "I hope they have been giving you nice scraps to eat."

"The beast does well enough. Ah, Meggie, ye ken your new duties, aye?"

Roslyn heard the scampering footsteps as the little maid rushed to join them. "Yes, Laird," she panted. "I am tae remain at Lady Roselyn's side at all times and help her tae get to know the castle."

"Excellent. See that ye do your work with diligence."

"The entire castle? I am to have the freedom to go where I please?" Roselyn was astonished at this new turn of events.

"I see no need to keep ye confined. 'Tis not as if ye could escape, is it? Meggie will be at your service. Ask her if ye require anything. And Elspeth too, of course, though she tends to spend her time in the kitchens which are situated below this room. Meggie will show ye the way if ye want to visit her."

"Thank you." Roselyn crouched to hug the large dog at her side. "And I have Freya too."

"Indeed. I must leave ye now as I have tenants to visit an hour's ride from here an' I want to be back before nightfall if I can manage it. Enjoy your afternoon, Roselyn."

"I will. I surely will. Thank you, Blair."

CHAPTER FIVE

What was it about the wench that captivated his imagination? Blair found he was increasingly bested by fantasies in which he visualised doing all manner of things to his lovely little English captive, acts which he knew to be both dishonourable and perhaps downright sinful. No matter, he was unable to exorcise the decadent images from his mind. He shook his head in frustration as he led his destrier back into the stables intending to see to the horse's needs himself rather than trusting the task to one of the lads. He found the labour therapeutic and it helped to clear his head. Or he generally found it to be so. Not on this occasion though.

He had been so certain of the facts of the matter when he'd ordered the English wench to be brought to Duncleit. He had planned to pursue the bastard who perpetrated the crime against his kin and bring him to justice too, then deal with the pair of them. He intended to deliver a clear lesson for any who thought to attack him or his.

But no longer. His plans for the Earl of Ingram had not altered at all, but as he came to know Roselyn better he was increasingly of the opinion that she was a victim of her brother too. The wench was not entirely without blame, but which of them was, after all?

His clan though, tended to think otherwise. They expected a hanging and he could not entirely blame them. Apart from Meggie and Elspeth they had had no opportunity to come to know Roselyn. His decision to allow her greater freedom was an attempt to counter that. Roselyn was unfailingly pleasant company, sweet and gentle and very, very contrite for her part in the tragedy which had befallen Mortain. By placing her among them he hoped that the rest of his household might soften their attitudes, though it had been three days since he granted her the freedom to roam Duncleit at will and he had yet to see the results. It was early days, he reminded himself, and however charming Roselyn might be, he still believed the corroborative testimony in support of her account would be essential to aid her cause.

He placed a bucket of oats in front of the snorting steed. "Aye, Bartholomew, ye may well paw the earth and complain. Ye'd have a lot more to moan at if ye had my burdens to carry." He patted the horse's neck and left the stall. He would see how the girl was doing. Maybe she had succeeded in charming at least some of his surly clan-members. The menfolk should be easy enough to win over, he mused, given the lass was quite lovely to look upon.

Not that this would sway his judgement, nor would her blindness. She did not deserve to hang, he was sure of that, though he had yet to establish the proper extent of her culpability.

His mind set, he strode across the bailey, stopping to exchange greetings with those he passed. Blair prided himself on knowing the given name of all who shared his hall. He was a stern laird when occasion called for it, but for the most part Duncleit was a happy, relaxed place and that was how Blair liked it.

He mounted the front steps and crossed the lobby. His gaze sought out Roselyn and found her at once, on the dais. She turned her head in his direction, as though she were aware of his presence. Perhaps she was, her sight may be gone but he had soon learnt that her other senses were acute. She smiled and took a step toward him, then another.

Blair saw the danger too late. Unknowing how close she was to the edge, she was about to step right off the dais. The drop was almost five feet; she would be injured, perhaps badly. He opened his mouth to shout a warning, then gaped at what happened next. The huge hound, Freya, an animal which as far as he was aware struggled to summon the energy to lumber out into the bailey to take a piss, bounded from the floor of the hall and up onto the dais. In one huge leap the dog shoved Roselyn back from the edge. She herself twisted on impact and tumbled down from the dais as Roselyn staggered back into the lord's table. Blair covered the length of the great hall at a sprint, but the hound beat him back onto the platform seemingly no worse for the adventure. By the time Blair arrived beside Roselyn she was patting the dog's head and congratulating the hound on a job well done.

"Are ye hurt, my lady?" Blair reached for her, unthinking and wrapped his arms around her shoulders. "I thought ye would fall, but—"

"But Freya saved me. Is she not a wonderful helper? I knew she was an intelligent dog, but she is quite magnificent, is she not?"

"Aye, she certainly chose the right moment to leap up onto the dais. You were lucky."

She shoved out of his embrace.

"Not lucky. I taught her to do that. Her task is to warn me if I step too close to the edge, though she is usually more gentle. She nudges me with her shoulder as a rule."

"Now Roselyn, I ken that ye like the hound, but don't be thinking ye can rely upon her. Where is Meggie, for that matter?"

"She went to the kitchens to fetch a mug of mead for me. And my Freya is very reliable. She knows her task. Watch."

"Now Roselyn…"

"Please, just watch."

Blair stood, helpless, as Roselyn called the hound to her. The dog stationed herself at Roselyn's left hip and gazed up at the young woman as though awaiting her next command.

Roselyn laid her hand on the huge dog's back, just between her shoulder blades. "Walk." Roselyn's instruction was crisp and clear, and the hound obeyed at once. Freya moved at a sedate pace and Roselyn followed, keeping her palm on the dog's back as the pair walked along the platform away from him. The edge was to Roselyn's left, and every time she veered toward the danger zone the dog planted her great paws and refused to budge, forcing Roselyn to shift direction. Several times the pair repeated this bizarre dance until Roselyn approached the end of the dais. Before Blair could call out another warning however, the dog had skirted in front of Roselyn to bring her to a halt before she could march right off the end. The young woman turned and the dog turned with her, this time moving to Roselyn's right to guide her back in his direction.

"Did you see?" Roselyn smiled up at him when she stood before him again. "She let me know when it was time to turn around."

"Are you sure you did not count the paces? I know that is how you judge your position in the room."

"I did, and I do, of course. But Freya does not know that and she got in front of me and stopped me before I could fall. She knows her duty."

"I am not convinced. You have Meggie to act as your guide."

"Of course, and now I have Freya too. You saw what she did. How can you doubt her?"

Blair eyed the hound with new respect, certainly, though he remained sceptical. "Aye, well, I suppose 'twill do no harm to keep her close. Her *and* Meggie."

• • • • • • •

It was late afternoon and Blair was intent upon drilling his men in the bailey when a shout from the east postern gate disturbed their practice.

"Riders, Laird. Approaching from the east."

Blair slid his claymore back into the scabbard which hung from his waist and sprinted over to the lookout post. It was past the time when he would have expected to see the search party return, hopefully with the missing travellers from Etal. Perhaps he would not after all need to send a larger force to investigate their disappearance.

"Can ye make out who it is?"

"They are ours, Laird. 'Tis the McGregor plaid about their shoulders."

Thank the dear Lord. "How many?"

"Seven, sir."

"Seven?" He had sent but four men in search of the missing folk. "Is Robbie among them?"

"Aye, I'd say so. Not many men that size..."

Ah, this day was going better than he had hoped. Not only were the search party back, hopefully with news, but God willing his captain-at-arms had also been successful in the quest set for him.

"Lower the drawbridge," he yelled. "Get ready to welcome our men home."

"Laird, there are more." The lookout called to him again. "Two carts, behind the men on horseback."

A broad smile split Blair's face. He bounded up the steps to the eastern parapet and leaned out, shading his eyes from the sun which was still high in the sky. The tartan-clad Highlanders were perhaps half a mile from his main gates and approaching at a brisk canter. Further back, maybe two miles distant, the carts made slower but steady progress. There looked to be four people in each wagon, five adults in all and three smaller figures. The folk he had spoken to at Loch Lomond had children with them. This must be them.

"See that Lady Roselyn is informed," he instructed the lookout at his side. "And Elspeth. We shall require food and shelter for our new clansfolk."

By the time Blair stood in the middle of his courtyard to welcome the first of the new arrivals Roselyn was at his side, her dog with her. Freya had become Roselyn's constant companion and it did not escape his notice that she crossed the bailey to join him holding onto the hound's shaggy coat, her step sure and confident.

"They are here? Is it them? Really?" Roselyn reached for his arm but missed. Blair took her hand and squeezed her fingers.

"I believe so. The men now dismounting are the search party I sent. There are carts behind, so the rest will be here very soon."

"Oh, I am so relieved. I had begun to think…"

He squeezed her hand again. "I know. But they are here now. Please, you must excuse me for a few moments." He disengaged his hand and stepped forward to greet Robbie. "Where did ye find Archie and his men?"

"We came upon them yesterday evening, close tae the fortress at Eilean Donan. The Ogilvie sends his regards, though he may yet seek recompense for a night's lodging."

"Mean auld skinflint. Still, I shall pay him if he asks." Blair did not seriously expect to receive a bill—The Ogilvie owed him a favour or two. "So, did ye see her?"

"Aye, Laird, an' we gave her your letter."

Blair nodded. "A reply?"

"'Tis here." Robbie reached under the thick plaid which enveloped his shoulders and pulled out a folded parchment which he handed to his laird. "She was right glad tae be of service."

"Thank you. Ye made quick time, there and back in not much more than a week."

"The roads are good at this time o' year. An' ye did impress upon us the urgency."

"Still, ye did well. Ye must be hungry. Go inside an' see

what Elspeth has laid out."

The captain-at-arms clapped him on the arm and strode off across the bailey, two of his companions at his heels. The other four men awaited Blair's attention.

"Archie, where did ye come across 'em?"

"They were skirtin' the southern face o' Ben Nevis but their cart had lost a wheel an' they were strugglin' tae fashion a replacement wi'out the proper tools. Between us though were able tae fix it well enough to get tae Fort William, though 'twas slow going. Once there we bought the two wagons ye see just coming over yonder meadow an' we made fast time from then."

"Are all who set out here?"

"Aye, Blair. All o' them."

"Their names? Please, do you know their names?" This from Roselyn who had approached to stand close behind him.

The man looked to his laird. Blair gave a curt nod. "Tell her who is with ye, lad."

"Aye, Miss. There's Ned an' Martha in the first wagon wi' their lad, an' another two wee bairns. In the second there be a John Cooper an' his wife, and her sister, Betsy."

"Oh. Oh, Blair, John is our steward, and Betsy too. I told you about Betsy. They can tell you what happened. They saw…"

"Aye, an' we shall hear their tale soon enough. Archie, will ye wait for them to arrive and bid them go into the hall for food. The little ones will be tired I dinna doubt. Meggie, would ye be sae good as tae ask Elspeth where there might be a quiet corner to lay pallets for them? I shall be in my solar, as will Lady Roselyn, but as soon as our guests are fed and rested I shall talk with them, in the hall."

"In the hall, Laird?"

"Aye. 'Tis best that all hear what is said and know the truth of their account."

"Blair, I would like to greet them when they arrive, if I may."

Roselyn turned her empty gaze on him and he stroked her cheek. "It is best that you do not, and that all here know that ye had no opportunity to explain what ye require from them. If their testimony is to help your case, it must be known to be true and not prompted by you."

"But I would not—"

"No, I daresay ye would not. But perception matters as much as truth in these affairs and it is of great importance what my people believe. This way is best."

He watched as her expression altered, as realisation dawned. He knew he was right in this and now so did she.

"Let us be away to the solar. I have correspondence to read which ye may find to be of interest."

He led her back inside and up to the solar, the hound loping behind them. Blair had managed to set aside his inherent dislike of dogs in his private quarters, though before allowing her into the chamber he had insisted that Freya suffer the indignity of a thorough tubbing to ensure she was clean and as fragrant as might be achieved.

Once in the solar he bid Roselyn make herself comfortable on the settle before taking his seat at the small table which also served as his desk. There he spread out the parchment handed to him by Robbie and started to read out loud.

My lord,

It is with the utmost gratification that I pen this missive to you, and I thank you for your diligence in seeking the truth where many would not.

Before offering my account of the events which transpired under this roof, I must express my deepest regrets at the dire and unwarranted circumstances which bring us to this pass. The Lady Joan of Mortain was a dear and gracious lady, much beloved here at Kelso. She and her family were cruelly used, and I am convinced that God will exact His divine retribution for the evil done to her and her kinfolk.

As to the events which took place in this very place, I cannot properly express my horror and condemnation. This is the House of the

Lord and was most vilely defiled. Lady Roselyn Beauchamp was in our charge, under the protection of Our Lord and Saviour and in a place offering His divine sanctuary, yet my lord of Ingram violated her rights and her person and in so doing affronted all decent sensibilities. He came to Kelso with armed men and forced entry to this sacred place at the point of the sword. He then proceeded to assault his sister, Lady Roselyn, most viciously and despite my pleas that he desist. His rage was most murderous and I feared for all our lives, though in particular I despaired that his sweet sister might not survive his attack. When he at last departed from this place the Lady Roselyn lay quite insensible on the floor of the refectory. She did not regain consciousness for several hours, and her injuries were most grievous I fear.

In response to your specific question, these dreadful events took place on the seventh day of July in the Year of Our Lord fourteen hundred and eighty-two.

It is with great relief that I have become apprised of Lady Roselyn's current situation, and I am given to understand that she has regained her strength. I trust her safety will be assured as she is deserving of care and gentle treatment, both in consideration of her unfortunate affliction as well as her sweet nature. I commend her to you, my lord, and to Our Great Redeemer in whose love and protection the dear child will forever reside.

With best regards and respect.
Sarah, Prioress and Reverend Mother

He set the parchment aside and turned to regard Roselyn. She sat quite still and outwardly calm though he knew her better than to be fooled. She raised her face to his and he saw moisture glistening in her deep violet eyes.

"You sent word to her? To the Reverend Mother at Kelso?"

"I did, aye."

"When?"

"That first evening, after I spoke with you and came to the realisation that there may be more to the story than I had at first supposed. You seemed so certain that the Reverend Mother would bear out your account, so I decided to pursue that on your behalf."

"But, it is such a long way, to Kelso…"

"I have good men at my disposal, and fast steeds. Robbie was there and back in barely a week. It is by coincidence that news from Kelso arrived here on the same day as the party from Etal. We shall be able to settle the matter once and for all this day."

"Yes, I…"

He noted that her already pale complexion was ashen and he left the desk to join her on the settle. The missive from Kelso alone was sufficient to enable him to spare her life; the testimony of Betsy and John would further bolster her story but they were no longer solely reliant upon it. He stretched an arm across her shoulders.

"This will end today, Roselyn. You have my word on that. With the statement from Mother Sarah there will be none who could doubt that you were coerced into revealing the details which helped your brother to ransack Mortain."

"But I still told him, and without that—"

"There will be a reckoning, but there is mitigation, and here is the proof of it. You will not pay with your life."

"But—"

"It is my decision, Roselyn. It always was and from the start I was minded to believe you. My people expect justice though, and they are entitled to see it done so I required this evidence to justify sparing you. And now…" He was interrupted by a knock at the door. "Come," Blair called out.

It was Archie. "The families from Etal are fed, Laird. You said you wished to speak with them in the hall."

"I do." He turned to take Roselyn's hand. "Come, we shall hear what they have to say."

• • • • • • •

The clansmen and others of his household shuffled back about their business. Blair watched them file out of the hall, his gaze pensive as he watched them leave. There were some mutterings but by and large they appeared content. Blair had believed they would be, the proof was plain enough, but until the matter was accomplished he could not quite shed the remnants of doubt. Now, though, he had proclaimed Roselyn innocent of the charge of murder and none had taken issue with that verdict.

She was, however, guilty of something though he was not entirely certain what name to put to it. She had revealed the existence of the fifty gold coins as a means to avoid a marriage she did not desire. That was not a matter of life and death, more one of preference and personal inclination. Though she had sought to retract her indiscretion the damage was done and from that moment on her brother had been intent upon availing himself of the wealth he then knew was to be had at Mortain. Roselyn had set those events in train and could not be totally absolved of the consequences.

He had but to take one look at her distressed countenance and he knew she viewed the matter in much the same way. She was racked by guilt for her inadvertent part in the tragedy. Punishment was inevitable, and it was without doubt required. Further, it needed to be swift and severe to satisfy the Clan McGregor, not to mention Roselyn's own troubled conscience.

"Lady Roselyn, would you stand before me, please?"

She had been seated at his left, but got to her feet and shuffled into position. As ever, her dog was at her side.

Blair lifted a hand to summon Aiden to him. The man had witnessed the proceedings in silence, though he no doubt had his views on the matter. He approached and waited for his instructions.

"Would you take the hound and secure her in the stables until I tell you she is to be released? Once that is done I would like you to return to me here."

Aiden nodded and produced a length of rope which he fastened around the dog's neck.

Roselyn lifted a hand as though to plead with him.

"What are you going to do with her? Please, Blair, do not hurt her…"

"For God's sake, Roselyn, what do you take me for?" He could not conceal the irritation in his tone. Had she learnt nothing of him over the days they had spent together? Had he not gone to considerable lengths to exonerate her of the major charges against her? Why should she imagine him to suddenly become mean and cruel now? "The animal needs to be out of the way, that is all, for I fear she might make an ill-fated attempt to protect you from what is to come next."

"Oh." She blanched, and he noted that she was again chewing on her lower lip, a mannerism he had not seen over the last several days.

Aiden tugged on the rope and the dog allowed herself to be led away as Blair continued to regard his nervous prisoner.

"I promised you that your life would not be forfeit for your part in this, but you have earned a punishment. Do you understand why?"

"Yes, my lord. I should not have breathed a word of what I knew. If I had not, Alan's attention would not have turned to Mortain and your family would not have been murdered."

"That is about the gist of it, though only God Himself knows what truly might have happened, regardless of your actions. Still, we find ourselves in a difficult position and I must deal with what is before me. I understand your reasons, but you were not justified in revealing private confidences shared by my sister, or the intimate knowledge you had of the castle and for those acts you will be punished." He paused to allow his words thus far to sink in. "You shall submit to a switching, at my hand."

"The… The switch, sir?"

"Aye, it is a fitting punishment. It will be painful, and humiliating, but you will survive it. And you will remember it, I can guarantee you that much."

"Yes, sir." She bowed her head, her submission already apparent.

"Do you still have any discomfort from your ordeal at your brother's hands? You know and accept what must happen, I see that, but it does not have to take place at once if you are not fully recovered. I am prepared to wait, to give you time…"

Roselyn shook her head, her expression vehement. "No! No, my lord, it must be now. I wish this to be done, over with."

"I appreciate that, but I intend to deliver a severe punishment and I would know that you are in a fit state to receive it."

"I am. I truly am. Please, do not drag this out further."

"Very well, provided your bruises have faded completely, we will proceed this day."

Roselyn's shoulders relaxed; she seemed relieved to hear this and he could understand her reaction. Grim though her situation was, her ordeal would soon be at an end. She tilted her chin up, her mouth trembled a little as she spoke next. "Will it take place in public, my lord? Are all to watch?"

Blair cursed as his cock twitched within his braies. This was to be a serious act of well-deserved discipline, he reminded himself, not a spot of rough bed sport. Now, if he could but get his randy ballocks to agree he might proceed with a modicum of dignity.

"No, the matter shall be conducted in privacy, I shall grant ye that much. When I ask you to, you shall proceed to my sleeping chamber, Roselyn. Meggie will assist you there if you need her. Once there you are to remove your clothing, all of it, and wait for me. If you require Meggie's assistance to undress you may have it, but then she must leave. I shall expect to find you alone, naked and kneeling at the foot of my bed when I arrive. Do you understand?"

"Your chamber, my lord? Not my own?"

"I believe I have made my wishes perfectly clear."

"Yes, my lord," she whispered. "And I… I believe I can

manage unaided."

"Very well. I have preparations to make and you may remain here until I ask you to go upstairs. You may be seated again if you so wish."

He watched her make her cautious way back to the seat she had occupied previously. He would have gladly helped her, but had to admire her growing independence as she managed to navigate the hall and those other chambers she knew well. She had just settled when Aiden reappeared from the main entrance at the other end of the hall, still with his length of rope but minus the dog. He strode up to the dais to receive his orders.

"Aiden, I require you to cut me a selection of switches from the coppice beside the loch. I shall need at least a couple of dozen, stripped and with all sharp twigs removed. Bring them to me here, soaked in cold water and lashed together in bundles of three or four."

His man had the grace to wince as he sketched a brief bow and left to do his laird's bidding.

Roselyn was silent, though tears streamed over her cheeks and she twisted her fingers together in her lap. He considered offering her some words of comfort, but thought better of it. There would be time for that later, after he was satisfied she had properly atoned for her misdeeds.

· · · · · · ·

An hour later Blair ascended his private stairs leading to his solar. Roselyn had gone up some twenty minutes earlier, at his bidding. She should be ready for him by now. Aiden had also completed his allotted task and the products of the man's labours now awaited the laird, suitably prepared and soaking in a bucket of water in the hallway outside his chamber door.

Blair halted to check the switches. Aiden had done his work well and Blair could detect no sharp edges which might cut Roselyn's delicate skin. He crossed the solar to the door which led to the smaller chamber where he slept.

Roselyn had obeyed his instructions to perfection, particularly considering that this was the first time he had required her to be naked in his presence. He had been tempted on many occasions and as his prisoner there would have been little she could do had he decided to take advantage of her vulnerable situation. When her very life hung in the balance his innate sense of honour would not permit him to stoop to such an act, but all had changed now.

She turned her head as he entered the room. "My lord…?"

"You will not speak, Roselyn, unless I ask you a direct question. You may of course scream—indeed, I believe my people will expect it."

She nodded and bowed her head.

He paused for a moment to peruse her slim body. Had there been the slightest mark remaining, any residue of her beating at Kelso, he would have insisted that this issue between them be deferred. There was not.

Very well then, we continue. He strode past her to fetch the bolster from the head of the bed and moved it to the foot. Blair considered the arrangement for a moment, then took a length of folded plaid from a chest and added that to the pile. It would do. He turned to regard Lady Roselyn.

"I shall require you to lie across the foot of my bed where I have placed pillows which will lift your bottom up for me. I expect you to remain still and in position until I am finished, and I have no doubt that you will find that difficult. If you move I shall be obliged to start all over again, so to avoid disappointment to both of us I shall tie you in place. Your wrists shall be secured, and your ankles." He moved to stand immediately in front of her and tipped up her chin with his fingers. "I will hurt you, Roselyn, for that is what I intend, but I will do you no lasting harm. Do you understand the difference?"

"I… I believe so, my lord. You are not at all like my brother."

"No, I am not. So, may I help you up?"

She nodded and reached for his hand. Blair helped her to her feet then paused to peruse her naked form. "You are quite lovely." He meant it, but now was not the moment to pursue that disruptive line of thought. Instead, he brushed his lips across her forehead then led her to the foot of the bed. "Lean forward and rest your body on the pillows. You may take your time to get settled, and when you are ready I shall tie you in place."

He stepped back to allow her the space to move, and moments later he was rewarded by the sight of her upturned, naked buttocks presented prettily for his punishment. His unruly cock stood to attention as Blair admired the vision before him. For several moments he did not move, but then he heard her whimper. She was afraid, utterly terrified. He should conclude this as quickly as he might and ogle her later.

"Spread your legs as wide as you are able, Roselyn. I shall secure your ankles first."

He crouched and fastened her delicate feet to the bedposts, his actions both swift and deft. He used leather straps, sufficiently flexible not to cause undue discomfort, but neither could she escape or kick. He had every confidence she would do her utmost to achieve both before they were done.

Next he moved to her side and took her right hand in his. He pulled it into the small of her back, then drew her left to join it. "I shall bind your wrists like this."

She lay still as he finished his preparations, her breathing rapid. Satisfied that she would remain quite still during the proceedings and not wishing to prolong her ordeal unnecessarily, Blair returned to the outer solar to select his first bundle of switches.

CHAPTER SIX

Was it possible to actually die of fear?

Roselyn contemplated that prospect as she lay, face down and tied in place, over the foot of her Highland captor's bed. Her eyes were closed, and since the moment she heard his footsteps approaching the sleeping chamber she had fought to control her terror but she was losing that battle. Perhaps it would have been easier to bear her punishment at his hands if Blair had treated her harshly, but he did not. He was gentle, courteous, considerate of her comfort as he prepared her for what was to come. And now, it was time.

His tread was soft as he moved across the room, and she knew the creak of the outer door. He was fetching something, and she knew what it had to be.

He had ordered her to be silent, but she had to ask.

"Sir…?" Her word was more of a sob.

"Roselyn? What is it?"

"How…? How many, sir?"

"I shall stop when I deem your punishment concluded. When I am satisfied that you have truly paid for your wrongdoing."

"Oh… but I—"

"It is over when I say that it is." His tone was hard, the timbre in his voice strict and implacable. She had known since she first encountered him on the steps at Etal that this Scottish warlord was a man to be feared. He would do what he considered right and just, and she had no choice but to accept his discipline. There was a part of her that would have it no other way.

"Are you ready?"

No! Never. Roselyn managed a small nod.

The sound of the switch slicing through the air was almost more awful that the sheet of white-hot pain which exploded across her bottom as he landed the first stroke. Roselyn let out a high-pitched scream, surprised by the intensity of the fire he lit despite her most fearsome imaginings. This was worse than she had thought. Nothing could have prepared her for this.

Almost before the agony started to dissipate he swung again. Roselyn jerked in her bonds, struggling to get upright but unable to because of the sprawled position of her feet. She could gain no purchase, and even if she could she would not be able to move from this position.

Blair shifted his position slightly in order to adjust the angle, and he delivered two more strokes in rapid succession, this time to her left cheek. He moved again to repeat the treatment on the right side. With every whoosh of the switch through the air, with every harsh, unrelenting slice to her poor, vulnerable buttocks, the agony built. The pain grew, bloomed, then exploded across her scorched flesh.

Roselyn shrieked and cried out, begging, pleading with him to stop. It occurred to her in a more lucid moment as her throat became raw with screeching that he need not have worried unduly about his clansmen knowing that justice was being done, she was announcing that loud and clear. Well, loud certainly.

She had attempted to count the strokes at first but soon abandoned that effort. There was no point, it was immaterial. He would stop if, when, he chose to. Oh, sweet Lord, he might never stop.

Roselyn wept, her shrieks subsiding to agonised moans as the blows continued to rain down on her unprotected bottom.

He paused, and for one glorious moment Roselyn believed it was over. But it was not, he had merely stopped to replace the bundle of switches which he had worn out on her punished flesh. He returned and resumed his attentions with renewed vigour, this time directing most of the whipping against the backs of her thighs. This hurt even more, though she would not have believed it possible. Roselyn was past struggling now, the fight sapping from her as blow after blow set her thighs alight and sizzled across the sensitive skin of her bottom. When he started to concentrate on her lower curves, the very spots where she would sit, she knew she would hurt for days to come.

"Sir, please, I am sorry. So sorry…" Her agonised whimpers were almost inaudible but were the best she could manage. She was utterly spent.

The pain subsided, a brief respite, she knew but she lay still, gasping through her agonised sobs.

"Again, please." Blair's tone was gentler now. He seemed to require something of her.

"Sir…?"

"Say it again, please."

"Say… what?"

"Your apology. I wish to hear your contrition and know that you do truly mean it."

"I do. I surely do. I am sorry and I beg your forgiveness and that of your people."

"You have mine, though I cannot speak for others. We are almost done here."

"Almost? My lord, I beg of you…"

"Now that I have your submission, and your true contrition, you will accept the retribution due for my sister's life, her family, her unborn bairn. Will you do this, Roselyn?

Can you accept your punishment and welcome the release it will bring to you?"

Long moments passed as she lay before him, in pain, scared, almost crushed under the weight of her remorse. Yet one word of his resonated in her head, one word repeated, over and over. *Release*. He could, would unshackle her from the bitterness of regret. She could move on. He would forgive her, so might his people. And she could, would, forgive herself.

"Yes, sir. I can. I can. Please, I want you to punish me and set me free."

He laid his palm on her smarting bottom and Roselyn flinched. He squeezed, not hard but enough to drive the pain deep into her body, as though he could caress the heat into her very core.

"Very well, I shall do as you ask. Ten more strokes, this whipping harder than before. You will count, and with every stroke know that your part in this tragedy is absolved."

Roselyn chewed on her lip and clenched her bound hands. She could do it. Surely, she could bear this. She must.

Blair covered both her hands with his and he squeezed her fingers. "It will be quick, I promise. You have only to count…"

She nodded and closed her eyes tight. *Please, let it soon be over.*

"One." Roselyn ground out the number as he resumed the switching. "Again, please."

"Good girl," he responded. The next stripe was laid across both buttocks but somehow Roselyn managed not to clench. She could absorb the pain, accept it, and allow it to cleanse her.

"Two, my lord. Three. Four. Five."

He struck her again and her body trembled under the onslaught. This time she remained silent, her powers of speech deserting her.

"Roselyn?"

"Five," she murmured soundlessly.

"Nay," he stated. "That was six. But it may as well be ten for all the good the next four will do. We are finished here."

"Sir...?" She was bemused, relieved yet disappointed. He had said ten, had promised her ten strokes and absolution. He could not fail her now. "No, it is not... I must... Please."

"I am satisfied. Clan McGregor has had its due."

Roselyn shook her head, oddly determined that they were not yet done and she could not leave here until the matter was properly concluded. "Ten, my lord. You said it had to be ten. I shall be satisfied with nothing less."

"I see. Very well, though I shall count from here on or we might be here the entire evening since you seem to be struggling to recall your numbers."

"Thank you," she whispered.

The next four strokes, the final ones, were delivered in swift succession. Roselyn did not cry out, nor did she struggle. She lay still, relishing each fresh wave of pain as it washed through her spent body. Even after he tossed the switch aside and released her ankles she made no attempt to move.

Blair untied her wrists and drew her hands up above her head. Roselyn clutched at the blanket beneath her stiff fingers as he massaged the stiffness from her aching shoulders. She yearned to crawl up the bed, to sink into the comforting warmth of the furs which covered the mattress but she could not shift so much as a muscle. She hurt, every part of her hurt and she could not muster the strength of a newborn babe.

Blair lifted her in his arms. She whimpered though he was gentle and took care not to touch her punished skin as he laid her face down on the bed. Roselyn lay motionless, concentrating on drawing in one breath after the next. She was exhausted, in pain, utterly spent and totally exhilarated.

She was alive, and she felt freer than she could recall in her entire life.

She stretched out her hand, seeking... something. Blair

laced his fingers through hers.

"Here, you must drink."

Roselyn attempted to protest but was too weak. Blair eased her up to place her weight on one elbow, her torso twisted to face him. He held the earthenware cup to her lips. "'Tis mead, your favourite. Take a little then you may rest,"

It did not occur to Roselyn to disobey nor even to question his instruction. She parted her lips and allowed him to tip a little of the sweet liquid into her mouth. It slid down her dry throat, the flavour rich and soothing.

"Thank you," she whispered.

"You are welcome." His response was low, his voice soft. She may have been mistaken as to what happened next. Could he really have smoothed her tangled hair back and kissed her forehead or was that just something conjured up by her fevered imagination? No one had treated her thus since her mother's death almost five summers ago.

Roselyn abandoned any further effort to grasp what might be happening around her, she no longer cared. Her usually acute senses were dulled, her reasoning confused. She buried her face in the fluffy softness of the pillow and allowed herself to drift off to sleep.

• • • • • • •

"Roselyn? Are you awake?"

No, too tired. Leave me.

"Roselyn, open your eyes."

Why? What would be the point?

"It will show me that you are awake and heeding my words. Obey me, please."

How do you know my thoughts?

"Ye're speaking them out loud, which suggests to me that ye might be awake."

She wrinkled her brow, puzzled, then fell back on the one certainty of which she had no doubt. "Leave me. I need to sleep."

"And so ye shall, soon enough. You are speaking to me, but I want to know that you are conscious and fully sensible afore I leave."

"Leave? Must you go?" A sharp pang of disappointment pierced her reluctantly dawning consciousness.

"Not at once. I have some time and wish to speak with ye, if ye're strong enough."

Roselyn parted her eyelids. "Is it morning?"

"Aye. Well, daybreak at least. Not quite light yet."

"How long have I slept?"

"A full twelve hours."

"I…" She reached for his face, knowing by the soft breath tickling her cheek that he was close. The movement was enough to rub her raw bottom against the sheet which covered her. "Oh, aagh!"

He chuckled. "Aye, ye will be sore for a while yet. Do ye ken where you are, Roselyn?"

She paused for several moments to consider his question. The events of the previous day rushed back to fill her consciousness and she groaned.

"You whipped me."

"Aye, it was amply warranted an' ye took it well. So, where are ye now? Do ye recall that?"

She nodded slowly. "Your bed. You left me to sleep in your bed. I… I am naked." She clutched at the blanket, intending to pull it up to her chin.

Blair stayed her hand, slowly drawing the covers down to her waist. "Aye, ye are. Gloriously so. And ye are in my bed, 'tis true, but I didna leave ye. I was here all night, beside ye."

"Oh." She stiffened, aware of his quiet scrutiny though less alarmed by it than she really ought to be. "You slept here? With me? Did we——"

He laughed. "Nay, we didna. I prefer my women to be conscious when I fuck them. Indeed, I insist upon it."

"When you… Oh, my."

She started to relax under the soft caress of his fingers

as they trailed over her collarbone. "Much as I might relish the turn this conversation of ours has taken, I must ask ye to contain your enthusiasm for bed sport if ye will and remain with the matter in hand. We need to discuss your future."

Though her head still spun and her bottom burned Roselyn was sufficiently shocked by his outrageous suggestions that she managed to ease herself up onto one elbow. "Bed sport? Sir, I would never…" She paused as the rest of his words sank in. "My future? What do you mean?"

"I mean, little English wench, that now your punishment is concluded you are free to leave here if ye wish."

"Leave?" Again, that cruel spear of grief and impending loss. "But, where might I go? Do you mean to send me back to Etal?"

"Nay, not there. I have no intention of returning ye to your brother's tender mercies in order that he might resume his negotiations for your marriage. He shall not have that benefit."

"Thank you," murmured Roselyn. "Then where…?"

"In any case, there is little enough left of your home," continued Blair as though she had not spoken. "From the tone of Mother Sarah's letter to me I would surmise that ye'd find a welcome at Kelso, but that is closer tae Etal than I would like and either your brother or Sir John would be able to snatch ye away at will. I find that not to be a prospect I can stomach."

She was glad enough to hear that. "Me neither. Also, my welcome at Kelso had much to do with the allowance granted by my brother to the priory in exchange for their care of me. He was convinced that my blindness would render me incapable of any useful role in the world, which was another reason for his wish to get me married off to any man who might be prepared to take me. I doubt the holy sisters' charity would prove boundless without a generous contribution to their coffers."

"Aye, perhaps. But I gather ye have entertained a desire

to take the veil, so if that is still your wish I could secure sanctuary for you at another house."

"You would do that for me? After what I did to you? To your family?"

"All is forgiven now, Roselyn. Was that not the point of yesterday's spot of unpleasantness?"

"Unpleasantness? Is that how you would term whipping me until I cried out for all in this keep to hear me?"

"Ye were never in danger. I gave ye my word an' I meant it. Ye're sore now, I ken that, but it is no more than a passing discomfort an' within a few days ye shall be over it completely."

"It hurts when I move," she retorted, a note of indignation in her voice.

"Then remain still. I have said that ye may stay here until ye feel like rising from the bed. Meggie can attend to ye an' I daresay I could be convinced to allow that hound of yours in here if ye insist."

"Is Freya all right?"

"I expect so. She'll come to no harm for spending a night in the stables. But enough of that, I shall be requiring an answer to my question. Do ye wish me to find a place in a convent for ye?"

"I…" Fond though she was of Mother Sarah and the holy sisters at Kelso, Roselyn had never seriously considered joining their blessed ranks. "Might I have some time to reflect upon that, if you please?"

He was not to be put off. "You do not wish to retire to the cloister? I detect little from you in the way of enthusiasm for the notion."

"I… I had not thought—"

"I was under a different impression. Did you not tell your brother that you wished to become a nun?"

"I did, but only as an alternative to marrying Sir John. Any fate would be preferable to that." She hesitated, unsure of his reaction were she to disclose what manner of future seemed the most desirable to her at this moment.

"Roselyn, tell me." He kissed her forehead. "Tell me what you really want to do."

"May I stay here?" There, she had blurted it out. She held her breath.

"I have said so."

"No, not here in your bed. Here, at Duncleit. In your castle. Might I not make my home here?"

"You would choose to stay, even though you are free to leave. You are no longer my prisoner."

"I do not feel like your prisoner, or at least, I have not for some time. Since you returned and... you have treated me like a guest."

"I do not tend to strip my guests naked and take a switch to them, not as a rule."

"Sir, do not pretend to misunderstand me. I have enjoyed more freedom in the few short days that I have been here than I have known since I lost my sight. My brother sought to lock me away but you have been considerate of my safety, my happiness. You have made it possible for me to move about unaided, though I have been glad enough of Meggie's assistance. And Freya. You allowed me to train one of your hounds—"

"A useless mutt, but I can see that she means a lot to ye."

"She means everything. With Freya I... I could make myself useful here, I know it. I could assist Elspeth and I know something of herbs and healing. I can play the lyre, though I confess I would require some practice before I might claim to be proficient. I would not be a burden on your household though, I swear that I would not."

"I know that, so ye may cease your babbling on the matter. All pull their weight here, according to their abilities, and ye shall be no different."

"Then I may stay?"

"Aye, if that is your wish we would be glad to have ye. Certainly I would, for I find I have developed a fondness for your presence in my bed."

"In your bed? Sir, do you mean…? That is, are you…?" Again she reached for the cover but Blair pushed it further from her reach.

"I intend to fuck you. Is that sufficiently plain?"

"Quite sufficient," Roselyn squeaked. "You have made your wishes perfectly clear."

"And what of your wishes in the matter, Roselyn? Might ye be in the least little bit willing?"

"What difference does that make?"

He took her chin in his hand and tipped up her face. She was aware of his gaze on her though she could not meet it. His voice was low, compelling, and she felt completely exposed. She started to lower her eyelids. "No, do not shut me out, lass."

She opened her eyes again.

"Thank you. Now listen and mind my words. Had I been minded to take you by force I could have done so at any time. None here would have lifted a hand in your defence. But I would not do that, not then, not now. I shall have you willing, or not at all."

"Willing? As what? Your mistress?"

"Aye, that's a good enough description."

"Not as your wife?"

"I have no plans to marry, but you must understand, when I do take a wife the union will be about politics, and about power. I shall have to ally the McGregors with another clan for mutual benefit. This, this thing between us, this is different."

She hung her head, dejected. "I know that you would have no wish to ally yourself with my family. You hate the Ingrams, and with good reason."

"There is that, also. But let me be very clear on one thing, my quarrel is with your brother alone, I do *not* hate you."

"And that is why you would… you would do that thing you said?"

"That thing I said? Ah, yes, allow me to be clear. I wish to fuck you because you are beautiful. You fascinate me and

I have desired you from the first moment I set eyes on you. I would fuck you right gladly. I have said so. Is it such a poor prospect?"

In fairness, Roselyn could not say that it was. She had been similarly drawn to him, her captor, her judge, and now her would-be lover. Would that matters were so simple.

"It is not a poor prospect, as you put it, but I could not become your mistress. It would not be proper, my lord." A poor excuse, given that even as they were having this conversation she lay naked in his bed, the blankets tangled around her thighs.

"Our situation is somewhat unique, I would suggest. I care not for your brother's opinion on the matter and his marriage plans for you are in tatters whatever you decide to do. Sir John might still be interested but you will find no other husband, not after having been abducted by a Highland warlord and held captive in his keep. But I promise that you will be treated with respect here, and I swear you will come to no harm at my hands."

"Will you beat me again?"

"Aye, if you deserve it. For disobedience or disrespect. I am master here and that will apply to all. But you would not find me cruel. Indeed, I believe you would find pleasure in what I offer."

"Pleasure, my lord? I do not quite take your meaning."

"Will you not own to the slightest stirring? You may deny your arousal but your body betrays ye, Roselyn. Your nipples are swollen, your eyes have darkened as you consider my offer. I believe if you were to spread your thighs for me now I would find you wet."

"Wet?" She drew in a shuddering breath. "My nipples… it is chilly in here."

"Nay, it is not. I banked up the fire afore I woke you. Stop making excuses and open your legs for me, Roselyn."

"I will not."

"Yes, you will, and you will do it now."

"I…"

He trailed his fingers the length of her body, tracing a path between her breasts and across her flat stomach to her mound. There he teased the auburn curls which protected her most intimate place.

"Open for me." He leaned in to whisper the words into her ear, his familiar male smell overwhelming her senses. He was spice, and he was musk, heather, pine, and something mysteriously unique, an essence which was only his.

Roselyn was lost, mesmerised. She rolled fully onto her back, even managed not to wince as her weight settled on her punished buttocks. Bending her knees a little, she allowed him to tease her thighs apart. His slid his hand between her legs and stroked her moist folds.

"Ah, so deliciously damp. Roselyn, you do indeed delight me."

"My lord..." She was lost, her words buried under the waves of pure sensation. "What are you doing to me?"

"I am pleasuring ye, sweetheart. Be still for me, and open wider."

As though in a trance, wrapped in fog of unaccustomed sensuality, Roselyn obeyed. She arched her back and let out a sharp cry as he slipped one long finger into her wet channel.

He paused. "Did I hurt ye?"

She shook her head. "No. It was... oh, please do that once more if you would."

He thrust his finger into her again, then added a second digit. Unfamiliar sensations assailed Roselyn, both confusing and exciting. And intense. It was incredible, unbelievable. Her head whirled. She felt tight, stretched, yet at the same time she wanted nothing other than to spread her body open, to welcome this intrusion. He was right, this *was* about pleasure. It was a strange sort of joy, but she craved it nonetheless.

"That feels good, my lord."

"My title is laird, not lord, but I believe we are on first name terms now. You will use my given name, most particularly when my fingers or indeed any part of my anatomy is lodged within your sweet cunt."

"Oh, God…"

"Nay, just Blair will do." He withdrew his fingers and resumed stroking her outer lips. He found a spot which brought Roselyn's hips right up from the mattress. "Ah, now I see I have your complete attention. Perhaps you might like to practice using my name." He paused in his sensuous rubbing and Roselyn moaned her need.

"Say my name," he urged.

"Blair." She whispered it.

He resumed the torturous caress. "Again. Say it again. Louder."

She raised her voice a little. "Blair."

"Better. And you will scream my name when you find your release."

"My…?"

He took that most sensitive nubbin between his fingers and he squeezed. Something clenched within, deep in her core, and Roselyn longed for his fingers to be inside her tight channel again. She yearned to be filled, stretched, owned.

"Could you…? Blair, I need…"

"I know." He continued to roll her sensitive flesh between his fingers, whilst he used his free hand to open that most secret place and plunged two digits into her again.

It was too much. Roselyn could no longer speak, could not even form a coherent thought. She could only feel as irresistible shudders rocked her slight form and her inner walls clenched helplessly around his fingers. She arched further, lifting her hips, pleading for something, anything…

"Oh, Blair. Blair, Blair, *Blair!*" She let out a keening wail as the sensations peaked and her body convulsed, then, gasping, she stilled.

Blair settled beside her and gathered her into his arms. Her bottom still hurt, indeed, her skin throbbed mercilessly from rubbing against the mattress but she did not care.

Nothing mattered in that moment apart from the need to burrow as close into Blair as she could, to seek his warmth, his strength.

He kissed her hair. "That was just a taste of what I can offer you. Will you stay? With me?"

"I…" She buried her face against his chest, realising for the first time in this entire encounter that he was also naked. "Oh. Oh…" She splayed her hand against his chest and curled her fingers in the light dusting of hair she found there.

"You fancy a spot more explorin'? I canna say I blame you, in the circumstances."

"May I?" Where did this unaccustomed boldness spring from?

"Aye, lass. You have spread yourself for me so 'tis the least I can offer in return."

"You are looking at me, but I cannot see you."

"You can, with your fingers. And you have other senses which I ken you use to good effect."

She smiled. "'Tis true that I can hear you, and I can feel you. I recognise your scent whenever you are close." She eased herself gingerly to her knees beside him, acutely conscious of his eyes on her nude and newly sated form. She leaned over and kissed his shoulder, then, on impulse, darted out her tongue to taste his skin. "You taste like wood smoke, and the forest at dawn."

"Indeed," he murmured. "Could I convince you to lie back and spread your thighs for me once more an' I'll tell you what you taste of?"

The very thought was scandalous. And wickedly enticing. Roselyn's head whirled and she actually swayed as she contemplated the forbidden thing he seemingly wished to do to her, but when she inhaled his heady aroma again it was with a renewed determination to make different discoveries.

"I believe, sir, that I should thoroughly understand the goods on offer before making my choice."

"I thought as much."

"You will remain still for me? As I did for you?" She hoped, but was uncertain of his response. The McGregor was accustomed to control. He was not a man who would readily obey.

"I shall, aye. You deserve as much."

"Thank you." She shifted and placed both hands on his shoulders. "May I straddle you?"

She thought his answer might be somewhat obscene, though the strangled epithet was purely Gaelic in origin.

"Sir? Blair…?"

"Aye lass, you may if you wish but I willna be accountable for the outcome."

"Just my hands. And my mouth."

"If you say so. I have no wish to rush you, but I'd be obliged if you might be getting on with it."

"You are in a hurry to leave. I understand, you have duties, as laird. Perhaps we might resume this later."

"And perhaps you might cease your prattling and let me fuck you. But failing that, please be assured I am in no particular hurry to be away."

She stifled a giggle. She had no need of the gift of sight in this moment. She knew by the growl in his voice that he suffered and could only surmise that she was the cause. "Then I shall continue."

Slowly, carefully, she lifted her knee and stretched her leg across his stomach. She was pleased to find him lean and sharply contoured and she was able to settle herself comfortably on his abdomen. The taut planes of his stomach pressed against her exposed core, reigniting her arousal. She rolled her hips to rub against him, conscious of her wetness, and she wondered at the unaccustomed pleasure to be derived from simple friction. Her palms found his shoulders again and she measured the width of them between her hands. Beneath her fingers the muscles and sinews flexed. He was solid, firm, and she detected both health and strength in his chiseled form. Despite his size and power though he had been gentle with her, almost from the moment they met.

"I know that you are tall, a full head taller than I am. Your shoulders are broad, yet your hips are not."

"I am built for fighting, and for riding."

"I suspect you have other fine qualities also." She shuffled back a little, intending to explore his sculpted stomach, but came up short as something large, thick, and very solid pressed between her smarting buttocks. "Oh! Your... er, I believe that your, your... Shall I move, Blair?"

"My cock."

"I beg your pardon."

"I hesitate to call attention to your limited vocabulary, madam, but the word you are flailing about in search of is 'cock.' My cock, to be exact. And yes, please do feel free to move, though now that you have discovered that part of my anatomy I would prefer if you remain in contact with it. If you find the current position a tad uncomfortable given your recent chastisement you might like to take my cock in your hands."

"But I do not know how..."

"I would be delighted to offer suggestions, my lady, if required. This is, after all, a voyage of discovery on your part and I would hate to hamper your quest for knowledge."

Her curiosity was fuelled by his comment. Roselyn knelt upright and reached behind her so that her fingertips grazed the shaft of his engorged cock. It was a word with which she was, in fact, perfectly familiar, though she had never before found the need to utter it in any context not concerned with poultry. The angle was awkward though, and she could not manage to do more than explore the smooth texture of the skin which covered his erect penis.

"You may find it easier if you turn around," suggested Blair helpfully.

"Of course," she murmured. "Quite so."

CHAPTER SEVEN

In fact Roselyn opted to settle back on the bed beside him, though her sole focus was the hard length of male potency now cradled between her hands. She had nothing with which to compare, but if she wrapped just one fist around it her fingers would not meet so she judged him to be large. She ran her hands the length of him, from the base of his cock to the rounded, smooth head, then back down again. He let out a long sigh which she interpreted as indicating approval. Accordingly, she repeated the action, then again for good measure. Blair's cock lurched in her hands.

Roselyn was startled. "Did I do something wrong?"

"Nay, lass. That was good. Mind, should you be moved to reach a little lower and cup my balls I should not complain over much."

Ever a diligent scholar, Roselyn was quick to heed his direction. She sought his balls and attempted to hold them in one hand though they seemed to possess a will of their own. Even so, she commenced a slow, steady massage whilst continuing to pump her other hand up and down the length of his shaft. She quickly realised that the head, that bulbous and smoothly rounded cap, was weeping with cool, slick liquid and becoming wetter with every stroke. Roselyn ran her thumb through the gathering moisture to spread it everywhere she could and she assumed that Blair's moans signified his approval of that strategy.

His aroma enveloped her, the air redolent with the scent of arousal. Was it his, or hers? She could not be sure but it did not matter. The musky tang clung to her and she bent toward him to better inhale. The odour was heady, addictive… she needed more.

An idea occurred to her. He had said he would taste her, but why should she not know his flavours too? The scent sang to her of spices and freshness, but with a quality she believed to be uniquely male. She would know it better, understand this new experience more completely if she were to make use of all her senses. It was practical, prudent even… She grasped him firmly in her hand and leaned down even more.

At first she was tentative, just drawing the tip of her tongue through the wetness which coated his cock.

Blair muttered that Gaelic word again, adding in several more before he wrapped a great hank of her hair around his hand. He did not pull on it though, nor did he force her head forward. He simply held it, held her.

Gaining in confidence, Roselyn savoured the salty taste on her tongue, then she parted her lips. She took him in, just the head at first. His cock stretched her mouth, but she managed. She sucked on it as though it were a sweetmeat, and decided the similarities were striking enough. The taste was exceptional, a spicy tang which grew stronger as she increased the suction. She turned her face to the side so the head slipped into the pocket of her inner cheek and she was able to take more of the shaft. She used her hand to pump that portion remaining outside, at the same time squeezing the heavy orbs which nestled against her other palm.

Blair tightened his grip on her hair, which heightened her arousal. She was powerful, in control of what was happening between them, but only so long as he permitted it. At any moment he could haul her off or ram her face down, forcing her to take him deeper. He did neither, though he twisted more of her hair around his hand.

He thrust up with his hips, not hard, but enough to signal that he wanted more from her. Roselyn found added momentum, squeezed a fraction harder, sucked that little bit more.

"Sweetheart… you need to stop now." His tone was muffled, pained almost.

Roselyn released him from her mouth. Had she done something wrong?

"Continue with your hands, harder, faster," he growled. "Yes, like that. Just. Like. That."

He jerked violently in her hands. "Let go of my balls and lay that hand over the top, right at the end."

She obeyed, just as a surge of hot, viscous liquid spurted across her palm.

"Oh!"

"Dinna stop. Not yet…"

She didn't, and more of the fluid coated her sticky fingers. The aroma was even stronger, headier, and without thinking Roselyn slipped her fingers into her mouth to lick them. Rich flavours exploded on her tongue, sweet and zesty flavours with a piquancy which spoke to her of intimacy, of heat, and of erotically wicked pleasures.

Blair's grip in her hair relaxed. He stroked her head as though to soothe away a hurt he had not caused. For long moments neither spoke.

Blair broke the silence. "Next time, you shall take my essence in your mouth and swallow it. All of it. For now, though, and since you so particularly wished to explore, I thought it best that you discover what you could expect to happen when you suck a man's cock."

"Thank you, sir. It was a most salutary lesson and I appreciate your… your…"

"My generosity?" put in her helpful tutor.

"Yes, that is it. Your generosity. Now though, I believe

I may be in need of a cloth."

"I shall summon Meggie."

"No!" The prospect of being discovered naked in The McGregor's bed, her hands covered in his semen, was not one she could quite face. Not yet. "I... I believe I might contrive to manage for myself."

He laughed. "And I believe you to be shy. Allow me, then." In moments he had produced a bowl of water, regrettably cool, and a cloth. He proceeded to wipe the remnants of his semen from her hands, then, she supposed from himself. There was a soft splash as he dropped the cloth back into the bowl. "I need to leave, and I will not press you for an answer at once regarding your plans. I hope though that I have managed to demonstrate that your role as my mistress would not be unduly onerous."

Roselyn could come up with no suitable answer for that, save a somewhat bemused, "Yes, Blair."

• • • • • • •

Roselyn sought her usual seat at the lord's table, her hound at her side. Her backside remained tender but she could at least sit with a modicum of ease. She would not have believed that possible just a couple of hours earlier.

Meggie had entered the chamber shortly after Blair's departure, Freya bounding ahead of her. The girl announced that she had instructions to see to Roselyn's comfort and since those instructions had come direct from the laird she was not about to be put off by any protestations from Roselyn.

With much sighing Roselyn resigned herself to the inevitable and allowed the serving girl to tidy the room and assist her in her ablutions. Although Roselyn tried to make light of the matter, the girl gasped at the sight of her new lady's punished bottom. Elspeth was summoned at once, and the cook brought with her a basket of unguents which she swore were guaranteed to aid healing and soothe the sting of a well-disciplined backside.

"Och, he has a firm hand does The McGregor, as did 'is father afore him. Her ladyship, the laird's mother, was a wild 'un at times an' I often had to apply a soothing balm tae her nether parts. 'Tis a tried and tested recipe I 'ave here an' ye'll soon feel the benefits, lass. So, let's be seein' what's up, then."

"Really, there is no need. I am perfectly all right." Roselyn clutched the laird's bedclothes beneath her chin.

"Ye shall be, soon enough. Now lie on your front an' just let me sort this out if ye would, lassie."

Roselyn saw no option but to comply and was soon glad she did. The cook exclaimed at the many shades of red and purple which apparently adorned Roselyn's tender skin, but seemed disinclined to take issue with the general principle. "It were a right serious matter, but our laird's a fair man, as I told ye afore. Still, all's done now. Keep still while I treat this."

The sticky mess which Elspeth pasted liberally across Roselyn's raw behind smelled vile, but within moments of application her bottom felt cooler and less inflamed.

The cook draped a sheet over her work and instructed Roselyn to stay still for an hour. "Then we shall pop ye into a nice, hot bath an' ye'll find it much easier from then on. Mind, ye may not wish tae tell the laird that. Ye'll still have the bruises tae show for your ordeal so he should be satisfied ye learnt your lesson an' not see fit to repeat it."

Roselyn was horrified. "What? No, he would not do such a thing. Would he?"

"Only you know that, lass. Is all well between the two of ye now, then?"

She pondered for a moment. Surely it must be; he would not have pleasured her as he had, nor permitted her such intimacies with his own person had he still been angry. He had told her all was forgiven, and she trusted him, in that at least. She nodded. "Yes. All is well."

"That's good, then. In that case I shall leave ye tae your

rest." The cook bustled off about her business, leaving Roselyn to ponder her new and very peculiar circumstances.

Now, much more comfortable than perhaps she deserved to be, Roselyn shifted in her seat as she scanned the hall. She felt considerably more relaxed today than she had yesterday when she had sat in silence beside Blair to hear the accounts of the newcomers from Etal. The rest of the household had been present too, and had listened with hardly a murmur as their laird questioned the English servants. Betsy and John Cooper, her brother's old steward, had offered testimony which supported the version of events she had described to Blair. John Cooper told of having had to lift Roselyn from the carriage which arrived from Kelso, then he explained how he carried the limp form of his mistress up to her chamber. Betsy described the horrific bruising and discomfort she had observed as she had cared for the injured young woman, and the utter lack of concern shown by the Earl of Ingram who had never even enquired as to his sister's health. Blair offered questions, probed here and there in search of greater clarity and Roselyn was near enough overwhelmed with gratitude, both for her Highland captor and her loyal friends.

Now she could tell from the hubbub of voices surrounding her that the great hall was its usual busy place, the heart of Duncleit. Servants and men-at-arms scurried about their business, visitors to the castle always waited in this chamber, and villagers seeking their laird's help or advice would wander in in search of him. The McGregor guarded his borders well, but closer to home he kept an open house. Roselyn tried to pick out a familiar voice from Etal but could not.

"Meggie, are any of the folk who arrived yesterday here in the hall?" The previous day others had spoken on her behalf. She owed them her thanks.

"Nay, milady. I canna see either. Is there aught I can do for ye?"

"I was hoping to speak with them. I wonder…"

"I shall go look, milady. Ye have the dog wi' ye if ye' need tae move from here."

At least Meggie trusted Freya. Blair would soon come around, Roselyn decided. "Thank you, but I am perfectly comfortable for now." An overstatement, perhaps, but she would do.

The maidservant's hurrying footsteps receded into the general din of the hectic great hall. Roselyn relaxed back in to her seat and absorbed the sounds of ordered domesticity. She could be happy here, she mused. She really could, so long as she and The McGregor could arrive at an understanding.

He had not said so, or even hinted it, but she could not help wondering if he would welcome her into his household with quite such relish were she not to agree to share his bed. And she could never agree to that, could she? The very notion was outrageous. How dare he even suggest it?

She flattened her lips wryly. The McGregor would dare just about anything, especially under his own roof. And she was no better. She had cavorted naked in his bed and as if that was not quite disgraceful enough she had actually taken his engorged cock into her mouth. She had performed that act quite unbidden, and in truth she had thoroughly enjoyed the adventure.

Blair had pointed out that her prospects for marriage, already slender, were rendered non-existent by her brother's crimes and his own actions in taking her prisoner. What did she have to lose? She did not blame Blair for her fate; he had treated her well, all told. His remarks had not been made in an unkind manner, he was simply being realistic and perhaps she needed to behave likewise. He had offered to provide for her, which he need not have. He had offered her choices, and really, would a life as The McGregor's mistress be such a poor route to take?

"Milady, I found her. Your old maid is here."

Meggie's return disturbed her from her musings. "Betsy?" Roselyn extended her hand.

"Aye, my lady, 'tis me. And right glad I am to see you. Are you well, my lady? Have they treated you kindly?"

"Yes. Yes, they have so please do not concern yourself with me. How many of you made the journey from Etal?"

"Well, there's me and my sister, with her man, John Cooper. But you know about John as he was in the hall yesterday. Martha came too, and her brood, though she has near driven me mad as we made our way here. I could have preferred we had left her in Mortain, but she was bent on a new life, so here we all are."

"What happened? Please, be seated and tell me all of it, from when I last saw you at Etal." She gestured to the empty lord's chair to her right.

"I'm not sure, my lady. This is the grand table, and the lord here, well, he's a powerful man and—"

"Blair will not punish you for sitting in his chair. Please, I wish to hear your story…"

"Aye, well, if you're quite certain…"

Roselyn waited impatiently as the other woman settled herself. "Would you like some mead? Or ale perhaps?"

"No, but thank you. Now, what is it you want to know?"

"Everything. When I was taken away you were in the courtyard with the others. I thought… I feared that the Highlanders would hurt you."

"Aye, as did we all, just like at Mortain. But that laird of yours, he came over and he asked us again if everyone was present. This time though he told us he needed to know because if there was anyone left within the buildings he would ensure they were found and brought forth before the torches were lit. He told us he was no murderer and we need have no fear of him provided we obeyed and caused no trouble to his men."

"Oh. So, were there more people still hiding?"

"Aye, plenty. We didn't know if we could trust him or not, but what did we have to lose, my lady? We told him that there were people who had fled to the storerooms and perhaps some in the loft above the stables. He sent John

Cooper with his men to search those places and to tell anyone still there to come out at once before the fires started. Everyone was safe, in the end, but the castle is beyond repairing. Just a shell now, my lady. It was terrible to behold but some decided to stay anyway and rebuild their cottages. There is much good stone to be had, you see…" She paused. "Well, you don't see, but you take my meaning."

"I do. And some went to Mortain?"

"Yes. Lord McGregor offered us the chance to go there to help restore that keep and the estate. Many took that option, because 'tis not so far distant and none of us had any wish to serve the earl any longer. That devil will lie low for a while but sooner or later he'll be back and demanding obeisance from the serfs still on the land. We were better away from there. He's a wicked man, my lady, your brother is. Wicked and cruel."

"I know that."

"Aye, that you do, better than most."

"But *you* are here, not at Mortain."

"Aye, that was the other choice. Lord McGregor said that his own keep was a safe and a prosperous place, and we would be welcome to make our homes there."

"But, it was such a long journey for you."

"Yes, but I was so scared for you that I ran after the Highland laird and I asked his lordship where he was taking you. I thought he might have me whipped for my impertinence but he did not. He stopped and spoke to me, said you would be taken to Duncleit to answer for your part in the massacre. Hearing that, I convinced my brother to set out for here as well. I could not leave you alone among those who might hurt you, my lady, it didn't seem right."

A disgruntled snort from Roselyn's left reminded her of Meggie's inquisitive presence. "I look after milady. Me and Freya," she announced indignantly. "And no one will harm her. The McGregor willna permit it."

"Thank you, Meggie." Roselyn reached to pat the girl's

arm, knowing she meant no disrespect to the newcomers. "You are right of course, but Betsy was not to know that. I am grateful to you, to both of you, for your help and your kindness."

"And Elspeth," prompted Meggie. "She was the one who 'elped ye with your poor whipped bottom."

"What? He whipped you? Why, that mean devil. I should ha' known better than to—"

"Hush." Roselyn interrupted the loyal servant's tirade. "It was a fair and just punishment and far more lenient than I might have hoped for." She paused, then continued, her voice low. "He would have been within his rights to hang me."

"No! Surely—"

"Yes. He could have done that, but he did not. Instead he sought out the truth. He waited until you arrived in order that you might speak out for me, and he even sent a messenger to Kelso to question the Reverend Mother there. I… I have no complaints at all about my treatment under Blair's roof."

"Blair? You and he be on first name terms then?"

Betsy's tone was sharp, knowing even. Roselyn recalled that the woman had never been one to miss much. "Yes, we are. He has been most, most… courteous."

"Except when he thrashed your backside? I daresay his manners may have been a little less than courtly then, my lady."

Roselyn considered that, but shook her head. "No. Even then he was not exactly unpleasant. It is difficult to understand, I know that, but—"

"Do you like the man, my lady?"

"What? Yes, of course I do. I respect him greatly. He is a fine laird, and—"

"You misunderstand me, Lady Roselyn. I asked, do you *like* the man?"

Roselyn clamped her lips together and sought to remind herself why she had even summoned this woman to speak to her this morning. Surely she did not wish to bare her very soul to a servant. Except—she badly needed to speak to someone and Betsy was at least a familiar presence. What was more, however blunt the maid might be, Roselyn knew the woman had her best interests at heart.

"Meggie, I wonder if you would leave us for a little while, please?"

"But milady, the laird said… I mean, he was most particular, like, that I was to look after ye."

It was clear that the girl took her duties seriously, though Roselyn also suspected that the little maidservant was riveted by the turn the conversation had taken. However, the confidences she was about to share were not fit for such young ears. "Please, Meggie. I am sure Elspeth could make use of your help in the kitchens and I shall call for you at once if I need your assistance. And I have Freya, or if absolutely necessary Betsy can aid me. I shall be fine."

The girl was less than happy but her mutterings of discontent were ignored. Roselyn just smiled, thanked her for all her help, and promised to tell Blair how diligently she had performed her duties. A disgruntled Meggie shuffled off in the direction of the kitchens.

"She is gone," announced Betsy. "So now, you can tell me all about this Blair of yours. And who is Freya?"

Roselyn opted to start with the simplest question. "Freya is my dog. Is she not a beautiful creature, and so clever?"

"This dog, my lady? The one at your feet?"

"Yes." Roselyn bent to scratch Freya's ears. "I have trained her to guide me. She is most adept."

"Is she? Well, I shall have to take your word for that, though I could not in all truth describe her as beautiful."

Roselyn tilted her chin in defiance. "She is beautiful to me."

"Then that is fine, madam. So, about the laird…?"

Yes, mused Roselyn… *about the laird?*

"He has invited me to stay here, at Duncleit. I may make my permanent home here if I wish."

"Duncleit seems to be a fine keep, and the people hereabouts speak well of the laird. And if you like him, well, I daresay you could do worse."

"I did not say that I like him."

"You dislike him?"

"No, of course I do not. It is—not so simple."

"In what way is it not simple, my lady? Do you intend to remain here? Where else might you go?"

"I could enter a convent. Not Kelso for I would never be safe there, but another house. Blair has said he could secure a place for me."

"That is considerate of him."

"Yes, and generous too since he would have to endow the convent with sufficient funds to convince them to offer me sanctuary. But I do not wish to take the veil."

"No, madam, I thought you may not. We are to remain here then?"

"I… perhaps."

"I am relieved. I do not believe I could have readily convinced my brother to follow you halfway across the country again."

"There would be no need, I assure you. I shall be fine."

"Lady Roselyn, this is Betsy you are talking to." The faithful servant's tone took on a quality Roselyn rarely heard. It reminded her strongly of her mother on those rare occasions when Roselyn had displeased her. Betsy took her hand and held on even when Roselyn might have pulled away. "Now please, quit this babbling and tell me what the problem is. You have said the laird is not a cruel man. He punished you but not unjustly. His home is a fine place. So, why do you hesitate?"

"He wishes to sleep with me. I would be his mistress, if I agree."

"If? Why would you not agree?"

"Betsy!" Roselyn was scandalised. "How can you say such a thing?"

"You may be blind, my lady, but I am not. Your laird is

126

a handsome man, uncommonly so, and it would seem he has other fine qualities also. I suspect there are many here who would readily share his bed. Indeed, were he to ask, I believe I might not kick him out…"

"Stop! Please, say no more. This is, is…"

"My lady, Roselyn, think about it. You have few other options, and none that offer better prospects for your safety and happiness. I believe the laird would please you, in the bedchamber, which is more than many women achieve. He has no wife, so…"

"But that's just it. What if he were to marry? I would be cast out, ruined…"

"And heartbroken?" The servant's tone gentled.

"Yes, that too I expect."

"Why should he ever send you away? He may never marry, especially if you have his children. I understand the Scots are less particular than we English on matters of legitimacy. You could be his wife in all but name, and you are already Lady of Duncleit."

"I am not. I am merely a guest. Until yesterday I was a prisoner."

"All here refer to you as Lady Roselyn and it is known you have the favour of the laird. The servants defer to you, the men at arms treat you with the respect due to your rank. You *are* lady here, whether you know it yet or not."

Roselyn could hardly believe what she was hearing. "You speak as though there was nothing at all wrong in sharing a man's bed just because he has a gentle way with him and asks nicely. I may have succumbed to his persuasive charms once, but—"

"You did? Oh, well, that is a relief. So you do at least know what you are getting. I take it he performed well enough? All was to your liking?"

"Betsy!"

"My lady?"

"Yes. Yes, all right. All was to my liking. It was… very nice. But I am still a virgin. At least, I believe so."

"I am quite sure you would have no doubt if you were not, though as I have never married I cannot claim extensive experience in such matters. Still, I expect we can rely upon the laird to address that issue soon enough."

"Yes," agreed Roselyn, "I daresay he will."

"So, you will become his lady—in or out of wedlock?"

Had there ever been any doubt? Roselyn acknowledged that probably there had not. Betsy had simply told her what she needed to hear, answers she should have articulated for herself. She wanted Blair, it really was that simple. There was no reason at all why she should not have him. Except...

"Why would he want me? I am blind, not even beautiful. He could choose anyone, any woman he liked. I have no lands, bring him no power or advantage. He told me he would expect that in a wife."

"And he could have negotiated an advantageous match at any time. Or his clan could. He has not so perhaps he sets less store by those matters than you think. He wants you. Your blindness is no impediment; indeed, you seem to be managing far better here than you ever did at Etal. As for beauty, my lady, there is none lovelier. Your Highland laird would be fortunate to have you beside him, as would any man. He has had the good sense to pursue you, so I can only assume he sees what everyone else does." She hesitated, then, "May I speak plainly, madam?"

Roselyn gaped. "You can be more direct?"

Her companion gave a wry chuckle. "Well, perhaps I have been a little forward, but it seemed warranted. I just want to say, do not let self-doubt cloud your decision. Take what is offered, if you want it. The opportunity may not come round again. Ah, I see our little friend returning. Meggie, was it? Shall I send her off on some errand?"

"No, she takes her responsibilities very seriously and will be upset if I do not allow her to hover about me. She is a good girl. But, thank you, Betsy, for your counsel and for your loyalty. I shall not forget what you have done for me, and how you spoke out in my defence."

• • • • • • •

Blair did not return for the evening meal. Roselyn made her own way down to the great hall at the appointed hour with just Freya and the handrail on the stairs to assist, and felt inordinately proud of her new independence. She took her usual seat at the table on the dais, and accepted Meggie's aid in selecting her preferred delicacies. Her companions at the high table, mostly Blair's senior men-at-arms, assured her that his absence was no cause for concern.

In response to her tentative enquiry the man to her left informed her that his name was Archie. "The McGregor will seek shelter where he needs it, there's many a cottage will offer him a welcome. He willna travel after dark if he can avoid it."

Another man, seated to her right, was already known to Roselyn. She remembered Aiden from Etal, and knew he had been the one charged with the task of gathering the switches which The McGregor later wore out on her unfortunate buttocks. Roselyn would have been embarrassed at the recollection but the man merely asked after her health and comfort and patted Freya. Roselyn learnt that her dog had not, after all, been confined to the stables but had spent that fateful night in Aiden's quarters.

"She's a fine animal," Aiden observed, "and ye're a fine trainer. Ye have a way with creatures, it seems."

"I do love dogs. Horses also, and I loved to ride when I was young. I fear I may never get over my nervousness about getting into the saddle again since I fell from my own little mare and lost my sight as a result."

"Ah, I can understand that, but ye really should try. We have several fine mounts here at Duncleit that ye might like. Quiet, gentle animals an' I daresay ye could train one tae your needs."

"My brother said that it would be too dangerous for me, I might be killed the next time."

"If ye'll pardon me sayin' so, my lady, but your brother is a fool. Ask The McGregor his opinion. If he permits it, I would be happy to select a mare from our stables for ye."

"I shall." Roselyn beamed at him. "I surely will. Thank you."

She now had more than just one cause to look forward to Blair's return.

Later that evening she sat on the edge of her bed having dismissed Meggie for the night. Freya snored softly beside the dying fire, clearly more than content with her new quarters. Roselyn was tired, but restless also and reluctant to clamber into bed quite yet. She wished Blair were here. She wanted him, needed him. They had much to discuss.

On impulse she stood and counted the paces to the door.

"No, you stay," she commanded as the dog stirred. Freya settled again, and Roselyn slipped from her chamber and out into the solar. She crossed the room to reach Blair's bedchamber, the one she had occupied with him the previous night. Perhaps she might draw comfort from being in this room, so steeped in his presence. She made her way cautiously to the bed and pulled back the rugs to climb in. She was asleep within minutes.

CHAPTER EIGHT

Blair edged his mount down the meadow in the direction of Duncleit. The castle lay before him, silhouetted against the night sky, illuminated in the thin moonlight. He had expected to be back hours ago but a badly swollen ford over the River Drynoch had caused him to make a lengthy detour on his return from settling a dispute in the village of Eynort. He had been tempted to accept the hospitality offered by more than one crofter on his route home, but he had declined. It was a fine enough night despite the recent rain which had caused the river to flood thus creating his current problem and he preferred to lay his head down in his own keep.

The lookout recognised him and lowered the drawbridge as he approached. Blair called his thanks to the man, still stationed on the battlements, and turned his stallion's head in the direction of the stables. He was glad enough to hand Bartholomew's reins to the tousle-haired lad who scampered out to meet him.

"See he is well rubbed down and given plenty of fresh hay."

"Aye, Laird, I surely will." The lad grabbed at the dangling straps and tugged the horse in the direction of his warm stall. The stallion took little convincing and Blair slapped his taut rump as he ambled after the boy.

"Right, now to see to my own rest," he murmured to the deserted bailey, "but first, food."

He entered his keep through the rear postern door, heading straight for the kitchens. He was careful not to step on any of the several servants who slept on the floors of the castle as he made his way to the cool cellar where he knew Elspeth stored cooked meats. Since being just a wee lad this had always been his favourite place to seek sustenance in the dead of night, and in all likelihood his faithful cook would have left something for him, just in case.

Elspeth did not let him down. A platter of succulent salted pork awaited him. He ate with one hip hitched on the edge of the huge oak table which dominated Elspeth's domain. A wee wench sleeping beside the cooling oven stirred. Frightened eyes peered up at him in alarm.

"Laird, is anything amiss?"

"Nay, lass," he whispered. "Go back to sleep."

"Is it time to light the fires? I was late last time, an'—"

"No, you are not late. Sleep now."

"Is that the pork ye're eatin', Laird? There's mutton either, but I like the pork best. I could get ye some ale too if ye like."

She shuffled into a sitting position, rubbing her eyes. Out of habit Blair tried to recall the child's name. Agnes, he thought, or was it Annie?

"I can shift for myself if I need aught. I didna mean to disturb you, lass."

The girl's response was a long, low growl from somewhere deep within her stomach. She clutched at her belly. "Ooh, I'm sorry, Laird. I was just… I mean…"

"Would you like some of this pork?" he offered.

She shook her head sadly. "I shouldna. The missus left it for ye an' I already had my supper, sir."

"There is no rule here that says a wee lassie wi' early fires to light an' a hungry belly canna have two suppers. Come to me, child."

She wriggled from her pallet and trotted to stand before him. Her dress was of rough linen, but serviceable enough, and the child was clean. Elspeth was most particular about such matters. Blair leaned down to offer her the platter. She gazed up at him, wide-eyed, then selected the biggest piece on the plate.

"Good choice. Annie, is it?"

"Aye, sir. Annie Drummond."

"Well, Annie Drummond, I'm right glad of your company this night. Would you like a morsel more?"

This time the child took two pieces, one in each hand. The pair of them chewed in companionable silence, and between them cleared much of the plate. After a few minutes Annie rubbed her eyes and yawned widely.

"Take some more pork an' go back to your bed, lassie. I'll be away to mine too."

"Thank you, sir." She took another couple of slices and he spotted her tucking one beneath her pallet before she settled down again.

"Goodnight, Annie," he whispered as he left to make his way up to his own chambers.

Annie did not reply. She was already fast asleep.

Blair entered his solar as quietly as he could in his heavy hide boots and whilst still bearing his claymore. He divested himself of both and cast an eye in the direction of the small guest chamber as he made for his own room. Roselyn would be in there, sleeping.

Would she be naked again? Well, a man could hope…

He lifted a torch from the wall to light his way as he entered his own chamber and stopped still. There, in the very centre of his huge bed, Roselyn lay curled up under his blankets. One slender shoulder poked out above the covers and that much of her at least was naked. His cock leapt to attention at the same time as he tried to make sense of this turn of events though her presence here could only really signify one thing.

He placed the torch in a sconce in the wall then undressed quickly and slid in beside her. Roselyn mumbled something in her sleep and turned to face him. Blair kissed her forehead and gathered her in close. She snuggled up to him, and as her soft breasts pressed against his chest he was delighted to note that she was indeed gloriously naked.

In the flickering torchlight he saw her eyelids flutter, a brief flash of brilliant lavender, then they closed again.

"You are home. I am glad." Her words were soft, heavy with sleep.

"Me too," he replied.

Roselyn was fast asleep again in moments. For the second time in almost as many minutes a female had nodded off in his presence.

Tis a gift, he mused. Now he had just to convince his rampant cock that they would both need to wait a while longer for gratification.

• • • • • • •

Roselyn was awake and perching on the end of his bed when he next opened his eyes. She had wrapped his plaid about her and looked very fetching indeed in the McGregor colours of green, yellow, and ochre, and bathed in the warm early morning sunlight which streamed through his window. Her head was bowed; she appeared pensive.

"Lass, are you all right?" He propped himself up on one elbow.

She turned in the direction of his voice. "Yes, I… I was thinking that perhaps I should return to my own chamber."

"Oh?"

She shook her head briskly and made to rise. "It would not do to be found here. Not fitting."

"Wait, Roselyn." He deliberately gentled his tone. "Why are you in here? I can hardly believe that you lost your way."

"No, I did not. But—"

"You think too hard, lass. The question before you is a

134

simple one… do you wish to share my bed or not?"

She stood at the foot of his bed, awkward, unsure, gnawing on her lower lip in a manner he found quite irresistible. "I do. That is not the problem, my lord."

"I have told you, my title is laird, not lord. And if sharing my bed be your wish too, then we have no problem." He paused, then, "If you still think you should leave I shall not stop you. But you might prefer to return to my bed and I promise you will find pleasure in it. I know which I would prefer." He turned back the cover and beckoned to her, but of course she did not move. "Roselyn, come back to bed," he commanded softly.

She hesitated for just a moment then scrambled back up onto the mattress. He guided her to his side then tucked the blankets around both her and the plaid.

"I like you in my colours."

She pressed her body up against his. "What are they? The colours?"

"Green, near enough the same shade as our bonny loch, and a fine, bright yellow to signify the sunshine. We get little enough here so we McGregors decided to capture some in our plaid. The dark amber colour is for the bracken on the hills surrounding Duncleit."

"It sounds beautiful."

"Aye. As are ye, my little English wench."

She tilted her face toward him. "You do not mind then? That I have no sight?"

"I tend to forget about it. It is a part of you, lass, an' I would not change you."

"There is naught amiss with my eyes. I believe I might yet regain my sight."

"Aye, well, that would be a fine thing. But just in case you do not, I shall ask auld Robbie the carpenter to erect a barrier along the edge of the platform in the great hall."

"You do not trust Freya to keep me safe?"

"I prefer to put my faith in a few planks of solid Scots pine. What about you, lass? Do you trust *me*?"

"I do, my laird. I truly do."

"'Tis just laird. And ye will not regret it."

He rolled her onto her back then slowly peeled away the plaid which covered her shoulders. Roselyn did not seek to prevent him baring her to his gaze, even when he pulled the tartan lower to expose her breasts. "Lady Roselyn, I find you have become most precious to me an' now that you are to remain wi' me here I shall make it my business to see you kept safe. And happy."

"Blair…?"

"Aye, lass?" He lowered his head to draw the tip of his tongue across her nipple.

"Oh!" She arched her back.

"You were sayin', Roselyn?" He licked the other swelling bud.

"Oh, dear Lord…" she exclaimed, grasping his head with both her hands. She tangled her fingers in his hair as she allowed her head to drop back against the pillows.

He moved back to her other breast and this time took her nipple between his lips and sucked.

"Blair, please… I… oh. Oh!"

He moved from one pebbled peak to the other, sucking, nibbling, biting gently. Her response was a keening frenzy of incoherent moans as she writhed beneath him. She was ready, willing, he knew it. Even so…

"Roselyn, I shall fuck you now. You ken this, aye?"

"Aye. I mean, yes." Her response was breathy but clear enough. And she was here, after all. Despite her doubts his little Sassenach had been most considerate in saving him the bother of having to seek her out.

Blair eased the plaid further down, and Roselyn was obliging enough to raise her hips so he could tug it from beneath her body and drop it on the floor. He maintained his play with her sensitive breasts as he trailed one hand down her belly to rest on the red-blond curls at the juncture of her thighs. "Open for me, sweetheart," he murmured.

"I have never… I mean, I may not be very… proficient."

"No? Then allow me to worry about proficiency. Your task in my bed is to obey. And to enjoy. Do you think you can manage that?"

"I can obey, certainly." She parted her thighs.

"Good enough," he observed, and stroked his fingers through her moistening folds.

"Oh, my goodness! What…? How…?"

"Hush. So far you have managed the obeying part tolerably well. This is the enjoying bit and since it may be new to you I expect you to make an effort by spreading your thighs wide for me, keeping as still as you may, and savouring what's to happen to you."

"So more obeying, then?"

"Quite so." He released her taut nipple in order to cover her mouth with his. The kiss was deep, intimate, and claiming. Roselyn parted her lips and he explored her with his tongue as she wrapped her arms around his shoulders. She shivered when he slid one finger inside her and made a sound deep in her throat as she thrust her hips up.

Blair laid a trail of hot, wet kisses along her shoulder then worked his way down her ribs before settling between her thighs.

"Blair, I do not understand. What are you doing?" She reached for him, groping, and he lifted a hand to lace his fingers between hers.

"Be still, sweetheart, and trust me. This will feel good for you, I promise."

"But what are you—oh!"

Roselyn's protests evaporated as he took her clitty between his lips and flicked at it with his tongue. Her hips soared from the bed and she let out a throaty moan as he increased the pressure. She was wet, and becoming more so with his every stroke of her pussy lips. He drove a second finger into her moist heat and curled both digits to seek out the sweet spot he knew would be there. A startled gasp from the wench beneath him was his signal that he had succeeded in his quest. He sucked on her clit and rubbed small, sweet circles on that pleasure spot. He would drive her to her release fast and hard this first time because that was needed in order to convince her that she was his to control, and that her pleasure was his to give. She was about to accept his cock inside her virgin channel and that would be eased if she was already aroused, already dripping with need for him. He intended to ensure both.

Roselyn shuddered. Her cunt tightened around his fingers, her inner walls convulsing as she shattered. She wriggled and panted, then finally let out a long, deep sigh and went still. He continued to suck on her clit until she was spent, and only then did he raise his head to regard her stunned expression. Her eyes were open, the irises a beautiful shade of dark violet, a hue he would never tire of seeing. Her mouth was slack, the very tip of her tongue swiping her lower lip. As he watched she quirked her lips in a slight smile, her expression somewhat surprised but undoubtedly content with proceedings thus far. He withdrew his fingers from her snug channel and shifted to position the head of his cock at her entrance.

"Roselyn, are you ready?"

"Ready?" She seemed perplexed, as though she did not entirely comprehend his words.

"I'm going to fuck you. Now."

"Yes, now." Clearly plain speaking was the most effective approach. She seemed to take his meaning well enough and lifted her hips as though she might somehow manage to impale herself on his cock.

Blair saved her the trouble by thrusting forward. Half his length slid into her hot sheath and she jerked hard.

"Am I hurting you?" She was tight. He knew he must go slow but she felt so fucking good as her pussy stretched around his cock.

She shook her head.

"Is that no, I am not hurting you, or no, you want me to stop?" He sent up a silent plea.

"Do not stop. Please, I need you to…"

It was enough. He withdrew a little, and adjusted his angle in order to achieve a long, smooth stroke. Without further preamble he drove his cock deep, sensitive to the moment her thin barrier tore under the onslaught.

Roselyn cried out. Her entire body tensed and went rigid, her hands grasping at his shoulders as she struggled to contain her shocked response.

He held still, allowing her the precious few moments she needed to shift and reshape around him. This was her first time and whilst he was better accustomed to romping between his sheets with more experienced wenches, he had fucked virgins on occasion and understood well enough his obligations in the matter. He would be gentle where he might but this first moment was not to be avoided nor unnecessarily prolonged. It was done now, and soon she would be over it. At least, he prayed it was so since it had been his observation that females could be an unpredictable bunch and a man was well advised to exercise caution.

"Has the pain gone, lass?" He nuzzled her hair with his lips.

"I do not know."

"If it had not, I believe you would notice."

"Perhaps. I wonder, might you move a little and I will tell you."

This struck Blair as an excellent plan. He drew his hips back just a couple of inches, then slid back to fill her again. "How was that, my lady?"

"That was perfectly fine, I believe. Rather nice, in fact."

Rather nice? He intended to do better than that. First though…

He caught her chin in his hand and turned her face to his. "Open your eyes, Roselyn. You may not be able tae see but even so your eyes are among the most expressive I have ever encountered. I have told you before I do not care for you hiding from me."

She lifted her eyelids and turned her unfocused gaze on him. He had never seen anything more beautiful. He sealed his lips over hers and sucked her sweet tongue into his mouth. She responded, raking her fingers through his hair as she explored his mouth. What she may lack in experience was amply compensated by her artless, open enthusiasm and willingness to please him.

He could love this little Sassenach.

"Ah, Roselyn," he growled, breaking the kiss as he withdrew his cock and readied for the first full stroke. "Ye delight me, ye truly do." He drove forward to bury his cock to the hilt, his full length and width spearing her. He was glad he had had the foresight to bring her to a climax already for this would not last long. This first time between them would be swift and intense, but still he was determined to ensure she had her pleasure too.

He thrust again, then once more. She lifted her legs to wrap them around his waist, hooking her ankles behind his back. Her fingers danced across his shoulders, touching, feeling, learning. She tested the texture of his hair, the planes and contours of his upper arms as he held himself above her. His muscles bulged and she pressed her delicate fingers against his tensing sinews. He watched her, his eyes never leaving her expressive face. Her features betrayed her wonder, her pleasure as he angled his cock to maintain contact with that sweet place he knew would drive her to her completion once more. He still discerned a lingering uncertainty, perhaps a hint of residual apprehension. He intended to dispel that with his deeds as well as his words.

She was his now, by right of conquest some might say but by her own consent also, her own free choice. Blair harboured no illusions about his dominant, controlling tendencies. He was a good laird because of it and he cared for those who depended upon him. The McGregor would be the master in his own keep and especially in his own bed, but her surrender would be freely gifted. He would earn it from her.

He shifted his weight to his left elbow and snaked his right hand between their bodies to find her swollen bud.

Where he had sucked earlier he now gripped the pebbled button between his fingers and rolled it. His touch was soft at first then he firmed his grip as she arched her neck. Her startled gasp spoke of pleasure and need and perhaps a little bit of astonishment. He squeezed, tugged at her clit, then pressed hard as she shuddered to another sweet climax.

He plunged his length in and out of her body, the friction delighting him. The involuntary clenching and convulsing of her quivering inner walls augmented his pleasure in her. She was hot, tight, wet perfection. His balls contracted hard, the sensation almost painful as his semen surged forth. He rammed his cock deep then stopped and held still as his seed filled her.

······

"Are ye quite all right, Roslyn?" He lay back on his pillows, the small, slender body of his little English wench curled into his side.

She nodded. "Yes, my lord. You did not hurt me. Well, not overly."

"I am gratified to know it, but that was not my entire meaning. Ye had doubts…" Passion spent, if she was regretting her decision he would rather be knowing that now. Had she behaved impulsively? Might she even now be wishing her virginity were not so freely given?

"I did, but no more. I feel… content."

He allowed himself a smile. Sensual satiation would leave a woman at her ease often enough and Roslyn certainly seemed suitably relaxed. He was relieved but not complacent.

"Will you be away again this day?" She wriggled closer to him, her soft, full breasts pressing against his ribs.

"No, I have duties here at Duncleit. Robbie does a fine job of keeping my men well-honed for battle, but 'tis a while since I drilled them myself. I shall be in the bailey most of the day."

She wrapped her arms around him. "I think I prefer it when you are here, even if you are busy. I listen for your voice, and I know when you are close to me by your scent."

"My scent? You find me smelly, my lady?"

She snuggled closer. "I find you aromatic, my vain lord. You smell of pine, heather, and sweet bracken, and more besides. You have a unique bouquet which is yours alone. You have a texture also, the supple softness of leather, the coarse warmth of wool, and the silky smooth sheen of your skin against my fingers. I learnt your taste yesterday and found it most pleasing."

Was she actually blushing? There was no mistaking the bright hue which crept up the back of her neck, the nape exposed as he toyed with her hair. "I forget how sensual you are, little Roselyn. I believe ye may open my senses too."

"I would like to try, my laird."

He dropped a quick kiss on her hair. "'Tis just laird. Now, I must go. The household is up and about already. Ye may remain here if ye like."

"I would prefer to make myself useful, Laird. Perhaps I might be of some assistance to Elspeth."

"Ye seem tae be getting the hang of our ways and I have nae doubt ye shall find your place, my lady." He untangled his limbs from hers and moved to sit on the edge of the mattress. Never a man given to lying in his bed much beyond daybreak, he found himself singularly reluctant to shift this morning. Still, he had a keep to protect, a clan looking to him for leadership. He'd best be about it.

"I missed you at the evening meal yesterday."

"Aye, I was delayed on my way home." He shoved first one foot then the other into his braies. Where had he dropped his shirt?

"I went down to the hall on my own. Well, with Freya…"

"I am pleased." He fastened the laces of his over-shirt and tucked the loose ends into his braies.

"I spoke with Archie, and with Aiden."

He paused as he hefted his sword belt around his waist. "Aye? I trust they were pleasant enough?" *They had fucking better be.*

"Oh, yes, perfectly. They were both most kind. I…" She paused, hesitant. He waited, knowing there was more to come. "Aiden asked me about whether I might ever like to ride again. I believe I told you about the accident which caused my blindness?"

"Aye, you did."

"He… he seemed to be of the opinion that I should consider getting back in the saddle."

"Oh?" Blair made a mental note to pummel Aiden to within an inch of his life. Get back in the saddle, indeed. "And what was your answer?"

"I made none. Aiden advised me to seek your view, but he said that if you were agreeable he would select a quiet horse for me."

If anyone was to choose a mount for Roselyn it would be him, not his second-in-command, though the fires of hell might well freeze solid before he would contemplate such folly. What if she were to fall? Or become disoriented and lost? It was bloody madness.

He regarded her closely, her expressive features a piquant mix of fear, hope, and perhaps the stirrings of courage. As he watched, fear seemed to gain the ascendancy. She shook her head, her demeanour becoming dejected.

"You are right, it is too dangerous."

"I did not say that." He may have thought it, but the words had yet to pass his lips. He sat beside her. "Roselyn, are you relying on me to forbid you to try this in order that you do not have to face your fears?"

She jerked up her head. "No! I would never…"

"Roselyn." His tone held a warning. He was right, he knew it.

"Perhaps I am. I apologise, I should not have—"

"It is natural enough, and you are wise to be cautious."

"You think it too perilous, then?"

Yes! Bloody hell, yes. "I shall consider the matter and let you know."

She nodded, seemingly reassured that he would see off this latest threat for her. As Blair left the chamber he knew it was not going to be so simple.

CHAPTER NINE

"My lady, might I trouble you to accompany me to the solar?"

Roselyn tilted her head at the sound of her lover's voice beside her. She had been aware of his approach and allowed herself to hope that she was the one he sought on this most unexpected visit to the hall in the middle of the day. Blair's days were usually spent out of doors and during the weeks since she had become his mistress she tended not to encounter him between breaking their fast together in the early morning, and sharing his trencher at the evening meal.

"Is something amiss, my lord?"

"No, but I would speak with you. Alone." The final word was murmured into her ear, intended for her only to hear.

Roselyn's lower body clenched and warmed. She had become accustomed to the familiar stirrings of arousal, and it took but a word or a touch from Blair to cause her to moisten for him. He was not above sliding a surreptitious hand beneath her kirtle at mealtimes to caress her inner thigh until she spread her legs for him. He would leave her aching with need and ready to pounce on him by the time he finally escorted her back to his chamber.

Their chamber now, she reminded herself. Roselyn's few belongings now shared the space. She possessed a bone hairbrush provided by Elspeth, four good kirtles made of fine Scots wool, and a pair of soft leather shoes which Blair had purchased for her from a travelling tinker.

That had been quite an occasion for the folk of Duncleit since visitors from further afield were rare. Roselyn had spent much time fondling the itinerant trader's wares, inhaling the aroma of herbs and spices, and enjoying the delighted chatter as the other women of the castle clustered with her around the barrow. She had particularly admired the texture of the shoes, but had no coin with which to make a purchase. Blair was not present as she admired the tinker's wares, but he had somehow learnt of her liking for the items and bought them for her.

He had even produced a lyre from somewhere and since then had demonstrated an impressive degree of fortitude as she sought to rekindle some semblance of competence with the instrument.

He took her hand and placed it in the crook of his elbow. "You may leave your hound here if you would, madam."

"Freya, stay." The dog turned, her nails clicking on the polished flagstones as she completed two tight circles before slumping back onto the planks beneath Roselyn's abandoned chair.

Roselyn followed Blair's lead to the foot of the stairs, then preceded him up the narrow steps. The route no longer bothered her; indeed, she could navigate the entire castle with relative ease. Every stairway now offered a stout rail to aid her, every fire had a screen before it, and there always appeared to be someone at hand to offer assistance or provide the information she needed to find her way. Blair's doing, she had no doubt, and she appreciated his kindness. She had never known such freedom, and with every day that passed her confidence grew.

Despite the uncommon hour it would not have surprised her had he led her right through the solar and into their chamber, but he did not. Instead, he steered her to the window where a wide, quilted seat afforded a comfortable place in which to sit. It was a favourite spot of Roselyn's.

"You know where you are?"

"Yes, my lord. Before the window."

"Aye. If you lean forward you can rest your elbows on the seat."

"Yes, I could. Is that what you would like me to do, Blair?"

"It is."

Roselyn's heart thumped but she did as he asked.

"Shoulders lower, if you please, and lift your bottom a little higher."

Was he intending to spank her? He did so, occasionally, but in play. Roselyn had found the sport to be to her liking, for the most part, though she knew Blair would have no hesitation in delivering another bout of serious discipline if the need arose. She hoped it would not. She nibbled her lip as she arched her back to raise her buttocks up as he required.

"Excellent. You do have the most delightful derrière, Roselyn. Have I mentioned that?"

"I believe the point has arisen in conversation, sir."

"Hmm," he murmured. "Even so, I believe a closer inspection would be beneficial." He took the lower hem of her skirts and raised the fabric slowly. He bundled it above her waist, then let out a low curse as the cloth refused to remain where he put it.

"Roselyn, I require your bottom to be bared so please be so kind as to gather the material of your kirtle before you and tuck it beneath your body."

She complied, the cool draught of early autumn air from the window wafting across her naked buttocks. "What if someone below were to glance up and see us, my lord?"

"They will see only you, my sweet, enjoying the fresh, clean air of the Highlands. As long as you remain quiet and do not alert those outside to your... plight, I see no difficulty."

"My plight, Blair? You mean to beat me?"

"Have you earned a whipping?"

"I had not thought so, but…"

"Not a whipping then. Open your legs, girl."

"Sir?"

"I shall fuck you, I believe, then I have a matter I wish to discuss."

"Should we not retire to our bed?"

"Such a creature of habit. No, my sweet Roselyn, not on this occasion. Are you wet for me?"

"I am not sure. I do not think so."

"Shall we find out?"

Roselyn gasped as he used his thumbs to open the lips of her most private place. He actually crouched behind her to examine the spot more thoroughly.

"Blair, please…" She was mortified, and exhilarated in equal measure. The sharp rap of his palm meeting her unsuspecting bottom and the sudden blaze of heat halted any further protest.

"You will be silent." His tone was stern. She knew this was one of his 'obey me, or bear the consequences' moments. Such occasions often frightened her initially, usually heralding some new and intense experience, but never failed to ultimately delight her.

She clamped her lips shut and sank into the submissive pose he demanded.

Her pussy quivered and she clenched around him as he drove two fingers into her tight passage. The sounds of her wetness reached her ears but she was past embarrassment. Arousal shimmered and swelled, her lower abdomen roiling with it. Her nipples hardened and rubbed against the coarse linen of her shift as she wriggled in her pleasure.

He slapped her again, harder this time. "Be still," he commanded. "I shall fuck you with my fingers first, and you will tell me when your release is almost upon you."

"Blair, I need your cock. Please…"

He chuckled and rose to stand behind her, his fingers still embedded within her slick passage. He reached around with his free hand to lay his middle finger over her engorged clitty and Roselyn groaned. It would take just a few deft strokes…

"Now," she squealed. "I am close."

He paused, his fingers still in her, on her. "Wait. Breathe in, then out, and wait." Long seconds passed, seconds in which Roselyn longed to shift, to rub against him, to lift her hips and thrust. It would take just the merest scrape of friction, the slightest stroke across her sensitised bud… She did none of those things though. Instead, she obeyed.

"Are you quite calm again? May I continue?" His voice was silky smooth.

"Yes, I…"

Mere seconds later she was begging him to stop again, her almost-release surging forth to tease and tantalise.

"Would you like me to spank you? I believe that might serve to ease your tension a little. You do appear somewhat overwrought just now, Roselyn."

"Sir? I do not know…please, I need—"

"Lift your bottom, and do not clench or I shall ask Aiden to seek out a decent switch for you. He performed the task to my absolute satisfaction the last time it was required."

Roselyn needed no further encouragement. She did as she was told and tried to make her bottom soft. She would accept, submit, and all would be well. Blair would make it so, she knew it.

Pain blazed, but she relished the sharp edge of it. He spanked her hard, the blows swift, covering her buttocks and thighs in streaks of flaring agony, but she lifted her bottom, raised herself on her toes and begged for more.

"Spread your legs wide, my sweet."

She did so, even knowing what he must intend. The blow when it came, landing directly on her swollen lips and clitty, brought with it a surge of white heat which tore through her, right to the very tips of her toes and the ends of her hair. She screamed, then sought to muffle her cries in the bundled garment which she still clutched in her hands. He paused for a moment, then struck her again. Then once more, and her release burst forth. She could not control it, nor could she manage to plead for respite. It was here, done, and she was swept up in it.

Only as the waves of pleasure receded, as her pussy throbbed with the residual shock of his treatment, as her inner walls clenched on nothing, only then did he sink his solid length into her.

She sighed, and rubbed her cheek against the upholstered seat as he leaned over her. His chest rested on her back, his arms encircled her. He was solid, powerful, and she was his to control. He would do as he wished with her, how he wished and where he wished, and she would not say no. She would never say no because he was her strength, her courage, her anchor. The McGregor was her master and she would have it no other way. She acknowledged that truth as he thrust into her. His thick cock stretched her entrance, he filled her utterly, and she felt safer, more secure than she ever had in her life.

Passion flared and she clawed at the seat. He took her hand in his.

"Easy, little one. I will not harm you."

"I know. I know that. I... I love you, Blair."

"Hmm, and I love you also. But you know that, too, eh?"

Roselyn turned her face, seeking his. He kissed her, then groaned as she tightened around him. "Little minx, you know better than to seek to take over. Maybe I need to spank you again."

"Maybe, if you believe it to be necessary, though I should very much prefer you to finish fucking me first." The words were out before she could clamp her lips shut. Where had such coarse desires sprung from, let alone the temerity to give voice to them? Surely she could not have uttered such a lewd remark, whatever the circumstances. She started to apologise but his low, sensual chuckle shut off her words.

"Ah, my love, we shall make a slut of you yet. I shall enjoy that greatly, my beautiful little English harlot."

"I am not a harlot for I shall only ever be with you." She did not deny his other observation.

• • • • • • •

"Roselyn, might I prevail upon your company this afternoon?" Blair lounged at her side at the lord's table, the remains of their slightly delayed midday meal before them. It had taken him mere moments to restore her clothing to a state of decency, following which he had led her back down to the hall.

Roselyn's head still swam from their earlier encounter. It had been so intense, and so intimate. She had bared more than her bottom to him, though that had been compelling enough. He had heard her avow her love for him, and he had declared that he loved her too.

Could it be? Really? And if it were truly so, then what might their future hold?

"Roselyn, did ye hear me? Are you busy this afternoon?"

"Me, my lord? No, of course not. Did you require me to do something for you?"

"Yes, I would like it very much if you would accompany me on an errand."

"An errand, my lord? Outside of Duncleit?" She could not contain her surprise. Roselyn had not ventured further than the castle and bailey in all the weeks she had been here.

"Aye. There is a world beyond and it is time ye experienced some of it, I think. My lands extend well beyond the burn a couple of miles to our east, and I am given to understand that the stream is partly dammed. Otters, no doubt, and debris from the recent rains, but it requires to be cleared before it causes problems for the crofters downstream who rely upon the fresh water. I shall ride there, along with a party of my men to aid the farmers. I thought you might enjoy the ride as 'tis such a fine day."

He leaned in to whisper in her ear. "And it has come to my attention that ye could likely do with the exercise. I do believe you may be getting a tad over-excitable and I can only put it down to being confined to the keep for overlong."

"Your concern for my health does you credit, sir, but I believe I might be able to offer an alternative explanation."

"Do not trouble yourself, Lady Roselyn. I have made up my mind, you are to have an outing and there's the end of it. I need to ready the horses but I shall stop by the kitchens and ask Elspeth to provide you with a warm cloak. Do you think you and Freya can make your own way to the stables or shall I summon Meggie too?"

The little housemaid's services were required infrequently now, and Blair appeared to have abandoned his initial mistrust of the hound's abilities to act as her guide. Roselyn relied heavily upon her canine companion. "There is no need to trouble Meggie, we shall manage perfectly well, my lord, and shall be there shortly. Is Freya to accompany us also?"

"I know better than to attempt to leave her behind. She would only trail after us so 'tis better that we keep her close. The bloody animal could do with the exercise too, come to think of it."

"He does not mean it, Freya." Roselyn bent to whisper in the dog's ear as Blair strode away across the hall. His footsteps faded to nothing as she rose to her feet and settled her hand on the hound's shoulders. The dog led her to the steps, then remained at her side as she made her way carefully along the length of the hall, then out of the main portal and down into the bailey. Here there was much more activity, but the dog had become adept at negotiating the bustling crowds, somehow knowing that she needed to allow the additional space on her left flank for her mistress. The stables were at the far end of the courtyard, close to the outer gate. Roselyn's preferred route was to make her way around the edge of the bailey, the curtain wall to her left. It may not be the most direct way, but she knew there to be no permanent obstacles on this side.

Several voices greeted her as she passed, cheerful and courteous all. Roselyn returned their good wishes and assured each who asked that she was perfectly fine and required no assistance.

It was true, she did not. She arrived at the stables to the sound of several horses already clattering on the cobbles, eager to be off.

"Excuse me." She caught the sleeve of a groom close to her. "Could you tell The McGregor that I am here, if you please?"

"No need, my lady, he approaches now, and my lord Aiden." The lad remained at her side until the familiar presence of her lord settled itself on her senses. She knew the moment he was close and reached for his hand.

"My lord, I trust I have not kept you waiting."

"You have not. Aiden is here, also."

"I know." She turned to where she knew the other man stood, a foot or so to her lord's right. "I trust you are well, sir?"

"Well enough, my lady."

"How did you know?"

"Know what?"

"That Aiden was with me? Do not tell me he smells also."

Roselyn laughed. "Alas, the truth is much more mundane. The stable lad told me. However he does have his own aroma, one of whisky and leather and something I could not quite name but which reminds me of the open forest. Apart from voices, which are all quite distinct also, this is how I know who is about me. I hope it is not disrespectful to make reference to it, for I mean no offence."

"The laird is just teasing, lass." Aiden's amused tone reassured her. "Open forest, eh? Are you ready to be away then?"

Blair responded before Roselyn could. "I believe she is. Shall we mount up?"

"Am I to ride with you, my lord?" Roselyn recalled vividly her first encounter with the huge stallion which Blair normally rode. She had visited Bartholomew in the stables once or twice since and believed the great beast to be affable enough, especially when a crunchy apple from Elspeth's kitchens was on hand to sweeten his mood.

"No, you shall have your own mount. Aiden and I have picked out a gentle mare for you and I believe she should suit you well enough."

"My own...? My lord, I do not think..."

He stepped in close to her. "I said I would give some consideration to the matter of your riding again, and I have. Whether or not you continue to do so after today is a matter for you to determine, but I am persuaded by Aiden that you should at least make the attempt. You will do so today with the both of us at your side and your dog at your mare's heels. That is as safe as it could be and I believe you will manage just fine. So, are you ready to meet your new mare? If you take to her I shall make a gift of her to you."

"You would give me a horse of my own?" She gasped. It was a generous gift indeed.

"Aye, I would. Young Will, bring Rosetta out if you please."

"At once, Laird. She is saddled up already, just like you said." A lad scampered off to do Blair's bidding, and Roselyn waited nervously as the clop-clop of hooves heralded the approach of her new mare.

"This is Rosetta? It is a pretty name." Roselyn extended her fingers, seeking the mare.

"Aye," replied Blair. "She is a fine grey palfrey with a smooth gait and a sweet temper. Come, give me your hand."

Roselyn required no further urging. Blair guided her to the soft muzzle and Roselyn smoothed her fingers across the velvety nose as the little mare nuzzled her palm. The horse snorted and clomped her hooves against the cobbles.

"Shall I help you into the saddle?" Blair offered.

"Thank you, my lord." Roselyn made her way to the horse's left flank and took hold of the pommel. She stopped and turned again. "This is a man's saddle."

"Aye, 'twill be safer for you, and more enjoyable too, once you get the feel of it."

"But, my skirts…"

"Elspeth will provide you with suitable attire for riding astride, if you choose to continue to do so after today. For now, you shall hitch up your skirts and I shall personally flog any man who dares leer. Is that quite plain to all?"

"Aye, Laird." The muttered assurances were freely forthcoming from those gathered about.

"So, you shall place your left foot in my hands and throw your right leg across the mare's back when I lift you. Is that clear enough?"

"It is, and, my lord… I used to ride astride when I was a girl. I believe I shall recall the skill readily enough." She lifted her foot and sprang up as Blair hefted her into the air. Other hands—Aiden's?—caught her right foot and guided it into the stirrup whilst Blair secured her left foot and arranged her skirts to maintain a degree of decorum. Roselyn gave no further thought to her modesty as the reins were placed between her fingers and she found herself atop a horse for the first time in years.

"I shall lead your mare, and we shall keep to a steady pace. If you tire you may ride with me. So, shall we be off then?" Blair offered her a companionable slap on the thigh, then suddenly they were in motion. Her knees instinctively tightened on the flanks of the mare, her heels nudged the animal into a smooth trot.

Roselyn laughed out loud.

• • • • • • •

"Am I to assume you enjoyed your outing today?" Blair draped an arm across her shoulders as they ate their evening meal with the rest of the Duncleit household. "Would you like to try some of Elspeth's roast cygnet? 'Tis one of my favourite dishes, especially with this apple and honey sauce."

"Yes, it is delicious, thank you." Roselyn captured a piece of the meat on the point of her small dagger and put it in her mouth. "In the priory we often laced such meats with cinnamon. You might like to try that too, my lord."

"Please feel free to suggest it to Elspeth. So, about the mare?"

"She was delightful, and yes, I had a wonderful time. Thank you."

"It is Aiden ye have to thank. He convinced me to allow you to try it, and Rosetta was his suggestion. Do you believe you might like to ride her again?"

Roselyn considered this for a few moments, then, "I would, yes. I was terrified at first, and nervous the whole time, but I enjoyed it and I did not fall off. I know that I slowed your progress, though."

"We were not in a particular hurry today. So, Rosetta is to be yours then and you may ride her when you please. But there are conditions."

She had supposed there would be. "Yes, my lord?"

"You never ride alone. Always with me, or Aiden, or one of my men to lead your mount."

It would never occur to her to do otherwise. She nodded, happy to agree.

"And you remain within sight of the keep."

"How shall I—"

"I will issue the necessary instructions, and you shall be sure to remind your escort of my orders whenever you go beyond these walls. Is that clear?"

"Perfectly clear, Laird. And… thank you."

CHAPTER TEN

"Ye chose well, lad. She makes a fine lady for Duncleit."
Elspeth plonked herself without ceremony in the empty seat
alongside her laird. "How long has it been now?"

"Five months," Blair replied, his gaze on the slender
form of his mistress as she flitted about his hall, her dog at
her side. "But she isna my lady."

Elspeth narrowed her eyes at him and he shifted in his
seat. He had learnt as a small boy that it was not usually wise
to gainsay the cook. "Nay? Is she not? How would ye
describe Lady Roselyn then, exactly?"

Elspeth's tone remained deceptively even. Blair was not
fooled for a moment and wondered if he might be well
advised to recall some urgent business requiring his
immediate presence elsewhere. Where in God's holy name
was Aiden when he needed the man?

"Laird? If not your lady, what then?" Clearly Elspeth was
not ready to drop the matter.

"She was my captive, now she is my mistress." Even he
knew that he sounded both surly and defensive.

"She shares your bed, aye, an' your hearth. There will be
bairns afore long."

"I expect so," agreed Blair. He fervently hoped so, but

was not about to share that confidence.

"Her children will be your heirs, she will be mother to the next McGregor. Or have I not got the right o' that?"

He turned to face her, his mood darkening. "Your point, if you please?"

"Ye should marry the lass and put an end tae any speculation."

He narrowed his eyes at her as irritation sparked. "What speculation? Who here would dare to question my actions? My decisions?"

The loyal servant was unmoved by the sudden flash of temper from the laird. Her gaze never wavered. "None would. An' everyone. We are your clansmen and women, this concerns us too."

"There is no 'this,'" he asserted in an attempt to maintain his authority, such as it was with Elspeth. "Lady Roselyn is my mistress. That is an honourable enough state and I shall take issue with any who dispute that or offer insult to her." He made as though to rise. He had heard enough.

Elspeth laid her hand on his arm. "Wait," she commanded. At his fierce glare she added a belated "please."

Blair knew better than to ignore her. He subsided back into his seat. "Go on, then, if you must. You have something to say so I shall be hearing it no doubt whether I wish to or no."

"Why will ye no' marry the lass? Do ye love her or nay?"

There was nothing of the shy and retiring about Elspeth. Normally Blair valued her forthright approach but on this occasion he might have appreciated a little more in the way of diffident reticence. It was not to be. Elspeth settled back to await his response.

"Of course I love her. She kens that well enough."

"We all ken it. So, I shall ask ye again, why are we not makin' ready for a Christmas wedding?"

"'Tis not that simple. Roselyn understands that I shall not wed her and she doesna mind. She is content."

"Is she? For most women would no' be? An' especially not a fine English lady such as she. Ye say that Lady Roselyn is fit tae run yer home an' birth your bairns but not tae bear the McGregor name? How do ye arrive at such a conclusion, lad?"

"There, you said it already. She is English, and she is the sister of my sworn enemy. She is no Highlander..."

"Ye mean tae send her from here then, at some point?"

He sent her an indignant glare. "Of course I do not. I love her."

"If she is tae remain then she is a Highlander now, whatever she may ha' been born. Do ye see her brother when ye look upon her, for I swear I do not?"

"You have never set eyes upon the Earl of Ingram."

"Have you?"

Blair dragged his fingers through his hair. "Nay, but—"

"May I speak plainly, lad?"

He peered at her in astonishment. Did this woman never listen to herself? "Aye, please do not let me deter you."

She let out a peculiar sound, somewhere between a cough and a snort. "Ye may save your sarcasm for them as may be impressed by it. I care about ye, lad, I care about all in this keep, so I shall have my say."

He was at once contrite. He knew Elspeth loved him no less than had his own dear mother, and he felt much the same way about her. Of course she was entitled to voice her opinion. It was he who reached for her hand now. "My apologies, Elspeth. Please, tell me what you think."

"I think if ye dinna marry our Lady Roselyn ye'll wed no one else. There are any number of fine Highland ladies ye could ha' approached an' I know ye've had your chances but ne'er shown any inclination. Are ye in need of a dowry? Is that it?"

He shook his head. The Duncleit coffers were tolerably full.

"Political alliances then? Are we under threat? Do we need to curry favour with the other chiefs?"

"No, we are safe enough." He paused. "That is what I told Roselyn, though. I told her that when I marry it will be to forge a political union and to safeguard my kinsmen."

Elspeth's gaze softened. "I suspect ye may ha' believed that at the time as I ken ye not tae be a liar."

"Thank you." He truly appreciated her faith in him.

"But ye should tell her, now that ye ha' changed your mind. 'Tis not fair otherwise."

"What about the clan? They would not accept a Sassenach for their lady."

Elspeth shook her head then gestured to the hall at large. "Look about ye, lad. Does that no' look like acceptance tae ye?"

His gaze followed her hand. Roselyn now stood close to the outer door, deep in conversation with two women from the village which lay just beyond his walls. One held a small babe, and Roselyn lifted her hand to caress the child's head. Both women curtsied to her, their smiles broad as they hurried from the hall.

"There is no problem here, lad, bar one o' your making. Now, ye think on what I have said." She got to her feet. "Eh, well, this'll no' get the parsnips i' the pot. I've wasted enough time on idle chatter." Elspeth dropped him a bob, which Blair considered ironic in the circumstances, but he refrained from commenting. On one matter at least, she was correct. He *did* have much to think about.

• • • • • • •

Roselyn turned back from the portal as the two village women hurried back in the direction of their croft. Their home lay a couple of miles beyond the village, an isolated farm where they scratched out a living from two cows and a few acres of arable land. She had learnt enough during her months in the Highlands to realise that theirs was a harsh life and crofters tended to be close-knit. She had been surprised therefore, astonished even, when the older of the two had asked her to stand as godmother to the latest little Drummond, a fine baby girl whom they apparently intended to name in her honour. Blair would be pleased, or she hoped he would. She must tell him straight away.

"Freya." She extended her left hand and at once the dog was there, the hound's thick, wiry fur between Roselyn's fingers as she turned to face down the length of the hall. Over the years since she lost her sight Roselyn had developed a keen sense of direction. She might be waylaid by obstacles she could not see, but rarely did she not know where she was going. The dog veered to the left or right as they made their way back to the dais, and Roselyn followed.

"Blair?" She knew his tread before he reached her. "Do you have a moment?"

He paused beside her. "I do not, my lady. Aiden is waiting for me in the stables."

Even as they spoke she knew that Aiden was with Robbie and a party of guards attending to a portion of crumbling masonry on their northern ramparts. Roselyn bowed her head and stepped aside to allow The McGregor to pass. Clearly he did not wish to speak with her and was making an excuse not to stop.

"Later, then, my lord?"

"Aye, later," he called as he hurried away.

Roselyn ascended the steps onto the dais and found her usual seat. Servants scuttled about her clearing away the remains of the last meal, sweeping, polishing, stoking the fire which warmed her back. It was November and the climate had turned distinctly chilly in recent weeks. Snow was expected, the roads would soon be impassable. Not since her initial incarceration in the chamber off the solar had Roselyn felt quite so trapped here.

Her palm drifted to her lower abdomen and she rubbed absentmindedly. Had she displeased him in some way? She hoped not, prayed it was not so because she needed Blair now. She relied upon his public affirmation of her place here, now more than she ever had.

"How far along, d'ye think?" Roselyn recognised Betsy's voice, turned to face her.

"What? Sorry, I was wool-gathering. Did you say something?"

"I asked how far along you might be."

Roselyn continued to stare blankly.

"The bairn," prompted her servant. "You be with child, am I right?"

Roselyn's heart sank. Was it so obvious? "How could you tell?" she whispered.

"By the way you are caressin' your belly, milady. My sister was the same wi' all o' hers."

"Oh." Roselyn folded her hands in her lap.

"Have you been sick? Many women are, at least in the early months."

Roselyn shook her head. Were it not for the lack of her courses in recent weeks and a distinct tenderness in her breasts she would not have known anything was amiss. She had not dared to acknowledge the possibility, even to herself, for the first month or so but now could deny it no longer. She was pregnant, and to a man who professed to love her but who could—would—set her aside at any time. Blair might not even provide for their child. He had never said that he would should this situation arise. Unbidden, tears formed behind her eyelids and within moments she was sobbing quietly.

Betsy acted without hesitation. She tugged Roselyn from her chair and hustled her up the narrow staircase leading to the solar. Freya padded along behind and as soon as the trio were safe in the lord's quarters Betsy shut the door. Roselyn heard the click of the lock.

"There, we shall not be disturbed. Now, you may tell me all about it. Is the laird displeased at the news, then, that causes you to take on so?"

Roselyn sobbed all the more, unable to form a response. Betsy was patient though, waiting quietly until the weeping subsided before pressing on.

"Milady, surely things cannot be so bad. The laird seems a fine man and he will not hold this against you. After all, it cannot be unexpected…"

"He does not know," wailed Roselyn.

"He will, soon enough," was Betsy's wry observation. "These things cannot be kept secret for long. What is more, your laird does not strike me as a fool without even the slightest knowledge of women."

"No, he is not." There was no denying that. Most assuredly Blair's knowledge of women was intimate, detailed, and extremely thorough. If anything, it was remarkable that he had not discerned her condition before she knew it herself. "I must tell him. Soon."

"He will be pleased."

Betsy sounded quite convinced, but Roselyn found herself a long way from being in agreement.

"What will happen to me? To us? What if he wishes to keep my baby, raise it as his own?"

"He will, surely, for it *is* his own."

"He will not marry me. He has said so."

"Ah, so that is it. Then, my lady, you must convince him otherwise. Why would he not marry you, especially now? It is clear to all that he adores you."

"He loves me. He said as much…"

"Do you believe him?"

Roselyn paused, then nodded. "Yes, I do. He is most kind, most… protective."

"Do you love *him*?"

Roselyn nodded emphatically.

"But, what about my blindness? I cannot run a keep or manage his household. I bring no wealth to his coffers, nothing but kinship to a man he hates."

"Then allow Elspeth to run the keep, she does it well enough. And you are blind from an accident, not from birth. There is no cause to worry about your child. Has the laird said he is in need of funds?"

"No, he has not."

"He will not hold you accountable for your brother's crimes. That was settled months ago."

"I suppose that is so, but—"

"If he still hesitates then you must make it your business to show him the error of his ways, an' you can start by telling him all about this little bairn you are carryin'."

"But what about everyone else? Those who live here, his clan…?"

"They will want what he wants, you mark my words."

"But, Elspeth…"

"Ah, well, that woman may be a tyrant in her kitchen an' it's true she and I do not see eye to eye on a lot, but I know she loves the bones of you. There will be no problem there, I'm sure of it."

Roselyn dried her eyes and attempted a smile. "Do you really think…? I mean… could it happen?"

"I have known stranger things come to pass. After all, half a year ago who would ha' thought any of us might end up here?"

Roselyn indulged herself with one last sniffle, then tilted her chin up. "You are quite right. We are here and… it *could* happen. I shall make it so."

· · · · · · ·

"My lord, I have something I must discuss with you." Roslyn stationed herself at the foot of the great bed she shared with Blair. She wore only her heavy nightdress and her hair hung loose and freshly brushed about her shoulders, just as he preferred it. She concentrated on controlling her agitation. It would not do to appear too nervous; she must be confident, convincing, every inch the suitable Highland chatelaine.

"Aye? Well, I too have a matter which requires your attention. Come to bed, lass."

"I… I should prefer to remain here, just for the moment. Sir."

164

"Roselyn? Is something amiss?" He sounded concerned now, and just a little bewildered.

"No, not amiss, exactly. It is just…"

"You are unwell? You do appear a tad pale, now I come to think of it."

"I am quite well, thank you. But… my lord, I believe I must ask you to reconsider your objections to marrying me." She halted, just long enough to hear the mattress creak as he moved. "No, please, remain where you are and listen to me. You owe me that…" Her voice was cracking, but she was determined not to weep. That would do no good at all; indeed, it would only serve to demonstrate that she was weak and emotional, not qualities revered in a sturdy Highland lady fit to be by his side and lead the people of Duncleit.

"Very well. Please, continue."

He sounded wary now and her heart sank. This was not proceeding as she had hoped. Still, best to get the hardest part done with first.

"I am with child, my lord."

No answer.

"Did you hear me?"

"I did. Is there more or are you done?"

More? What more need there be? Still, it was clear to her that he required to be convinced so she ploughed on. "I recall that you have entertained reservations regarding my suitability, but I know that I could be a good wife for you, and a good mistress for Duncleit. I have some skills in the arts of cooking—herbs and flavouring, that sort of thing. I can supervise the management of the household, and with Betsy to assist, and Elspeth, of course…"

"I expect Elspeth can manage without supervision. Betsy too, for that matter since she strikes me as amply capable. In any case, would you not be fully employed in the nursery? Or in my bed?"

"I did not mean to imply… What?"

"What?"

165

"What did you say, my lord?"

"I merely wondered whether, as my wife and, I gather, the mother of my future heir, you might not find yourself more gainfully occupied with duties that only you could properly fulfil. I would advise that you allow Elspeth and Betsy to continue as they are."

"Your wife? So, you would consider it? Even though I have no dowry, no powerful family to pledge their aid and support?"

"I daresay you might contrive to convince me of the merits of such a selfless sacrifice on my part."

Was that laughter in his low tone? Was he teasing, or, or… "Sir, please, I am not sure…"

"Then stop wringing your hands and get yourself over here now. Lay your fingers on my face, Roselyn. I want you to see me, to know what I am thinking just as I can read you, as clearly as I can discern the next day's weather from the evening sky."

"Can you really do that?"

"Roselyn, here. Now." His tone had hardened, it was time to obey.

Roselyn scrambled across the mattress to reach him. He took her hands in his and guided them to his face. "See me," he murmured. "Know what I want, what I need."

Her nimble fingers fluttered across his features. She observed the curve of his full lips as they lifted in a smile, the firm set of his jaw angled toward her. He closed his eyes as she stroked his eyelids, his unfurrowed brow.

"You are not angry."

"No, I am not."

"You do not mind, about the baby?"

"Madam, you have never struck me as a fool. Why did you think I might? I like bairns well enough."

"I was unsure. I…"

He took her hand in his and turned the palm up, then kissed the centre of it. "Have you seen enough? Are you convinced yet?"

"I am convinced that you are teasing me, my lord."

"Good. And I am convinced that you will make an excellent Lady of Duncleit. Even if I was uncertain, I can be sure Elspeth would soon set me right on the matter. She holds you in high regard, my little Sassenach."

"You call me that often. At first you meant it as an insult."

"It is Gaelic, my mother tongue, and it means Saxon, though as I told ye afore, in the Highlands we use the word to refer to any lowlander or one from the borders, such as ye."

"Is it an insult?" she asked warily.

"Not when applied to you, lass." He rolled her swiftly onto her back and kissed her.

Roselyn wrapped her arms around the solid width of his shoulders. Could it be true, that this fine and handsome laird would be her husband? It was not so long ago that she had feared herself doomed to a loveless match with the likes of Sir John of Hexham. She welcomed his hot, questing tongue, sucked greedily on it as she returned his kiss.

"Ah, my demanding little English," he murmured. "I do believe you require a decent fucking to quiet you down."

Roselyn was quite convinced he was right, at least about the decent fucking. She mewled in frustrated disappointment as he eased his weight from her.

"Are you quite well, my love?"

Roselyn had believed she was, though she was starting to harbour doubts. Unassuaged lust could be somewhat debilitating, she was finding. Could he not just deliver on his promise? "Blair, are you still teasing me? I wish that you would not."

He buried his face in her hair then trailed kisses along her shoulder which was still decently concealed within her prim nightdress. "And I wish that you would not come to our bed wearing quite so much. I meant, wi' the bairn. Do you have any ill effects I should be knowin' about?"

"I do not believe so, not exactly, but…" She hesitated,

could she tell him? She had come this far, after all. "My breasts are very tender of late. I wonder if perhaps you might be a little less—exacting—than usual?"

"Ah, no squeezing your nipples then? Is that what ye had in mind?"

She nodded, grimacing. Normally she loved such play, but now the very thought caused her to wince.

He smoothed her tangled hair back from her face to kiss her again, though this time he merely brushed his lips across hers. "I shall be your husband and you my lady. You ken well enough that I enjoy rough bed sport and I ken that you have a liking for it too though you may prefer not to say so, delicate English flower that you are. But if ever I hurt you, scare you, do something that displeases you, I would have you tell me, aye? Pregnant or no, but especially now. Are we in accord on this, my lady?"

"Yes, Blair. Perfectly."

"Good, so shall we be rid of this then?" He tugged at the ties securing the neck of her gown and succeeded in loosening them.

Roselyn got to her knees and caught the lower hem between her hands. She lifted the garment and dragged it over her head. "I am yours, Laird."

"Aye, lass, and let none forget it. Now, if you would be so good as to lie back and spread your legs for me...?"

His fingers were gentle, almost reverent as he traced the outline of her aching breasts. He licked her tender nipples, first one, then the other. Roselyn sighed; the sensation was soothing, and so intimate she believed she might weep.

He cared about her, he wanted her. She, and their precious child.

Blair shifted lower. His lips travelled across her still flat belly, kissing the spot beneath which she believed her tiny baby to nestle. He continued on to draw the tip of his tongue around her wet lower lips, then he gently parted her entrance with his fingers. She gasped, and waited as he blew on her hot, wet core. Roselyn stiffened, her body poised and expectant as she held her breath. The sensation when he at last drove two fingers deep caused her pussy to convulse, her inner walls quivering around his slow, probing digits. He found that special place and pressed there, at the same time as he took her clitty in his mouth and sucked on it. Was there ever a feeling so delightful, such a joyous sensation, such sublime pleasure?

Her body trembled, every part of her was alive, clenching, writhing as he played her, drew her response from her amidst shudders she could not even start to control. Her arousal swelled and she knew she was close. Would he allow her her release?

"My lord…?"

"Take it. Take all of it, my love."

So she did. All of it and more. Her climax peaked and she had barely finished shaking before he slid his solid cock into her hot sheath. Roselyn managed to utter his name but would have been hard put to recall her own when he withdrew and drove forward again. She lifted her hips, seeking more, urging him deeper, then she clamped her legs around his waist and simply hung on.

I love you, I love you, I love you. The words reverberated around her head as he drove her higher still, his body stretching hers, his cock filling her.

"I love you too, my beautiful Sassenach," he murmured.

Roselyn cried out as her release seized her again. A kaleidoscope of remembered colours exploded behind her eyelids and she believed she might be flying. He thrust again, hard this time, then harder still before he stopped and held his body motionless. Only his cock moved, jerking hard within her tight body as he sprayed his seed into her womb.

CHAPTER ELEVEN

"'Tis a fine sight, would ye no' agree?" Aiden stood beside his laird on the Duncleit battlements, his hand shading his eyes from the sun which hung low in the sky this early spring evening. The mists which had earlier in the day smothered their glen in a thick, impenetrable blanket had lifted at last to reveal the stark, wild beauty of the landscape which surrounded the McGregor keep.

"Aye, none better," agreed Blair, though his gaze was not on the distant hills. Rather he regarded his wife of the past four months, Lady Roselyn McGregor, as she made her heavy way across his bailey. Roselyn's belly was gloriously rounded, her pregnancy now in its seventh month. The bairn was a strong little thing too, he mused quietly, if the hearty kicks the pair of them endured most nights were any indication. He wondered that Roselyn ever got a wink of sleep, though she did appear to be blooming.

Aiden cleared his throat and Blair returned his attention to the matter in hand. "I ken that you are concerned about Mortain? What news do you have?"

"Ingram has been seen at Etal, seeking to retake his stronghold there."

Blair was already aware of his enemy's return. Aiden's

impeccable sources had brought the intelligence to them several weeks earlier but Blair refused to risk his men and horses in a foolhardy midwinter dash across Scotland. His old adversary would still pay for his crimes, but there was no rush.

"We did a good enough job there. He will find little comfort in his old seat."

"True, which is why I fear he may turn his attention to Mortain. The estate is near enough to Etal to be tempting, an' he will anticipate little in the way of resistance, especially as most of those who now dwell within the estate are Ingram's old retainers. He will expect loyalty, perhaps even a safe haven."

Blair's brow furrowed. He knew well enough the implications of such a threat. "You believe we should be ready to defend our lands at Mortain?"

"Aye, Blair, I do."

Blair pondered that for several moments. He was sorely tempted, but he was never a man given to precipitous action. "'Tis still early in the year and the route will be arduous. Also, I am loath to leave Roselyn at this time."

His comrade nodded. "You should remain here, Laird. I can lead the force sent to defend the garrison. A couple of dozen well-trained men should be ample, but we would need to maintain a presence there I fear, at least until we can be certain that the English cur presents no further threat to us."

Blair nodded. Aiden was only stating what he, too, had concluded after the reports from Etal. The bairn soon to make an appearance would be his heir and if a wee laddie the boy would eventually be The McGregor and would lead Duncleit, but Mortain was Blair's domain too and he owed those people his protection. More, he was planning ahead and hoped for many more bairns after this one. He wanted to ensure the lands in the borders remained intact for his next lad to inherit. There would be enough to go around, but he had to act now to safeguard their interests and those of his dependent clansfolk.

"When will you leave?"

"Within the sennight, weather permittin'."

Blair nodded his assent and thought that to be the end of it, but Aiden did not move to commence the preparations for departure. Instead, he shuffled awkwardly at his laird's side, a demeanour most unlike that which Blair had come to expect from the hardened Scots warrior.

"Aiden?"

"Your lady looks well, Laird."

"Aye, that she does." Blair waited.

"She is close to her time, aye?"

Blair shrugged. "'Tis a few weeks yet, I gather."

"She will ha' need of Betsy?"

"Betsy?" Blair was fast losing the thread of this conversation.

"Aye. She will require Betsy tae attend her at the birthin' I daresay."

Now Blair was truly baffled. When did his second-in-command develop such a fascination for the mysteries of childbed? "I suppose so. We have not discussed that an' I doubt I shall be consulted in any case."

"Perhaps Elspeth will be sufficient tae see the bairn safe into the world…?"

Blair had heard enough. "God's holy balls, man, what are you blatherin' about? Why this sudden concern about midwives?"

His companion bristled, then stiffened beside him. Aiden fixed his chief with a defiant glare. "I had thought to ask Betsy to accompany us—me—to Mortain."

Blair tunnelled his fingers through his hair. "Has the woman developed some skill with the bow of which I am unaware? Might she fend off an attack from Ingram by brandishing her needle?"

"I wish to wed her. We had thought to remain at Mortain for it is closer to her home, and we could be of use there."

Blair gaped. "Shit. I didna see that comin'. You… and

Betsy?"

"Aye, Laird. Me an' Betsy." The man's expression was bordering on belligerent.

"How long has this been brewing?"

Aiden shrugged. "A tidy while. 'Tis what we both want an' I'm hoping ye'll raise nae objection to the match, Laird."

"Objection? Why would I object?"

"I am your clansman an' therefore I require your permission to wed. Betsy too, since she joined our household."

Blair collected his wits sufficiently to formulate an answer. "Dinna be such a fool, of course I'll nae stand in your way. I wish ye joy, the pair of ye. But, is she not a wee bit older than ye?"

"Just a couple of years, no more. I am five and thirty, Laird and she not yet forty summers. We are both past the age where we might have expected bairns, and we do not long for such in any case. I believe we shall do well together. We... suit."

Blair considered that. His dour captain-at-arms was not a man given to effusive sentimentality and he suspected a degree of passion to underlie that innocuous word. *Suit indeed.*

"My felicitations, Aiden. So you wish Betsy to come with you then, to take up residence at Mortain? Am I to gather the pair of you intend to set up your home there?"

"Aye, Laird. We had thought tae hold the place for ye, until such time as ye may wish to make other arrangements."

"You would act as my steward?" It was a decent enough plan, Blair thought.

"I would, an' Betsy could run the household. She and Elspeth, well, ye must ken that they dinna see eye to eye..."

"Do they not?" He made a mental note to ask what Roselyn knew of such friction around his hearth, though he supposed it made sense. From what he had seen of the woman he knew Betsy to be no retiring English flower and Elspeth had been accustomed to running Duncleit for more years than he could recall. Perhaps the place was not quite big enough for them both, especially now that the castle had a lady also. "Never mind, I shall take your word for it. So, we will be needin' a priest then, and quickly. I would not wish to delay your departure, but neither will I forego the chance to dance at your wedding." He clapped the other man on the back. "I shall summon Father Edmund. He should be here the day after tomorrow, especially if my missive makes it clear there's a flagon or two of fine ale in it for him."

"We should be most obliged, Laird."

"Aye, well, off you go to tell your bride the good tidings. I suppose I had better mention it to Roselyn."

"I believe she has an inkling already."

Blair shook his head. For a woman with no sight his wife saw a great deal more than he, it would seem.

· · · · · · ·

Later that same day he sought out Roselyn and found her resting on their bed. He settled beside her.

"Are you well, my lady?"

"I am, but I find I soon tire these days. And my feet always seem to ache dreadfully."

He shifted to sit at her side and pulled her feet into his lap. Her shoes had been discarded beside the bed but he now peeled her thick woollen stockings off as well. In recent weeks he had developed some considerable skill in the art of massaging his wife's feet, and the intimacy also afforded him an opportunity to speak with his wife alone.

"I spoke to Aiden today. He is to leave soon, within the week. Your brother is on the prowl in the lowlands and we fear for the safety of Mortain. Aiden will take men to garrison the fortress and hold it safe."

"That is a sound plan. I wonder, my lord, if you might move your fingers just a little to the left. Ah, yes, just there." She sighed and settled back against the pillows.

Blair lifted the bare foot he held cradled in his lap and shifted further onto the bed. He applied pressure to the sole of his wife's foot, just behind her toes and she whimpered in ecstasy. It was a sound he was accustomed to hearing and swore he would never tire of, though of late she had been more appreciative of his efforts when applied to her feet than her dainty little clitty. Well, perhaps not *more* appreciative, but certainly she welcomed such attentions at the end of the day. Such were the vagaries of women, he supposed, especially in the final stages of pregnancy though it was not a state of which he had much experience. He flexed the delicate toes between his hands and pressed on her instep. Roselyn groaned.

"Aiden tells me he wishes to wed your maid, Betsy and have her accompany him to Mortain. I trust this will not inconvenience you, Roselyn?"

"I shall miss her." Roselyn stretched and lay back, her eyes closed. A beatific smile settled upon her calm features.

"You do not appear unduly distressed at the news."

"I am sure we will manage. She loves Aiden."

"Does she?"

"Of course. Is he not quite the most lovable man?"

"Eh?" Blair quite lost his grip on her foot.

"Please do concentrate, my lord. Now you shall have to start over."

He grasped her heel and started to flex and rub all over again. "Aiden has many fine qualities to be sure, but I would not have described him as lovable."

"Then it is good that you are not to marry him. Betsy is quite besotted."

"You knew of this, this… association between the pair of them, I assume?"

"Of course. Everyone knows."

Not quite everyone. Blair cleared his throat. "I have sent for Father Edmund. The wedding will take place as soon as he arrives."

"Excellent. I shall talk to Elspeth in the morning. We

must provide a decent feast for them."

"I gather Betsy and Elspeth are not friends."

Roselyn chuckled. "It will be more peaceful here, once they no longer share a kitchen. Elspeth is your loyal servant, I know this, but you must agree she can be quite fierce. I daresay though that she will find cause for rejoicing in this news and will be more than happy to prepare a table laden with the best she can offer. It will be a splendid feast."

Fierce? He supposed that was a fair enough description of his faithful cook. Blair decided to let the matter drop.

• • • • • • •

"I wonder, would you object, my lord, were I to visit the Drummonds this morning? I have a small gift for my goddaughter and had hoped to deliver it myself."

Roselyn smiled at him from her cosy nest in their bed. A month had passed since the wedding feast for the departing couple and his wife had grown even more huge. Blair found her state utterly fascinating and would spend as much time as he could merely resting his hands on her belly and marvelling at the bumps and wriggles from within. He was both entranced and terrified in more or less equal measure. He would prefer that she not leave the sanctuary of his chamber until the bairn was safely birthed, but in this the last month before her confinement she seemed more energetic than ever. His attempts to persuade her to do nothing but eat and rest had proven fruitless. Delightfully obedient, his wife simply became morose and bored if she was instructed to remain indoors, particularly since the spring that year continued to bring so many pleasant, balmy days. She adored the warm caress of the sun on her face and the play of the breeze in her hair, and he supposed he could understand that. His wife was wondrously tactile, of necessity, and he would not deny her her pleasures.

"Very well, but please be sure to return in good time, well before dusk. You should take Meggie with you, and one of the grooms to drive the cart." He had forbidden her to ride her little palfrey as soon as he knew of her pregnancy.

"I shall have Freya to guide me."

"And Meggie," he insisted, his tone stern.

"And Meggie," she agreed.

Blair ate his noontime meal alone that day, and sorely missed Roselyn's cheerful chatter by his side. He had become used to her presence, loved to listen to her observations of the people and events around her. She brought with her an awareness of new and different impressions which she shared with him, the myriad sounds and scents of his bustling home, the nuances of conversation between his rowdy clansfolk. She enriched his senses with her own and he could hardly recall a time she had not been here. He adored her, 'twas that simple.

"How was the roast pigeon, Laird?" Elspeth clattered more plates before him, one laden with steaming carrots, the other with fresh-baked bread.

"'Tis fine. As ever."

"I flavoured it with pepper, Lady Roselyn's suggestion."

"Ah, yes, I had wondered." His palate had been introduced to a range of new delicacies of late. Many of them were enhanced by the spices brought back from the Holy Land by crusaders and which Roselyn had urged him to purchase in order to augment their fare. It had been expensive but he did not begrudge the investment.

"We have saffron, too."

"Indeed?" He took another slice of the aromatic pigeon.

"Aye, 'twill be grand with the mutton. Lady Roselyn says so."

"I am sure she is right. You do not miss Betsy, then? She has been gone a month now."

Elspeth let forth a derisive snort. "That woman had a heavy hand wi' pastry an' could never manage to produce a half-decent broth, however good the meat. We're best without her if ye ask me, Laird."

"I see." Blair reached for another piece of pigeon and

wished he had not ventured into this conversation. And why had he allowed Roselyn to go out for the day? What was he thinking? He swallowed his final mouthful, swilled it down with a half-mug of ale, and left the table.

"My lord, I see something." The voice of his lookout on the western battlement halted Blair's progress across the bailey. He paused to squint up into the lowering sun.

"What is it, Hamish?"

"I dinna ken, sir, not exactly."

Blair took the stairs at a run and strode around the stone parapet to where his guard stood. "Show me."

"Over there, just this side o' the brow o' yonder hill. Moving slow, in this direction."

Blair saw nothing at first as he scanned the expanse of heather, only just reawakened by the new season and starting to regain its golden glow. Then he picked it out. A small, dark silhouette emerged from the shade of a copse of trees. One figure, or perhaps two but he could not be certain. He peered into the distance, his concentration intense.

"'Tis a child, surely…" he murmured, more to himself than to anyone around him. Others had gathered also, and all eyes were trained on the distant hill. Long minutes passed as the row of fighting men focused on the small figure.

"Not just a child, he has something beside him. A pony or donkey? A goat, perhaps?" No, even as he breathed the words Blair knew it was not a pony; the gait of the animal seemed wrong, uneven somehow. And the pair were making ridiculously slow progress.

Blair made up his mind. "Saddle my stallion, I shall ride out to meet them." A man rushed off to do his bidding and meanwhile Blair remained where he was, his gaze locked onto the two incongruous figures making their torturous way to his keep.

The light shifted, a beam illuminated the pair, and at last he saw. Blair recognised the tiny, shuffling form.

"God's holy bones, 'tis wee Annie Drummond. And she

has Freya at her side." His heart lurched in his chest then sank. What the fuck was the little scullery maid doing out there on the glen with his wife's dog? And where in God's name was Roselyn?

Blair took the stairs down from the battlements two at a time and sprinted across to the stables just as the lad emerged with Bartholomew. He leapt into the saddle and turned the stallion's head.

"Open the gate," he yelled as he charged for the main portal. "Robbie, you are to follow me. Bring men with you." He had no idea what might have happened, but it could not bode well that Roselyn's constant companion, her shadow, was hobbling down his hillside alone but for a skivvy from his kitchens.

He reached the huge oak gates just as they parted and galloped through. Once in the open he kicked his mount into a gallop and together they ate up the mile or so which separated them from the unlikely pair.

As he got closer he could see that Annie was weeping, and that she was urging the dog to keep moving. The hound was dragging her rear left leg behind her, and he could see at a glance that the limb was broken.

"Sweet Jesus," he muttered as he thundered up the hillside, urging Bartholomew to even longer strides.

Annie saw him coming and stopped to wait. As soon as they stopped moving Freya collapsed into the heather. The hound lay panting on her side as Blair hauled the stallion to a skidding halt and slithered to the ground.

He crouched beside the stricken dog as Annie flung her small arms about his neck. "Laird, they took 'er. They took Lady Roselyn an' they killed Harry."

Harry? One of his stable lads, and probably the one who had been driving Roselyn's cart. Blair dislodged the sobbing child from his neck and set her before him. "Annie, ye must tell me what happened. Who took her? What did ye see?"

The scrawny little wench could barely speak to him for her sobbing and the child was clearly terrified. Of him? He could not quite think that, not after she had hugged him so. He needed to calm her or he would get nowhere. Still kneeling in the heather, Blair took the slight figure in his arms again and stroked her matted hair.

"'Tis all right, Annie. No one will hurt ye, and ye did well tae come home. Now, can ye tell me what has happened tae Lady Roselyn?" He adjusted his usually more cultured speech to match that of the tiny scullery maid in an attempt to put her more at ease.

She gulped, sniffed hard and nodded against his jerkin. Blair eased Annie from his embrace and tipped her chin up. Hooves thundered behind him, his men were coming.

"So, tell me, hinny." He could not quite muster a smile but he did succeed in calming his features enough not to alarm her all over again. "Tell me all that ye saw."

"The lady came tae our croft. I was there, Elspeth said I could spend the day wi' me ma an' the new young 'un..."

Right, so his cook had sent the wee lassie home for the day, Blair could piece that much together. It wasn't unusual for families to send their younger children into the care of their laird to earn their way in the castle, it was one less mouth to feed on the croft, but Annie had clearly been homesick and under all that ferocity he knew Elspeth to be a kindly soul. "So Lady Roselyn reached your family's farm then? She arrived there safe?"

"Aye, Laird, an' she played wi' the bairn. She shared our meal, but she brought flour an' apples an' a fine side o' pork that Elspeth had nae use for. So there was plenty tae go around."

"Right, then what?"

"The lady said it were time for her to go as she had to be back by nightfall. I wanted to see the kittens in the barn so I ran off to have a wee look, an' I forgot that I was supposed to hurry..." Tears started again and the little girl's shoulders hunched over. "I am sorry, sir, so sorry. I shouldna ha' been so slow..."

"Annie, please, tell me the rest."

She sniffled a bit more, then peered anxiously about her as the men from Duncleit dismounted and clustered around them. "I came out o' the barn just as the lady's cart was leavin'. I ran after 'em as otherwise I would have to walk all the way back an' the lady had said as how I could ride i' the cart wi' her an' Meggie."

"They didna wait for ye?"

"Meggie was lookin' tae the front an' talkin' tae Lady Roselyn. Harry ne'er saw me neither. They didna ken I was behind them, runnin' after…"

"Why did ye no' shout? Lady Roselyn couldna see ye but she would have heard."

"I did, but the wind was in the wrong direction an' they was so far ahead. But I kept on runnin' in case they might stop an' I could catch up…"

"Right, I understand. So…?"

"It were over by Dunisburn woods, where the trail goes through the trees an' it be dark overhead. I dinna like the woods, Laird, there's all sorts o' goblins an' such livin' in those dark corners."

Surely she was not about to tell him his wife had been spirited away by woodland pixies? "Annie…"

Annie clutched at his arm. "There were men there though. A lot, maybe a dozen. They jumped out o' the trees an' onto the cart and some were on horses. They was yellin' at each other an' the dog was barkin' an' snarlin'. I heard the lady scream so I crouched in the long grass at the edge o' the wood an' I tried to see that was goin' on but I couldna. There was noise though, a lot o' din. Men shoutin'…"

"Did ye see who they were? What colours they had on 'em?"

"They were no' another clan, Laird. They were English, or lowlanders perhaps by their speech. The lady knew 'em though. I heard her call one o' them by his name."

"What name? What name did she say?"

The child screwed up her face in concentration. He schooled himself to wait.

"Alan."

"You are quite certain?"

"Aye, sir. It were Alan she called 'im."

Alan. Alan, Earl of Ingram. It had to be.

He had no idea how this had come about, but there was no other explanation.

Blair rose to his feet, consumed with self-loathing and disgust. How could he have been so stupid, so bloody complacent as to think they were safe, far away from Etal on the Isle of Skye? That conniving, greedy bastard had come after him. Ingram had followed him across the Highlands and now he had Roselyn.

His Roselyn.

"Laird, we shall be after them, aye? They canna ha' got far." Robbie was at his elbow and itching to be off.

Fear served to sharpen Blair's wits. Bone-deep terror seized him and served to concentrate his thinking. At once his mind was racing ahead. "Annie, can ye say how long it has been now, since this attack happened? What did you do next? Did you see where they went?"

"Nay, Laird, not really. I hid until all was quiet again, then I peeped out. The cart was still there i' the middle o' the track, but there was no one else. I was scared but I kenned that I had to look so I crept forward."

The child was shaking. Blair laid his hand on her shoulder. "You were very courageous, wee Annie. I am proud of ye, but I need ye tae carry on being brave now so we can aid Lady Roselyn. D'ye think ye can manage that for just a wee bit longer?"

The small head nodded, though tears continued to stream down her cheeks. Blair crouched to kneel before her again, his eyes now level with hers. "You told me that Harry was dead?"

"Aye, sir. I found 'im, by the cart."

"The men left on horseback?"

"I... I think so. Like I said, I didna see them leave but they had horses. They took the pony from the cart an' all."

"Aye, an' they left the wagon behind which suggests they intended to cross rough territory rather than remain on the beaten tracks." This from Robbie who stood behind him. "We need to be in pursuit."

"So, you left the cart where it was and started to walk home? Is that right?"

Annie nodded again. "But I was too scared to come through the woods, which is the quickest way, so I skirted around the edge. 'Tis further, but nae shadows."

"I see."

"An', I found the dog."

"The dog? Freya? Where did ye find Freya?" He glanced back at the wolfhound which was now being attended by two of his men.

"Round at the far edge, where the burn runs down the side o' the trees there. She were lyin' i' the grass, pantin' an' squealin'."

He could imagine. But somehow this brave wee thing had managed to get the injured hound back on her feet and moving again, and had brought her home.

"How long? How long have the pair o' ye been walking?"

"Two hours, perhaps more. It was just after the noon meal when we left me mam's farm."

He glanced at the sun, well in the west now and likely to set in the next hour or so. They had precious little daylight left in which to mount the search, but he would make the best of what was there.

"Right, Annie, I shall need ye tae help me just a wee bit more yet. I need ye tae show me where the cart is, and Harry, and the place where you saw the men jump out. Then, we shall go back the way ye came an' ye can show me exactly where ye found Freya. Can ye do that, d'ye think?"

"'Tis a long way, an' I am tired…"

"I dinna mean ye tae walk, lassie. Ye shall ride wi' me, on my horse."

The tearful eyes widened, whether in fear or excitement

he could not quite say though she regarded Bartholomew with a fair degree of apprehension. He was not surprised; the huge black warhorse was meant to inspire respect. Blair knew he could rely on the animal to play his part now though and he whistled softly. The cluster of clansmen parted to allow the stallion ample space as he approached in response to the summons, then stood quietly over the pair who crouched on the ground. Blair reached up and the horse nuzzled his palm.

"See, he is quite gentle. He does nae eat wee girls either."

Annie's small hand moved, though she kept her fist clenched.

"Open your hand, like I do, see. Lay it flat an' he will just rub his nose on your palm."

The stallion played his part impeccably, and in moments the small girl was patting his wide muzzle. "I wish I could have a pony but me ma says we can only have cows, an' a few chickens. An' now I live at the castle so I would have nae time tae ride one I daresay."

"I shall teach ye tae ride, Annie, and ye will be very good at it, I ken. Ye shall help tae lead Lady Roselyn's palfrey when ye're a wee bit older but first, we must find her and see her safe."

"Aye, Laird." Annie managed a watery smile.

Blair remounted, then reached down for Annie's small hand. He easily pulled the child up onto his horse and settled her before him.

"Angus, ye will remain here an' do what ye can tae ease the dog's pain. We'll find the cart an' send it back here so ye can use it tae take Freya the rest o' the way back tae Duncleit. I'll be needin' your mount since the English took the horse that was pulling the wagon."

The man, Angus muttered his agreement and handed the reins of his horse to another clansmen. In moments the rest had remounted and formed up behind Blair. He kicked the stallion into a gentle canter and started back up the steep hillside.

When the green mass of Dunisburn woods came into view he paused. "We shall ride through the woods, along the track, and you say that we shall find the cart at the far end, just at the spot where Lady Roselyn entered the trees. Is that right, Annie?"

"Aye, Laird, I last saw it there."

"And after, when you started for home, which side of the wood did ye come around, Annie? Was it the left or the right?"

"The right-hand side, from here, Laird. I followed the burn."

He nudged his mount forward again and led his men into the cover of the trees. No one spoke, all were alert for any sound to betray that the attackers might still be secreted in the thick woodland, waiting to ambush them. Annie shivered within his arms.

"Fear not, wee lassie. No one shall harm ye."

She settled, clearly ready to trust in his promise. He hoped that her faith was not misplaced but he had no other choice. He had to find his wife… and quickly.

A few minutes later they arrived at the site of the attack. The scene was much as described by Annie: the cart deserted in the middle of the track, the traces dangling loose where they had been slashed to release the pony which had drawn it. Blair cursed under his breath when he caught sight of the body of his stable lad face down in the dirt. The boy was but thirteen summers and his mother worked with Elspeth in the Duncleit kitchens.

The McGregor horsemen reined in but remained mounted. Blair twisted in the saddle.

"Hamish, I need ye to drive the cart back to Duncleit. Ye should take the lad's body too, and stop on the way to pick up Angus and my wife's hound."

The man dismounted with a curt nod and strode to where the youth lay, half under the cart. Blair also slipped from his saddle to aid his man in lifting the body onto the back of the wagon. He unwrapped his own plaid from about his shoulders and covered the boy with it then he helped Hamish to secure Angus' horse between the shafts.

"We shall see ye back at Duncleit."

The man nodded and clicked on the reins. Blair watched, grim-faced as the cart trundled back the way they had come, his equally sombre clansmen parting to make way for it. He swore once more for good measure before swinging back into his saddle behind Annie.

"So lassie, now we shall see where ye found Freya, aye?"

They departed the cover of the trees and Blair was soon able to pick out the tracks left by the small girl as she had made her way homeward. "Now Annie, 'tis very important that ye show me the exact spot where ye found Freya." He was relying on the assumption that the dog had followed the attackers and had perhaps even savaged any she might have been able to seize in her instinctive desire to protect her mistress. Whilst she had clearly come off worst in the end he could hope Freya had given a decent account of herself before she fell. Injured men left tracks. He might discover some trail he could follow. Blood would be nice. He slowed Bartholomew to a walk and scoured the edge of the woods with Annie.

"There! 'Twas there, sir. I know it, just beside that log." Annie bounced up and down in the saddle in front of him. "Ye can see it, just in front. The grass is flattened where Freya was lyin'."

The signs were clear, unmistakable. Blair pulled his stallion to a halt and signalled for his men to remain behind him. "No one is to trample anything. Keep the horses back so we dinna confuse our own tracks with those of the English. Annie, ye may stay here if ye would."

"I am no' scared now, Laird." she affirmed, clinging tight to the pommel at the front of the saddle.

Blair squeezed her shoulder then dismounted. He bent to examine the crushed grasses, the trampled undergrowth at the edge of the woodland, and the hoof prints which led away from the spot, due east. Just as he had surmised, his adversary was headed back to the mainland, and from there no doubt their route would take the raiders south to the border. They had a decent head start on him, but the English were still a long, long way from home and in hostile territory. He knew this terrain though. He knew it intimately and could travel at speed, and through the night, whereas they would need to stop or at least pick their way with some care. He would have the bastards yet.

He stood and looked about him. Blair gazed to the east across the empty expanse of Highland landscape, and behind him, back into the oppressive darkness of the woods. And it was there that he saw what he had hoped for. A hand, bloodstained and dirty, just poking out from the undergrowth. And it was moving. He had one of them, but there was no need for Annie to witness what would come next.

"Annie, you have done well. Now I need ye tae go wi' Duncan." He beckoned another of his men forward. "He will take ye to find Freya and Hamish, and ye can ride back to Duncleit on the cart. Elspeth will take care of Freya, and of you. Oh, and be sure to tell her I said ye're not to be lightin' early fires anymore. Someone else shall have that task now because you are to be my maid of the horse."

He reached up to help the beaming child from the stallion and saw her safely ensconced in the saddle before Duncan. "See the lassie safe, then come back to join us." He patted the horse's rump as the animal turned to skirt around the flattened area of grass.

"Robbie, Alastair, I shall be needin' your aid, if ye please." He waited until Duncan and Annie were out of sight then he drew his dagger from his belt.

CHAPTER TWELVE

The bobbing gait of the horse almost caused Roselyn to gag. She hugged her abdomen with one arm and clung to the pommel with her other hand as she twisted her neck to glare at her brother who was mounted behind her.

"Are you quite deranged? How can you even start to imagine you can escape with the abducted wife of a laird? The McGregor will hunt you down, and—"

Her brother's fetid breath almost caused her to gag as Alan leaned in close. His arms tightened brutally around her chest as he dragged her hard up against his body. "Shut your mouth, slut, or I shall be pleased enough to shut it for you. Sister or no, you could yet meet the same fate as that other Scottish whore."

Rage drove Roselyn's tongue, and mounting terror caused her to fight his grasp, her struggles becoming ever more frantic as he carried her from the home she had come to love. "You must be utterly deluded if you think you can get away with this. I am wife to The McGregor, I am to bear his babe in just a week or so. He will never let you escape, not this time."

"He may try. He did before, but I eluded the fool and I shall again." He grabbed her chin in his hand and twisted cruelly, forcing her face up toward his. "Christ's blood, I had forgotten how those empty eyes haunt me. Sir John must be mad to still want you, but I am thankful that he does and in return for your worthless carcase I shall secure him as my ally."

"You cannot force a match now. I am already wed."

He cackled with mirth, the unnerving giggle ringing in her ears. Was he always so repulsive? Or quite so deranged? Her brother managed to curb his glee enough to gloat. "You might fancy yourself wed to a Highland savage but it is a marriage made without your family's agreement and under duress. The union is already annulled under English law."

"You have no right, this is lunacy." Roselyn jabbed her elbow backwards to catch him in the midsection, causing his merriment to cease in a sharp 'oof' of pain.

Moments later her ears rang as he slapped her hard on the side of the head. "There will be more where that came from. I was ever too soft with you, lenient because I felt sorry for you in your affliction, but no more. You will obey, bitch, or I shall teach you something of the consequences. And have no fear, your future husband will not be perturbed by a bruise or two, though I doubt he'll be minded to give house room to another's bastard. Still, a Scottish whelp should be easy enough to be rid of and most will be none the wiser."

Roselyn's struggles increased anew as terror seized her. "You cannot harm my child. Blair will kill you. Better still, I shall kill you myself."

Her threats elicited more callous chuckling from her brother. "You, madam, will do well enough to hang on to your own miserable life let alone be fretting about some worthless barbarian brat. And your so-called husband, your precious Highland warrior scum, is nowhere to be seen. He will never catch us. We shall be at the crossing to the mainland in a few hours, and once we cross the water there is all of Scotland for us to hide in. Your Highland mongrel can scour this Godforsaken barren wasteland for as long as he cares to and he will never find you. You are mine now, and soon you shall be wife to my friend and ally, John of Hexham. Be glad of it, Roselyn, for matters could go far, far worse for you. The fools at Mortain discovered that, to their cost. They might have been spared but they would insist on seeking to protect their miserable few coins."

Bafflement loosened Roselyn's tongue and she blurted the question which had plagued her since learning of her brother's heinous acts. "Why? Why did you do as you did? Why be so brutal when the taking of hostages would have been the more lucrative course? If you needed funds so badly, why squander that opportunity? You must have known that Blair would have paid a fortune for the safe return of his sister, as would her husband."

Alan let out a snort of disgust. "Aye, and I should have had that chance but for that vicious hellcat. My men had bested her husband but the bitch would not let it be. She insisted on retaliating. At first she wept, crouching beside him, cradling his head in her lap as he died. I would have taken her hostage, guaranteed her safety, and I told her as much. She had but to surrender. Instead, she seized her dead husband's sword and came at me, screaming and heaping vile curses upon my head. I had no choice but to strike her down. She deserved the end she met."

"She was pregnant, close to her time, just as I am. Are you really asking me to believe that you could not subdue a woman in that condition without recourse to such brutality? Are you even a man at all, brother, that you make war on women and children?"

He ground his teeth. "The shrew grated on my nerves," he snarled. "I had had enough of her. Ransom or not, I needed to be rid of her, to silence her screeching, her vile accusations. She brought it on herself."

"You hit her with your mace. You cracked her skull open..."

"Her fault," he spat. "All of it hers. I was ready to be merciful, to spare her and that mewling rabble of miserable, filthy peasants who surrounded her, but she would not let it be. The screaming, the howling, the fucking din… So loud, so shrill… it had to stop. It had to just fucking stop…"

"You are mad," Roselyn breathed. "Quite deranged."

"You think so? Yet still I have succeeded in outsmarting you and that slack-wit you think you married. I had only to wait in the hills and watch his rat-hole of a castle for less than one day and you trotted out, right into my arms. He never suspected a thing."

Roselyn opened her mouth to issue another angry retort but was silenced by a second ringing blow to her right ear which left her head spinning. She felt sick, her back ached, her neck hurt from his cruel grip, and her belly felt heavier than it ever had. Harsh, gripping pain seized her and she stifled a scream.

She could not go into labour now. She absolutely refused to do so. As long as her baby remained within her body she could protect it. Her maniac of a brother would not harm her, at least not seriously, not as long as he saw the prospect of marrying her off to his equally delusional crony. But she had no doubt at all that he would toss her newborn child into the nearest burn the first moment he could.

The horse jolted her cruelly as her brother kicked it into a gallop. The beating of hooves on either side told her that he had several men with him. She would estimate at least eight, all mounted and riding hard for the ferry crossing which linked the Isle of Skye to the Scottish mainland. She vaguely remembered the short voyage when she had been brought to Duncleit, the gentle swaying of the small boat, the splash of oars. She had clung to the edge of the tiny craft and had heaved a sigh of relief when firm but capable hands had aided her back onto dry land.

Her brother was correct in his ramblings, up to a point. Pursuit would be more difficult once they crossed Loch Alsh, the strip of water which divided Skye from the mainland, but if Alan imagined that a mere couple of miles of brine would defeat The McGregor he was sorely mistaken. Her husband knew this land, he had friends scattered the length and breadth of the Highlands, allies who would gladly aid him in his search. No one would hide her brother, there would be no help anywhere, no shelter, no haven. She never doubted that Blair would track Alan down and he would rescue her. But would he reach her in time?

Helpless for now, Roselyn clung to the horn of the saddle, gritted her teeth with each wave of clenching pain as her abdomen cramped, and she prayed.

She lost track of time, but was aware of the cloying chill in the air, a sure sign of evening. It would be dark soon, if not already. She had been seized perhaps three hours ago, Blair must be aware of her abduction by now. He would without doubt lead a search party when she failed to return by dusk, and they would find the abandoned cart. What of her driver, young Harry? And Meggie? Where were her companions?

More time passed, and Roselyn could no longer contain her moans as her labour progressed. She had heard that a first babe took a while to arrive, so perhaps she had time yet. She swayed in the saddle and would have fallen but for her brother's vise-like grip.

"What's the matter with you? Be quiet or I shall ram a rag in your mouth. If you think to attract any to your aid you may think again, for there is no one for miles about us."

Roselyn bit down hard on her lower lip. "Where is my maid," she ground out. "I have need of her…"

"She is well enough and has the sense to remain silent."

Poor little Meggie, she must be terrified. "Please, I must stop. I need a moment or two…"

"The crossing is just a few miles away. We shall stop there and not before." Her brother was breathless now, the strain of his headlong dash across the Highland countryside taking its toll. She supposed his fondness for pastries and fine wines played their part too. His flabby clumsiness and crude violence would be no match for the lean, supple strength and finely honed skills of her husband. If only Blair was here…

A few miles? How long would that take? How much more could she bear before she could conceal her labour no longer, regardless the greed-fuelled self-absorption of her brother? Roselyn might be blind, but he was the one who chose not to see what was happening, literally right in front of his stupid nose. She clamped her jaws shut and resolved to hang on to the bitter end.

Another half hour passed and even the insensitive Earl of Ingram became aware that something was amiss. Roselyn was writhing in his lap, and she screamed out loud as her womb contracted sharply.

"Lady…?" The wavering tone of an anxious Meggie. "Are ye all right?"

"Quiet, brat," snarled Alan. "I shall have no whimpering from you. And you…" he seized a hank of Roselyn's hair and wrenched her head back, "you shall keep your mouth shut, you treacherous bitch, or I shall be giving you something to scream for."

"Ye be hurtin' her. Let her go." Brave little Meggie was not giving up.

"Hush, sweetheart. I am fine, just a little tired is all." Roselyn managed to grind out the words, not wishing to risk allowing Meggie to draw her brother's wrath. "We shall be at the ferry soon, then we may rest."

"I see it, ahead." Alan slowed the mount and his grip in her hair slackened as he raised himself up in the saddle to better peer through what must by now be the pitch dark of a Highland night. Was there a moon? How much could he see? Would those who must by now be in pursuit be able to find their way also?

She was convinced that Blair would know to head for Loch Alsh, and perhaps there was a speedier route by which he might reach here. If there was, her husband would surely take it. He might yet catch them up before the English could cross, especially if she could find some means to slow their progress.

Her brother dug in his heels and the horse lurched forward into a gallop again. Roselyn felt the slight shift in her brother's relentless grip and knew they were charging fast downhill. She considered throwing herself from the horse's back but did not dare for fear she might injure her baby that way.

Time was running out. Her mind raced furiously as the steed slowed. She could smell the tangy scent of the water close by, could hear the gentle lapping of the waves on the shingle beach.

"I need to dismount. Now."

Alan ignored her. "Hey, you, boatman. Over here. I have need of your craft and there's gold in it for you. You shall be handsomely paid for a swift passage." He grabbed at the purse by his side and rattled the coins as though that might entice the ferryman to greater efforts.

Perhaps it would. She needed to do something, anything, to disrupt his plans. Roselyn retched, then deposited what remained of the midday meal she ate so long ago all over her brother's hands and sleeves. Her fastidious sibling let out a roar of outrage and flung his reins aside.

"The vile bitch has cast up her innards all over me. Christ's piss, what a mess." He pulled the now walking horse to a standstill and shoved Roselyn roughly to the ground. "You shall walk the rest of the way, you foul piece of slime. Gagh, look at this mess. A rag, someone…"

Roselyn lay on the rough shingle beach as her belly contracted. She panted hard until the pain passed, then rolled onto her knees. The sounds of hooves seemed to be all around her, and everywhere she heard her brother's whining tone as he complained to all who might listen about the piteous state of his fine tunic.

Why had she not thought to deposit the contents of her stomach earlier? Roselyn grimaced as a second wave of nausea seized her and leaned forward to retch into the damp sand. Soft hands smoothed back her hair.

"My lady, are ye ill? Is it the bairn?" It was Meggie's voice, thank the dear Virgin.

Quickly, Roselyn shook her head. "No, it is nothing, just the strain of… of… everything. Are you unharmed, sweetheart?"

"Aye, my lady. They just threw me onto a horse an' I clung on."

"Harry? Where is Harry?"

Meggie was silent. Roselyn clutched at her hand. "Tell me."

"He… they hit him, my lady. With the flat of a sword I think, but then that man, the one who took ye, he took out his dagger an' he… he…"

"The vicious bastard. Alan killed Harry? But he was just a lad…"

Meggie sniffled beside her, shock and grief perhaps only now starting to take their toll. Roselyn grasped her maid's small hand and would have uttered something intended to calm the lass, but was seized with another contraction which swept all other considerations aside.

"My lord, I believe we need to attend to Lady Roselyn or she will deliver her child right here on the beach." It was the voice of a stranger, the gruff dialect English rather than Scottish.

"What? No, she is not about to give birth. I forbid it. Do you hear me, you stupid wench? You shall not thwart me now. If you want to drop the whelp here then do so, but we'll leave the brat where it falls."

"My lord, I—" The English guard seemed less than willing to support such a course but his protests were drowned by her brother's roar of pure fury.

"Fucking shut up. All of you, just do as you're fucking told. God's balls, you are paid well enough to obey a simple command. Throw the slut into the nearest boat, and as soon as she births that heathen's spawn toss it overboard."

"No!" Roselyn's wail of anguish was lost in another agonised scream as her womb tightened brutally.

"You. Yes, you, the boatman. Come here, now." Ingram's autocratic command rang out across the beach.

There was a crunch of wet gravel and heavy footsteps reached Roselyn's ears, then the chink of coin as her brother hurled the purse at the ferryman. "Yours. All yours if you carry her to your boat. Take her snivelling servant as well, and row them across to the other side. Sir John of Hexham is on the opposite shore and he shall take her from there."

"Aye, my lord, right gladly." The lilting tone of the man's Highland brogue sounded achingly familiar. Roselyn started, tilted her chin and held her breath. Beside her Meggie also gasped, but Roselyn grabbed her hand and squeezed it hard. She may be mistaken, but was rarely wrong in her ability to recognise those close to her. She trusted her senses and incredible though the possibility might be, the man into whose keeping her brother was about to hand her was indeed her husband's captain-at-arms.

Aiden should not be here. He should be in Mortain, guarding that stronghold for Blair, not posing as an oarsman in the pay of an English murderer.

"Be still, Lady Roselyn, and calm. We shall soon have ye safe again." The familiar scent of her husband's close friend reached her nostrils as the man bent to lift her from the wet pebbles. He murmured his gentle reassurance in her ear, and Roselyn understood at once that her brother was not to know the true identity of the boatman. She nodded and gripped her maid's hand tight, wordlessly conveying the warning to Meggie, too.

Gentle hands eased her from the hard ground and in moments she was lying on her side in the bottom of a boat, Meggie huddled at her side. The craft bobbed merrily on the choppy waves and Roselyn felt her stomach heave once more.

"Sweet Virgin, she's about to cast up more filth." Alan's disgust dripped from his tone. "Get her out of my sight. Let her husband worry about her now, I have done my duty in the matter."

"Take Lady Roselyn across tae the other shore. Ye ken well enough what tae do when ye reach there." Aiden issued the instructions now, to some unseen man already waiting at the oars

"Aye, sir." Roselyn could not place a name to the owner of the second voice, but she knew the tone to be familiar. She was with one of her husband's guards. She felt the motion as the boat she lay in was shoved out onto the waves, then the rhythmic splish-splash as the man bent to his task.

"Meggie…" she whispered. "Where are we? Who is here?"

A male voice replied. "Ye may speak freely, my lady. We are out of earshot of the shore now and 'tis just we three. I am Alexander, madam, one of The McGregor's archers. We have nae spoken before now, but—"

"I am delighted to make your acquaintance, Alexander. I… aaagh!" She doubled up in agony as another contraction overwhelmed her. Roselyn was dimly aware of Meggie's squeal as she gripped her poor maid's hand mercilessly. Her baby was coming, and it was too early. She was giving birth weeks too soon, but there was no stopping the inexorable force of nature as her womb laboured to expel the tiniest McGregor into a hostile and uncertain world.

Roselyn wept, whether in relief or sheer desperation she could not say. She longed for Betsy, or even the gruff efficiency of Elspeth to help ease the pain of the coming ordeal. But most of all, she needed her husband.

• • • • • • •

Blair got to his feet and wiped the blade of his dirk on his braies. The English soldier had been near enough to death when they discovered his worthless carcase, but the matter was completed now and no one here would lament his passing. Blair had, however, managed to extract the intelligence he needed before dispatching the man to meet his maker.

"We ride for Loch Alsh, and with all speed. Ingram is making for the ferry crossing, and has left the bulk of his English force to await him on the mainland. We need to prevent him from reaching them." He swung back into his saddle. "He has almost two hours' head start. Alastair—which is the quickest route?"

The man nudged his horse forward. Alastair Salmon was son to Blair's ghillie and had grown up on these glens and hills. He knew every inch of the McGregor lands. "Straight over the summit of *Sgurr na Coinnich*, Laird. 'Tis the highest peak on the Isle and a hard ride. A perilous way but 'twould slice a good half hour from the journey time."

"We shall do better even than that. I need to reach Loch Alsh in less than three hours. Who is with me?"

The roar from his men was all the response he needed. "Alastair, ye shall lead since ye ken the route best." Blair waited just a moment to let the man hit the front, then kicked Bartholomew into a gallop. His men streamed after him. They had an enemy to defeat and a lady to save.

Darkness fell within minutes of leaving Dunisburn woods but the small force of Highlanders never broke stride. From his interrogation of the dying soldier Blair now knew that Alan of Ingram had eight men-at-arms with him, so his own force outnumbered the Englishman. There was little doubt of the outcome should they succeed in overtaking the raiders, but that was not the greatest of his worries.

Roselyn was strong and in good health, but she was a woman close to her time and the danger to her and their unborn babe was grave. He would never forgive himself if he failed to bring her home safe, but there was too little time to formulate a plan that would guarantee her well-being. He could only ride like the devil himself was on his heels and pray they reached her in time.

Bartholomew's hooves ate up the miles, pounding across the springy grass and soft heather. The ground began to rise and their progress slowed, though only marginally. Blair knew they needed to make swift progress, but they also needed their horses to remain sound. He paced his own mount and his men matched his speed. The incline grew steeper, and the animals laboured beneath them, but none dropped back. Mercifully they had the benefit of a clear, moonlit night or they might well have lost a horse to a tumble or an unseen rabbit hole, but they managed to avoid such hazards.

Blair's jaw tensed. Any advantage they enjoyed was similarly bestowed upon their quarry. He urged his mount to ascend the peak even faster.

At last they crested the summit and the landscape opened before them, sloping away in a much gentler descent down to the sea. Blair could not yet see the loch, but he sensed the end of his journey and the proximity of his foe. Ingram had not crossed yet. Blair knew it, could feel it, could actually taste his revenge which was tantalisingly close, almost within his grasp. But his first priority was to see his wife out of danger and returned to his home where she belonged.

"Well done, Alastair. My thanks to ye for seeing us safe here. Come, we shall have the bastards on our swords afore long now."

Blair led the charge as the Scots thundered down the hillside, heading for the shore.

The final rise fell away and they could discern the shimmering water below. The moon cast her soft illumination over the glen and Blair slowed to peruse the scene beneath.

He saw boats bobbing about on the gentle waves, but all were still moored at this side of the crossing. Blair offered up a silent prayer of thanks. They were not too late. Not yet.

Men and horses milled about on the beach. The scene was chaotic and confused, but Blair counted more than a dozen figures. He could pick out the figure of the man he assumed to be Ingram, and his eight remaining guards, as well as Roselyn who lay motionless on the sand.

Dear Lord, was she hurt? If that bastard had harmed her…

Even as he watched, the small figure of the maidservant flung herself down at Roselyn's side and he saw his wife lift her hand as though to offer comfort to the child. So like his own Roselyn, always aware of the needs of others, putting them before her own.

Apart from Ingram and his guards there were others among the throng on the shore. They must be locals, the ferrymen, and from the looks of it they were ready to convey their unexpected cargo across the narrow strip of water. These were Scots, loyal men who would never usually aid an enemy of The McGregor but all had their price and they were not to know what was happening, what evil they were abetting. He kicked his stallion back into a full gallop, but was still more than two miles distant. Ingram would have ample time to bundle Roselyn and the rest of his tattered band into the boats and set off for the mainland, and would no doubt scuttle any craft they did not use in order to ensure their pursuers could not continue the chase.

Even now one of the men was lifting his wife and placing her in the first of the small craft. She appeared ill, unable to shift for herself. Her maid scrambled after her and the pair disappeared from sight as they huddled together on the floor of the boat. The man who had carried her there shoved the boat out onto the waters of the loch then turned to wade back to the beach. The lone oarsman beside Roselyn leaned in to his work and his beloved lady was carried away from him on the glimmering tide.

"What the…?" Robbie's incredulous exclamation sounded from beside Blair's right shoulder. "What the devil is going on down there?"

It was a fair enough question. The man who had launched Roselyn onto the waves had now regained the shore and stood before Ingram. For a peasant the man bore himself with a degree of authority and uncommon courage.

Ingram appeared surprised, took a step in retreat, then he reached for his sword. The boatman was quicker and drew a claymore from within his voluminous cloak. Ingram had apparently seen enough. He turned and scuttled for higher ground.

The now sword-wielding ferryman did not give chase. Instead, he lifted his left hand to his mouth and let out a piercing whistle. At once the rocks and vegetation surrounding the small stretch of beach erupted as men leapt from hiding places to surround the confused and bewildered English troop.

The battle was brief. The English were overwhelmed in moments and were soon herded into an ineffectual huddle beside the boats.

"Who…? I do not…" Blair slowed his mount as recognition dawned.

"Holy bones, 'tis Aiden," breathed Robbie. "What the fuck is he doing here?"

What the fuck, indeed? Blair had never been happier to see his old friend. There would be questions later, but for now he would just offer up thanks that somehow Aiden's sources had once again not let him down.

The boat out on the lock was turning, heading back for the shore. Blair reined in to watch, his relief almost overwhelming him. Their headlong dash might still have been in vain but for Aiden's unlikely intervention. As he surveyed the now calm scene on the beach, a movement to his right caught his eye. He turned in time to spot a shadow disappear between two large rocks.

It was Ingram. The coward had abandoned his men in order to save his own skin. So he thought to get away, did he?

Blair swore softly under his breath. "Not this time," he murmured, "not this fucking time."

"Robbie, go lend aid to Aiden, should he require it. And to Lady Roselyn. I shall be with you soon enough." He saluted his men and turned his mount in pursuit of his adversary.

The chase now was leisurely enough. Ingram had fled on foot, and could only scramble in desperation up the slippery hillside. As the moon dipped behind a bank of cloud he lost what sliver of light he might have benefited from and stumbled face down into the bracken. Blair clucked at Bartholomew who ambled slowly on.

Blair might have allowed the sport to drag on longer had he not been eager to return to Roselyn. She was safe now, he knew that much, but still he would be easier once he was at her side. But not whilst this cur lived. Not whilst this murderous wretch drew breath and there was even the faintest chance he might threaten any of them again. He owed his wife that, and he owed it to his clansmen, both the living and the dead.

This was about revenge, and about justice, but mostly in Blair's mind the fate awaiting Alan, Earl of Ingram was a matter of cool necessity. This had to be done, it was quite that simple.

He approached to within five paces of his adversary then slid from his mount. Blair drew his claymore from the scabbard and jammed the tip into the soft earth. He leaned on the sword as he waited for Ingram to turn and face him. The ignoble lord seemed more intent on scaling the harsh and rugged outcrop of rock which the fool must fondly assume stood between him and his escape.

There would be no escape, and no mercy. Not this time.

"Fight, Ingram, and perish doing so, or die the snivelling coward you are. Those are your choices."

The earl ignored Blair's invitation, seeking another tenuous foothold on the smooth rock face.

Blair shrugged. "Very well. In that case, allow me to assist you, my lord." He stepped forward, reached up to grasp Ingram's ankle, and gave a sharp tug. The man tumbled to the ground to land in a sprawling heap at Blair's feet. "I shall offer you one more choice, but that is all. You may get to your feet and draw your sword, and face me like a man, or I shall send you off to your eternal rest here and now. Which shall it be?"

Spittle dripped from Ingram's mouth as he tried to scramble backwards. "You dare not harm me; I am an earl, a member of the English aristocracy. Your king will have your hide for this, you stinking barbarian. I shall——"

"You shall die, that is all. I have merely sought to offer you some choice in the manner of it." Blair stepped forward to position the point of his sword at his enemy's throat. "I confess, I had expected more resistance, given the 'courage' you showed at Mortain. Perhaps it is just the unarmed and defenceless who bring out such fine qualities in you."

"You... How dare you speak to me of courage? You are nothing more than a Highland savage. You defiled my sister. You took her by force and planted your whelp in her belly. I should——"

Blair had heard enough. "You speak to me of defiling women? You, who would slay defenceless ladies, and mere bairns? Get up. Now." He stepped back to allow Ingram to do so. At last the man seemed ready to put up some semblance of a fight. Ingram clambered to his feet and reached for his weapon.

Better late than never, mused Blair. He circled the earl warily. Ingram was clearly a bully and given to ordering others to do his dirty work, but Blair had learnt as a lad of just twelve that it never paid to underestimate an enemy, especially one who was cornered, desperate, and facing certain death.

Sure enough, Ingram lunged at him in an attempt to pierce his chest. Blair sidestepped easily and slapped the flat of his sword against his opponent's shoulder to send him to his knees again. He waited, immobile, as the earl regained his feet.

Ingram tried the same move again, with a similar result. Again, Blair allowed him time to recover, and was rewarded by a determined attempt to hack off his sword arm. This time Ingram's blade connected and sliced through the leather of Blair's sleeve. No blood was drawn, but it was clear that the cornered rat was dangerous. Time to end this.

Blair sidled around his adversary as Ingram swung at him in wild, uncontrolled arcs. Had the man never been taught even the rudiments of swordplay? Seemingly not, because the earl lunged again, leaving his entire left side undefended. Blair's claymore swirled about his head, the air shifted with the force of the blow, and blood spurted from the Earl of Ingram's neck.

His enemy collapsed to the ground, gasping for air and Blair knelt beside him. It had been a clean enough blow and would prove fatal, though death may be minutes away.

Blair was tempted to leave him there to die alone, but knew he could not. This was after all his brother-in-law. His enemy was beyond help, and could harm them no more so justice was served. The McGregor could afford to be merciful now, even if the bastard deserved much less. Blair drew his dagger, the same blade with which he had seen off the wounded guard back at Dunisburn woods, and he finished the task before him.

Satisfied, Blair stood. He cleaned his blades, replaced his claymore in the scabbard, and jammed the dirk back in his belt, then he whistled for his horse.

· · · · · · ·

"I was never more glad tae see ye, my friend, but I confess to being baffled. How did ye ken that ye were needed here?" Back at the beach Blair leaned down from his stallion to grasp Aiden's outstretched hand. "Do ye have a man spare to go an' recover the earl's body?"

Aiden grinned up at him. "Aye, I shall see to it at first light. But for now, I suggest ye attend to Lady Roselyn. She needs ye, unless ye would prefer tae allow me and the wee lassie there to deliver your bairn."

"What? But the child is nae due for weeks yet." Blair flung himself from the horse and set off at a sprint in the direction of the boat where Roselyn still lay.

Aiden kept pace alongside him. "Ye may tell the child that, when he arrives. I daresay ye shall have that opportunity soon enough."

"Shit."

CHAPTER THIRTEEN

Roselyn panted hard, her body gripped with another crippling contraction. Her entire being was consumed with an overwhelming urge to push. Was that the right thing to do? She had no notion how to birth a bairn, but surely she must...

"Blair, where are you? I need my husband," she wailed. "Is he here?"

"The laird is coming," assured Meggie. "There, I see him now."

"Tell him... tell him I... aaagh!"

"I am here, sweetheart." There was a clatter of booted feet as The McGregor vaulted to land beside her in the tiny boat which had been dragged up onto the shingle beach. He grabbed her hand, then smoothed back the tangled and matted hair which covered her face. The evening was chilly, but heat consumed Roselyn. Sweat erupted from her brow, her limbs felt clammy, but all those discomforts were as nothing when set beside the agonising squeeze and twist of her distended belly. Her contractions were rapid now, unceasing it seemed as her womb strove to propel her child into the world.

She groped in the darkness for her husband's hand. "It

is time. The baby is coming…"

He grasped her fingers, turned her hand and kissed her palm. "I know. He will be here with us very soon."

"I need Betsy. And Elspeth."

Blair let out a groan. "I know, my love, but you shall have to make do with me. And Aiden."

Roselyn stifled a whimper. "I mean no disrespect, my lord, but you know nothing of midwifery."

"What is there to know?" As ever, The McGregor was ready to rise to the challenge. Confidence and self-assurance were all well enough, she would readily concede, but were a poor substitute for experience and knowledge of the intricacies of childbed. Her husband continued unabashed. "We have between us seen more foals birthed than either of us cares to recall. I daresay we can manage a mere Sassenach."

"I am not a mare, my lord."

"So I have observed. Nevertheless, we shall contrive to—"

Roselyn knew his intention was to reassure her, and in truth she was ready to place her trust in him. She was a pragmatist at heart. The McGregor was the best help to hand, and he had never failed her yet, but any further discussion on the matter was forestalled by another wrenching contraction. She doubled up and let out a scream which pierced even her own ears. As the wave of pain receded she emitted a string of curses which would cost her hours of contrite penance on her knees in the Duncleit chapel. Roselyn was beyond caring, past any semblance of dignity as she surrendered to the urge to bear down.

"I cannot… I cannot… I, oh, oooh." She tightened her grip around his fingers, and pushed for all she was worth.

"My darling, I need to check—"

When Blair would have loosened her grip she just clung on harder. "Do not leave me. Please, I need—aaagh!"

"We must lift her legs and bend her knees thus." Firm but gentle hands grasped her lower limbs and spread her legs wide. It was Aiden, his tone calm and capable. But he was kneeling between her legs and had a perfect view of her most private parts. Roselyn opened her mouth to protest, but was seized by another relentless contraction and lost the will to do anything but push.

"Shall we exchange places, Laird?" The voices were distant now, Roselyn could barely make out the words let alone make sense of them. But the instant her husband started to shift she grabbed at him and clung on as though her very life depended on it.

"Stay with me, I need you, I love you."

He kissed her damp forehead and smoothed back her hair again. "I love you too, my wee Sassenach, and I shall remain right here. But Aiden shall have to attend to the other end of matters, aye?"

She nodded, defeated. She needed their help, she and her helpless baby, and would take all that was offered.

"We must protect him. My brother, he will harm him. He will throw our child into the sea…"

"No, sweetheart, he shall not. I promise you that. He will nae harm you or our bairn."

"He said… I shall kill him. I will not let him—aaagh!" She bore down again, and this time she swore she felt something move.

"Yes, I see the head. Hold now, my lady, hold for a few moments, then with the next contraction he will be here." Aiden's quiet, competent tone calmed her, and her husband's gentle encouragement lent her the strength to continue.

"'Tis almost done, my love. Just one last push. We are here, we shall help you." Blair wiped her hot brow with a cool cloth, then kissed her forehead. He glanced over his shoulder at Aiden. "How goes it?"

His friend's expression was serious, intent. He met Blair's gaze and offered a curt nod. "A few moments more, Laird. Ah, yes, now. Push now, Lady Roselyn. Push. *Push!*"

Roselyn did as she was bid and let out the loudest scream

yet as she swore her entire body split apart. There was a rush of warmth, wetness beneath her, then sudden and blessed relief. She lay still, gasping, her body heaving with the effort she had expended.

All seemed to cease, it was as though time was suspended for those few brief, sweet moments of utter calm. There were some muttered words she could not decipher from Aiden, then her husband exploded into action.

"Give her to me. You see to my wife."

"Blair…" she whimpered as he got to his feet.

"Soon, my love. First I must see to our daughter."

A daughter? A baby girl… A wave of joy washed over Roselyn. She would never have said as much but throughout the months of her pregnancy she had secretly longed for a daughter though she knew her husband required sons.

"May I hold her? Please, give her to me…" Roselyn ignored the intimacy of Aiden's deft fingers still working between her thighs. She reached into the darkness surrounding her, desperate to hold her newborn daughter.

Something was wrong. Missing. She listened hard. Why did the child not cry? She would be able to locate the babe if she would only let out her first wail.

"Blair? Where is she? My baby… aagh!" Another contraction seized her, less intense, less painful than the previous ones but still sufficient to halt her pleading.

"'Tis just the afterbirth, my lady. All done now." Aiden remained close as he completed his gentle, capable ministrations. She was comfortable, dry, her belly no longer hurt like she was on fire within. But her husband was not beside her, and her baby remained silent.

Roselyn began to sob. This was bad. This was very, very bad. The child had come early. Was it too soon? Had her precious daughter not lived?

"I am sorry, I am sorry, my lord. I shall produce a boy for you next time. Please, just let her live. Let me keep my baby girl…" She was sobbing, screaming her entreaties to any who might be within earshot.

"My lady, the laird is with her. He will save her." Meggie sounded frightened, stunned even, but Roselyn gathered herself enough to realise that the wee girl was trying to be brave and she could do no less. The child's words made no sense though.

"Save her? What do you mean? What has happened?"

"The baby is nae breathin', my lady. Our laird is blowing his own breath into her…"

"Oh, Sweet Virgin, please, help my baby. Help her now. I shall pray every day. I shall spend my entire life upon my knees on cold stone if you would just—"

The still night air shimmered with the sudden cry of a newborn babe. The shrill wail hung there in the chill night as all fell silent. The child quieted too, there was not a murmur to be heard. Roselyn turned her head in the direction of the sound and struggled to rise up on her elbow. Aiden's strong arms supported her, as Meggie clutched at her shoulder.

There was a muffled gurgle, a snuffle, then a high-pitched and angry shriek as the babe filled her tiny lungs properly at last and let the waiting world know her displeasure at the recent turn of events. Her cries were almost drowned out by the cheers of the assembled men, but Roselyn heard only the sweet sound of her baby's shrill voice. In moments she held the squalling child at her breast as the little one instinctively whimpered and groped as she sought the nipple.

"You should try to feed her, my love. We have fashioned a screen of sorts from our plaids and ye shall have a little privacy now." Blair was again by her side, his arms around both her and the baby.

"Is she all right? She was not breathing…"

"That happens sometimes, with foals as well as wee McGregors it would seem. The cure is much the same in either case. I believe our wee lassie has a fine pair of lungs in her and she should do fine from here on. I daresay she would appreciate her first meal."

Roselyn allowed Blair to assist her in loosening the front of her kirtle and lowering the bodice to reveal one breast. Blair assisted her in guiding her nipple into the tiny mouth, then Roselyn winced as the little one latched on and set up a powerful sucking.

"Oh, that feels like…"

Blair chuckled. "I envy her, but must own that her need is currently greater than mine. And how about you, my Sassenach? How do you feel?"

In truth, Roselyn did not know. How ought she to feel moments after giving birth? She was sore, tired, and completely elated. Most of all, she yearned for her safe, warm bed back at Duncleit.

"I want to go home, my lord."

"So ye shall, my sweet, so ye shall, as soon as I can procure a bloody cart."

• • • • • • •

"Are ye quite comfortable, my lady?"

Blair tucked yet another plaid around his wife and baby daughter as he arranged them, and Meggie, in the back of the cart which Alastair had obtained from one of the local crofters. He had dispatched the man to find some means of conveyance whilst Roselyn slept off the worst of her recent exertions, but now the thin light of a new dawn began to bathe the inhospitable landscape and he was keen to make for the safety and comfort of his keep.

He had had no option but to allow his tiny daughter to pass her first night out under the stars, but the sooner he got his new family into the warm haven of Duncleit the better he would like it. The danger posed by Ingram might be gone, but wolves still roamed the Highlands and even in the late spring he could never rule out a sudden and unexpected snowfall which might block the tracks and trap them out on the glen. It was not only nature which might threaten them; these lands were wild and there were always lawless brigands more than willing to set upon the unwary or vulnerable.

Blair intended to be neither. Itinerant outlaws posed little threat, he was surrounded by heavily armed troops, but there was no reason to tarry here. Blair itched to be off.

He mounted Bartholomew and brought the patient stallion up alongside the cart. He would ride beside his wife and daughter. Aiden positioned his mount on the other side of the wagon, and Blair gave the signal to move out.

"Please, we really do not require so many blankets. The men must be cold…" Roselyn smiled up at him from her cosy cocoon.

"There is none here would begrudge the lady of Duncleit the use of their plaid, nor our wee Joanie here." He leaned over to beam at the tiny infant, seemingly none the worse now for her precipitous entry into the world. Little did the child know how much she had scared him in those first moments when she had refused to take her first breath. He adored his wife, and that was fair enough, but in that instant when he had feared for the baby's life he had known what it was to feel absolute and unconditional love as well as bone-deep desperation. Nothing and no one would be permitted to do the little one harm, and he had no regrets whatsoever at having permanently solved the deadly threat posed by her demented uncle.

He hoped Roselyn would see it the same way—after all, Alan of Ingram had been her brother.

"You are sure about taking the English prisoners with us?" Blair glanced across at Aiden. "I will not tolerate any further threat to my family or clan."

"They are ready to swear allegiance to Clan McGregor, Laird, an' I shall have need of strong men at Mortain. They had little enough desire tae serve Ingram in any case. I doubt we shall see any bother from them."

"We had better not." Blair remained cautious but would allow his captain-at-arms the benefit of the doubt. He turned to Roselyn who cradled their baby in her arms.

"Thank you for agreeing to name her for my sister."

Roselyn bent over the child to nuzzle the soft cap of downy hair. "It is a fine name, and Lady Joan was a wonderful woman. Tell me, does our daughter favour your family?"

Blair took a moment to consider. "Wee Joan has my dark hair, but I believe she has your beautiful lavender-coloured eyes."

"I mean… can she see? Please, is it possible to tell so soon?"

Blair leaned in to caress his wife's shoulder. "My love, we spoke of this. You lost your sight by accident, there is no reason to suppose the infirmity would be passed on to your children. But if it helps to ease your mind, be assured that whist she might be a tad unfocused, our baby sees well enough for a mite of less than a day old."

"You are sure?"

"Aye, I swear it. She is looking at me now." That may have been stretching the truth a tad for in fairness he could not swear that the child actually saw him, though he had taken the precaution of checking her most carefully whilst Roselyn still slept and knew that the baby was sensitive to light and would blink at a sudden movement close by. Those were good enough signs in Blair's opinion and he was happy to set his wife's fears to rest.

Silence followed for the next hour or so as the procession made their way cautiously back across the glen in the direction of Duncleit. They would skirt the hills this time, the route longer but safer for the cart and more comfortable for its occupants. Blair knew he needed to raise the issue which hung between them. He swallowed hard, but the matter could not be put off.

"Do you understand why I had to do as I did?"

She made no pretence at not taking his meaning. "You killed my brother. Yes, my lord, I understand perfectly."

"He was mad, dangerous…"

"I know that. He said some dreadful things to me whilst he held me captive, his account of what took place at Mortain. He said it was all Lady Joan's fault because she fought him and screamed at him. My brother was a coward and a murderous devil. He was deranged, 'tis true, but he was evil too and had you not accomplished what needed to be done I would have sought to kill him myself. I swore I would, when he threatened to drown my baby."

She had said as much last night when he first informed her of her brother's demise, and Roselyn had recounted Alan of Ingram's demented justification for his brutality. Blair had listened, his jaw clenching as he'd learned of his sister's final moments. He was proud of Joan and regretted nothing of his treatment of the perpetrator of such wickedness. Still, he could not be certain that his wife fully grasped what he had told her, the import of the deed he had committed against her kin. Emotions were raw, none of them thinking straight exactly. Now, in the cool light of this spring dawn, would she still feel as she had then? Blair was not finished yet so he ploughed on.

"It was quick, I could at least grant him that. But I could not, would not allow him to live. It was done for Mortain, for Joan and Edmund and their babe, and for you."

"My lord, please let us not speak of him. He is gone, and I say good riddance. We are lucky he did not do us more harm, certainly he intended to. But we are safe, all of us, thanks to you and to Aiden." She turned in the direction of the other man, silent thus far. "We owe you much, Sir Aiden. I cannot thank you enough for what you did. I… I thought all was lost, and then…"

"I am only glad that we were in time to intercept your brother on his flight back to England. It was an opportune moment, and we took it."

"Opportune, my arse." Blair fixed his loyal comrade with a look. "How did you come to be there?"

"You would have wished me elsewhere, Laird?"

"Do not test my patience. I was never so fucking glad to

see anyone in my life, but I still want to know how it came about. You should have been a week's ride away, in Mortain. What were you doing loitering on the shores of Loch Alsh and playing at being a ferryman?"

Aiden shrugged. "Very well, I shall explain. We arrived in Mortain about three weeks ago, as planned. I set the men to repairs, although the people who went there from Etal have made much progress and you will be pleased to learn that the keep is at least habitable. We planted some early crops which will feed the community by the early summer and I am confident within a year or two the estate will recover. Your bondsmen there told us that Ingram had been already to Mortain and had demanded their loyalty, but none were willing to return with him to Etal. There was no bloodshed and he left, but they knew it was not the last of it. Sure enough, he was back, five days after we arrived. This time he came with an English force of about twenty men, and had thought to lay waste to Mortain again. He had a shock when he met with us and we sent him on his way, his troops depleted by at least half."

"Vicious bastard. He would never have left Mortain be."

"Nay, Laird, I believe not. When he failed to take the castle itself he set to destroying the crops we planted. For several nights he and his remaining men would wreak what havoc they could, but Ingram was not satisfied with that. He came to our gates seeking to parley so I spoke to him. He accused you of abducting his sister, a defenceless woman, and threatened to mount a raid upon Duncleit to rescue his beloved sibling. Naturally, I told him he would be better advised to return to Etal and abandon all thoughts of further forays into Scotland. There was much swearing and bluster, but ultimately he rode off, his men with him. As you might imagine I despatched men at once to bring word to Duncleit."

"None arrived," announced Blair.

"No, I ken that. Jamie an' Duncan were set upon by thieves afore they even got out of the border lands, their horses stolen."

"Did they survive? Please, do not say that they perished…" Roselyn struggled to sit up, her expression stricken.

"Nay, we came across them on foot, at the head o' Loch Lomond. They are wi' our force. Luckily I had also planted spies in Ingram's ranks…"

"Naturally," agreed Blair.

"Quite so, and my efforts bore fruit. I soon learnt that the English bastard had hatched some hare-brained plot to ride to Skye with the intention of retrieving that which he thought was his. The matter was made more pressing for him when Northumberland turned down his requests for aid in effecting the rescue of Lady Roselyn and Sir John of Hexham threatened to commence negotiations to obtain a bride elsewhere."

"But surely he knew of Roselyn's marriage to me. The match to Sir John was no longer possible."

"He did know that," broke in Roselyn. "My brother said as much, but told me he had had our marriage annulled in England and that Sir John would still marry me."

"God's blessed balls, they are as mad as each other." Blair would not have credited such idiocy, but then, he had met the man last night and was convinced Alan had been quite deranged.

"Sir John was waiting at the other side of the loch. He was to take me from there to England," continued Roselyn.

"Well, that was your brother's plan," agreed Aiden. "Unfortunately for him, it was not mine."

His companions remained silent, waiting for him to complete the account. Aiden continued.

"I gathered the force you see here, left just a handful at Mortain since I perceived the danger there to be at least temporarily suspended. We were a day or two behind Ingram and Hexham but we rode hard for the Highlands and arrived at Loch Alsh just a few hours after them. By the time we got there Ingram and some of the men had already commandeered boats at sword-point and crossed onto Skye, but we encountered Hexham and his group still on the mainland shore. They were easy enough to overpower, and took little persuasion to tell us the finer details of their leader's plans. I got the impression Hexham was by no means convinced that the annulment was valid, and in any case he had been looking forward to a virgin bride—beggin' your pardon, my lady—so he was right glad to be allowed to withdraw and return to England where I expect he is even now planning to petition Northumberland for the hand of his niece."

"Bloody fool," muttered Blair.

"Who? Northumberland?" enquired Roselyn.

"The whole fucking lot of 'em," Blair clarified. "So, Aiden, why did you not pursue Ingram onto the isle?"

"Aye, I could ha' done so an' I might have been able to prevent him ever laying hands on Lady Roselyn. I regret that I did not do that, but at the time I could only guess at his plans and might have missed him. Had he managed to seize her, and if he had clear passage back onto the mainland and then on as far as the border, we might not have caught up with them in time. As it was, I knew with certainty his intended route back once he had Lady Roselyn, so I opted to lie in wait for him and claim the benefit of surprise. The rest you know."

"It was a quite splendid plan," declared Roselyn. "It worked beautifully. He thought he had outwitted us all by lying in wait until I emerged from Duncleit, then he seized me at the first opportunity he had. He was sure he had bested us, and never suspected a thing. Neither did I, until I heard your voice. Meggie recognised you, of course, but she is a clever girl and remained silent."

"Ye have excelled yerself, wee Meggie, and there will be a reward in this for ye," promised Blair. "Ye have served your lady well this last day."

"What would you like as your reward?" enquired Roselyn. "Name it, and if it is in our power you shall have it."

"May I be your lady's maid, my lady? Just that, an' no kitchen work? I could help wi' the bairn too, o' course."

"Well, I—"

"Excellent notion," declared Blair. "We shall be needing a nursemaid, and I know how much my wife values your help. We shall use the small chamber off my solar as the nursery, and you may have your bed in there also, to be sure you are close at hand if required."

Meggie squealed with satisfied joy, which disturbed the baby but wee Joanie soon settled again.

"So, Laird, now ye ken how I came tae be at the Loch, but what about you? It would ha' been nightfall afore ye realised Lady Roselyn was nae home safe so I can only think ye must have had wings on your stallion to reach the coast so quickly."

"Yes," agreed Roselyn. "I had been wondering much the same thing."

"We learnt of the attack much earlier in the afternoon. Little Annie Drummond was following your cart when you left the Drummond croft and she saw the attack. The poor wee thing was too frightened to show herself so she stayed hidden, but as soon as the English left with you she started to make her way back to Duncleit to raise the alarm."

"Annie was there?" Roselyn frowned. "But, I had thought she intended to remain at her family's croft until the next day."

Blair broke in. "Aye, well, it is for the best that the girl was running along behind ye, as it turned out. We spotted Annie from the battlements and I rode out to see what was amiss. She had your dog wi' her, you see…"

"Freya? But, I thought that they had killed Freya!" Roselyn grasped her husband's arm. "She was wonderful, so brave, so ferocious. She had one of them, I am sure of it. But I heard… I heard—" She broke off, sobbing.

"Well, certainly they tried to put an end to her, but she's a fighter, that hound of yours. The dog was injured though, and Annie came upon her on her way back. We saw the pair of them in the distance and realised something was badly wrong. Annie was able to lead us to the abandoned cart, and to the place about a mile away from there where she found the dog. From there I could determine the heading they were on and knew they were making for Loch Alsh and not the crossing further south to Mallaig." Blair chose not to dwell on the matter of the wounded English guard he discovered in the woods, the man's throat badly torn by the wolfhound's powerful jaws. "We rode right over the summit of *Sgurr na Coinnich* to make the best time and arrived in time to see your men, Aiden, rise up out o' the shadows and overpower the English. Ingram attempted to slip away in the confusion though, the coward. He sought to escape and save his own skin and we might ha' missed him but for the fact that we had the vantage point high up on the glen and could see everything in the moonlight."

"So you went after him?" whispered Roselyn.

"Aye," affirmed Blair, "that I did."

No one spoke for several moments, then his wife's voice broke the silence. "Was Freya very badly hurt?"

"Her leg was broken, I am certain of that, but I know no more. She was taken back to Duncleit."

"I do hope she will be all right, for I have need of her."

"I hope so too, sweetheart. She is a far finer animal than I ever allowed credit for."

EPILOGUE

Duncleit Castle, Isle of Skye, June 1487

"You wished to speak with me, my lord?" Lady Roselyn entered her husband's solar, her fingers grasping the wiry coat of the huge wolfhound by her side. "Hold, Odin. Sit." The dog hesitated, causing his mistress to repeat her command. Then he planted his heavy haunches on the solar floor and waited.

"I see he is improving. It took four times of telling the last time." Her husband sounded amused, but there was a hint of admiration in his tone also. It was warranted; training this dog was not the easy matter it had been with his dam but the hound was getting the hang of it. Eventually.

"Odin is willing enough but he lacks Freya's intuitive grasp of my needs." Roselyn paused as a wave of sadness washed over her. "I do miss her so."

Her husband's arms were suddenly around her shoulders. "I know it, sweetheart. I do too for she was a fine companion to all of us. The bairns loved her too, but it was time, and you did her a kindness in letting her go."

"I know that, and it has only been a month. I shall become used to Odin, and he to me…" She brushed away a tear. Her old dog had recovered from her injuries sustained as she'd battled to save her mistress from the Earl of Ingram, only to die in her sleep five years later. Roselyn had discovered the still, cold hound early one morning and had wept for the best part of a week at the loss of the animal which had been so dear to her and had helped to transform her life. Despite his gruffness she knew that Blair had developed a fondness for the old dog and shared her loss. The faithful hound now lay under a carved stone in the corner of their bailey.

Roselyn would never forget her for the dog had been almost the first friend she had made when she arrived at Duncleit as a prisoner and had freed her from the confines of her blindness in a way she had never dreamed might be possible. Freya had been her eyes, her constant companion for almost six years, but now she was gone. She had left behind a rich legacy though, not least in the intelligent hound Roselyn had selected to be her successor when she first realised Freya was growing old and would not be beside her forever. She and Odin had work to do together, but she knew now that she could put her trust in a dog and it would not be misplaced.

The same could be said for a husband. She turned in Blair's arms and kissed his mouth. "I missed you at the noontime meal, Laird."

"Yes. I had word of a messenger from England so wanted to receive him without delay."

"What news did he bring? Is all well at Mortain?"

"Aye, as far as I know. Aiden is a fine steward, and Betsy manages our household there well enough, though I daresay that wee devil of theirs is a handful, more demanding than even the most barren acres."

Roselyn laughed. "Yes, little Archie is a boisterous lad. I would have never imagined they might have a baby, not at their time of life."

"I happen to know it was not on Aiden's mind either, but they all seem content enough. I gather young Archie will be the first and the last though." Betsy had barely survived childbed, and the physician sent by Blair to attend the birth had announced that there would be no more children of their union. Neither of the new parents had any quarrel with that.

"So, if not Mortain, what news did the messenger bring?"

"Harry of England has agreed to my petition that our little Jamie be pronounced your brother's heir."

"What?" Now this she had never expected. "I did not even know you had made such a proposal. Are you saying my son is to inherit Etal? After you… after you…"

"*Our* son. And aye, after I killed the previous earl. It seems Harry Tudor is not squeamish about such matters and in any case the new English king cares little for northern squabbles. He just wants to secure peace in his kingdom after so many years of civil strife in England. The Tudor reign is far from secure and times are still turbulent. The last thing Harry needs is unrest in the borders. He wants an ally in these parts, and as I am laird of Mortain he sees the value in my son being the Earl of Ingram, since Etal lies just on the English side of the border. It is a pragmatic decision on his part, but one which will benefit us too."

"But Jamie is so young, not yet three years old."

Blair chuckled. "Aye, he has some work to do yet afore he can rule his own keep, but I am minded to ask Aiden to act as his steward at Etal also, until our boy is of an age when he might take control. What do you think, my love?"

"I consider that an excellent plan." She hesitated. "But, there is more you have to say, I think…"

"Aye, there is. We now have a second boy, wee Robbie."

"I had noticed that, my lord. Robert is now half a year old and still wailing fit to raise the dead most nights."

"Aye, the same. A fine, lusty boy. Just like his brother, and his sister, come to think of it. He would make a fine laird also, in due course."

"But Jamie is the elder…"

"Duncleit, Mortain, and now Etal? I fail to see how James would hold all three and do justice to them, especially given that it is the better part of a week's ride between Skye and our other holdings in the borders. That is in part the reason I petitioned Harry Tudor. Now, James shall have his uncle's title and the lands in Northumberland. It is a fine future for him, and at least as grand as leading Clan McGregor here on Skye."

She paused for a moment as the implications of her husband's words sank in. "You intend for Robbie to be the next McGregor, and not Jamie?"

"Aye, I think that would be best. But I need you to be in agreement for it affects you too."

"It is your decision, my lord."

"They are *our* sons and I would have your blessing on this afore I ask the scribes to record any of it. I will also need to consult with my clansmen for it will only come to pass if they see the sense in what I am putting forward. I will need them to support Robbie and agree to let Jamie go to England when the time comes. I may be The McGregor, but ours is a clan ruled on consensus."

"You will convince them, for it is a fine notion. It is fair."

"Aye, and it is practical. Mortain would never have been laid waste as it was had help been closer at hand. Etal and Mortain are neighbours and by allying them I am hoping to strengthen both. As you know, I have never sought to extend my lands and influence, I would have been content to remain laird here on Skye and not to expand my borders further. But events have a habit of overtaking us and I came by Mortain, and now Etal, as a result of matters outside of my control. Well, more or less. I want to do what is best for all, and this seems to be the right solution. We have enough sons already to go around, and who knows, we may have more yet…"

"My lord, it has not yet been a year—"

"…or daughters. I believe Joanie would love a baby sister."

"Babies are not dolls."

"Indeed they are not. Dolls are quieter and make less mess. Are you quarrelling with me on this, my sweet?"

"Not quarrelling exactly, I just—"

"I have warned you, have I not, about gainsaying me in matters pertaining to the bedroom?"

"My lord...?"

"You will bid that lumbering hound of yours to remain here whilst you accompany me into our chamber. There, you will oblige me by laying yourself across the foot of our bed and raising your skirts. I daresay once your bottom is suitably punished and glowing a delightful shade of crimson that you will soon enough reconsider your objections to providing me with another daughter. Or a wee boy, for I am not particular, though a girl would be favourite."

"You intend to spank me? Now?"

"Aye, right now. Then I shall see to the matter of my new daughter by fucking you as you so richly deserve. Do you require me to lead you through into the bedchamber?"

She tilted her chin at him. "I believe I will find my own way, Laird."

• • • • • • •

Roselyn lay still, her hands tucked beneath her. Her bottom was bared, the skirts of her kirtle bundled up around her waist as her husband had instructed. The cool air of their chamber wafted across her buttocks as he moved around the room, passing close to her. He did not speak further but she was intensely aware of his presence, his perusal as he viewed her naked backside from all angles. Already her arousal dampened her core and her inner thighs. She spread her legs a little, longing for him to touch her. He often did, prior to a thrashing.

Although she had expected it, Roselyn flinched as he laid his warm palm on her right buttock. He curled his fingers, digging the tips into the fleshiness there. Three children had left their marks; she was no longer the slender little thing he had married but he appeared to find her even more desirable now.

"Christ, wench, but ye make a lovely sight, bared and ready for me."

"Thank you, Laird." Roselyn's breath hitched in her throat; she dreaded the pain which would shortly seep into her deepest tissues, yet she longed for it too. Her husband seemed to know just how to unleash her most basic, her most carnal desires. The exquisite joy of this play between them never faded. She prayed it never would.

"My sword belt, I think."

"Oh." That would hurt. That would *really* hurt. Instinctively she lifted her bottom higher, pressing her rounded cheek into his hand.

"Ah, my sweet, eager little wife. Am I keeping you waiting?"

"I do not wish to seem impatient, my lord, but…"

"But?" he prompted.

"But please, I want…"

He slid his hand around, into the crevice between her buttocks, then down to explore the moisture between her thighs. He slipped his fingers through her folds to stroke her entrance, then further still to rub her swollen clitty. Roselyn groaned in pleasure and turned her face toward him. "Please, may I have my release first?"

"You may," conceded her husband. He proceeded to thrum the pad of his middle finger across her engorged nub, at the same time inserting his thumb into her tight channel. He angled it to press on that sweet inner spot which always drove her to distraction and he rubbed there also.

Roselyn stuffed a lump of the blanket into her mouth, determined not to cry out and alert any who might be within earshot to their daytime pleasures. This was private, their own time, their own secret thing which they did and they both loved. She had not long in which to stifle her moans of delight. Her release came upon her swiftly and without fanfare. She tumbled happily into that familiar oblivion, her juices weeping all over her thighs and the rug beneath her.

As she settled Blair withdrew his fingers from her heated body. "Now," he announced. "Now you shall learn the consequences of your insolence."

"I meant no disrespect, Laird."

"Did you not? In that case, this is just for our enjoyment. Do you agree, Roselyn?"

She nodded as her lower abdomen clenched in anticipation. "Yes, my lord, just for fun."

The first stroke of his belt across both buttocks brought her up onto her toes. The second had her dancing in place. The third caused her to cry out, the sound muffled in the blanket she clutched within her fist. Heat built with the next three, each new stripe placed parallel to the one before. When he moved lower and started on the backs of her thighs she whimpered in agony but she did not ask him to stop. He would, at the first time of asking since this was not a punishment, but she wanted this as much as he did. Roselyn had come to crave a decent whipping as much as her husband adored delivering one. They were the perfect match.

"Oooh, oh, that hurts, that hurts…" she panted as he dropped more scorching strokes over her thighs.

"Too much?" He paused to lay his hand on her sizzling flesh, pressing hard as though to push the heat deeper. "Do you need a rest?"

"No. No, it is good. It is just so… oh, yes, yes…" she sighed as he caressed her throbbing thighs, then widened her stance as he moved behind her and pushed her legs apart. Blair inserted two fingers into her pussy and she contracted around him, gripping hard as he thrust twice, then three times.

"Ah, such a wet and needy lady. Are you ready for me to fuck you yet, do you think?"

"Yes. Yes, please, I want you—"

"Oh, no, I think not. I believe you might require a few

more strokes yet, to create quite the right level of need. Of… desperation. You will beg me to fuck you."

"I will! I am! Please, Blair…" She tightened her inner muscles as he made to withdraw his fingers. "Do not stop, I beg you."

"You wish me to fuck you with my fingers?"

"Yes. No! Your cock. Your fingers. Anything…"

He leaned over her to whisper in her ear. "You shall have my cock, and my fingers. You shall have everything, my love, just as you deserve. But first, you will accept five more strokes. Hard ones this time. I am done being gentle with you."

Roselyn groaned as he stepped away. There was a swish as his belt split the air, then it landed with renewed fury against her already tender buttocks. She abandoned any attempt to stifle her scream.

"My love, you will wake our baby."

"I apologise. I will be quiet."

"Thank you." He repositioned himself, and landed the next stripe, this time across the backs of both thighs.

Roselyn swallowed her agonised squeal and stamped both feet rapidly as the pain sank in, then dissipated.

"Three to go. Shall we do this quickly now?"

"Yes," Roselyn ground out. "Yes, please, sir."

Blair was as good as his word. One stroke wrapped itself around her right buttock, the next fell to the left. He paused and Roselyn held her breath. She knew this last one would shatter her already scrambled senses.

"You have tensed up. I shall wait until you are quite relaxed, your gorgeous bottom soft for me again. I would like you to spread your legs wide also. Then we shall finish."

It took an effort of will, but Roselyn managed to compose herself in readiness, softening her taut muscles enough to satisfy her husband. She widened her stance and actually arched her back as though to offer her delicate lips up for this most brutal of kisses.

Blair swung the belt one last time, and caught her across

both lower curves and her exposed pussy. Pain exploded, pleasure drowned everything. Roselyn's body convulsed as her release rocked her, shattering her control and shimmering right out to her fingertips and her toes. She collapsed onto the bed, clinging to the blankets as wave after wave of pain-tinged pleasure surged through her.

Then she was in Blair's arms, his lips in her hair, his soft, beloved voice murmuring his love, his encouragement, his adoration. She reached for him, found the scratchy stubble of his jaw. He kissed her palm, then tumbled her onto her back. Her upper body was fully clothed still, her lower limbs naked and hurting, her bottom throbbing in agony as he pressed her into the bed.

Blair lifted and spread her legs, shoving her knees over each of his shoulders as he loosened his braies and drove his cock deep into her. Roselyn thrust her hips at him in her frenzied response, seeking more, seeking deeper, harder, faster.

Blair leaned over her, forcing her legs higher and wider, then he withdrew his cock and surged forth again, and again. He filled her, stretched her, claimed every inch of her as he answered her desperate, keening need. It was quick, this coupling. It was primitive and ancient, animalistic almost, but this was what they both wanted, what they needed.

Roselyn buried her face in Blair's shoulder, tried in vain to stifle her cries of fulfilment when her arousal peaked again. He made no such effort as he shouted his pleasure. He slammed into her one last time then remained motionless as his semen rushed forth to fill her with its wet, life-affirming heat.

A daughter. Yes, we shall have another daughter next. That was Roselyn's final conscious thought before she stopped thinking altogether and her body went limp.

THE END

STORMY NIGHT PUBLICATIONS WOULD LIKE TO THANK YOU FOR YOUR INTEREST IN OUR BOOKS.

If you liked this book (or even if you didn't), we would really appreciate you leaving a review on the site where you purchased it. Reviews provide useful feedback for us and for our authors, and this feedback (both positive comments and constructive criticism) allows us to work even harder to make sure we provide the content our customers want to read.

If you would like to check out more books from Stormy Night Publications, if you want to learn more about our company, or if you would like to join our mailing list, please visit our website at:

www.stormynightpublications.com

Made in the USA
Monee, IL
05 September 2021

77450935R00134